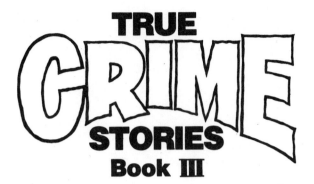

TRUE CRIME STORIES
Book III

TRUE CRIME STORIES
Book III

MAX HAINES

The Toronto Sun Publishing Corporation Limited

Other works by Max Haines

Bothersome Bodies (1977)
Calendar of Criminal Capers (1977)
Crime Flashback # 1 (1980)
Crime Flashback # 2 (1981)
Crime Flashback # 3 (1982)
The Murderous Kind (1983)
Murder and Mayhem (1984)
The Collected Works of Max Haines, Vol. 1 (1986)
That's Life! (1986)
True Crime Stories (1987)
True Crime Stories, Book II (1988)

Published by the Toronto SUN Publishing Corporation Limited
333 King Street East, Toronto, Ontario Canada M5A 3X5
Distributed by Penguin Books Canada Limited
2801 John Street, Markham, Ontario L3R 1B4

Editor
Glenn-Stewart Garnett

Copy Editor
Maureen Hudes

Cover Art and Book Design
Vince Desai

Cover Photo
Hugh Wesley

Project Co-ordinator
Joe Marino

First printing: August 1989

Canadian Cataloguing in Publication Data
Haines, Max.
Max Haines' True Crime Stories, Book III

ISBN 0-919233-29-5

1. Murder. 2. Crime and criminals. I. Title.

HV6515.H356 1989 364.1'523 C89-094940-9

Printed and bound in Canada

Acknowledgments

When I wrote my first book, *Bothersome Bodies*, in 1977, I had no idea that over the years ten more volumes would follow, all but one devoted to true crime. Someone out there is fond of the grisly and gruesome.

The police forces of two continents have been most cooperative in providing me with documentation, and in many cases, first-hand knowledge of crimes they have investigated. Fellow journalists have been more than generous in their assistance concerning crimes they have covered for their newspapers.

Certain individuals contributed greatly to this work. Vince Desai, Glenn-Stewart Garnett, Maureen Hudes, Joe Marino and Hugh Wesley. The Toronto Sun Publishing Corporation Limited librarians have continued to surprise me by digging up little-known information of crimes committed long ago. I am indeed indebted to chief librarian Julie Kirsch and her staff: Rebecca Cowan, Susan Dugas, Julie Pistacchi, Robert Smith, Glenna Tapscott, Joyce Wagler, Katherine Webb Nelson and Barbara White.

Special mention must go to a woman named Marilyn, who cajoles, scolds and aggravates until the sentence reads just right. She is also a terrific wife.

So I urge you once again to put out the cat, turn down the lights, and curl up with a good crook.

M.H.

Contents

For Gussie Haines

THE BEAUTY AND THE MISSIONARY

Joyce McKinney has the unique distinction of being one of the most interesting defendants ever to stand accused of a major crime in England. She achieved this lofty status without benefit of knife, axe or gun. Joyce never hurt a fly. Quite the contrary. She was an extremely loving creature.

Joyce was one of a kind. You see, she was accused of kidnapping a Mormon missionary and forcing him to have sex with her. Honest. Settle down, this could prove to be downright titillating.

Joyce was brought up in the village of Minneapolis, North Carolina. She graduated from Cranberry High School in 1967 and proceeded to further her education at East Tennessee State, where she obtained her B.A. degree. Obviously thirsty for knowledge, Joyce received an M.A. from the University of Tennessee, after which she pursued a doctorate at Brigham Young University.

These cold academic achievements fail to portray a complete picture of Joyce. The fact is, she was a gorgeous blonde, with all her physical attributes distributed in all the right places. Her outstanding beauty did not go unnoticed. Joyce entered beauty contests and won several. Her major accomplishment in this field was winning the title of Miss Wyoming and being entered in the 1973 Miss

1

World Contest. Joyce didn't win, but you get the idea. There were no plain Janes in that contest.

Joyce's first crush was, would you believe it, Wayne Osmond. Yes, Wayne of the real honest-to-goodness, pure as the newly driven snow Osmonds. While Joyce was at Brigham Young's School of Theatre and Cinematic Arts pursuing her PhD, she also pursued Wayne. She made a nuisance of herself by following him everywhere. Wayne, like all the Osmond clan, had the agonizing problem of coping with love struck fans. There is no hard evidence that he ever knew of Joyce's existence.

Who can explain the mysteries at work in the universe which allow boy to meet girl? It happens every day. Kirk Anderson met Joyce when she pulled up in her Corvette in front of an ice cream parlor in Provo, Utah. Nature took its course. Before you could say "The locusts are coming, the locusts are coming!" Joyce and Kirk, to put it in its plainest terms, had intercourse.

Although the act had its moments, the couple was somewhat distracted when Joyce's father walked in on them at or around the middle. Joyce was downright hurt when Kirk later informed her it had all been a terrible mistake and that their unofficial engagement was definitely off.

Without going too deeply into Mormon religious beliefs, it is safe to say that the church forbids sexual intercourse before marriage. It also forbids smoking and drinking alcohol, both before and after marriage. It's a strict religion. Kirk was ridden with guilt at the earthy way he had succumbed to the wily Joyce.

As a practising Mormon about to embark on his stint of missionary work for two years, he was deeply disturbed. The matter took on some measure of urgency when Joyce not only expressed undying love for the now reluctant Kirk, but also informed him through her lawyer that she was pregnant and was just itching to marry him. This rather tense situation was alleviated somewhat when Joyce claimed to have had a miscarriage. I stress the

word claimed because we only have Joyce's word for the pregnancy, as well as the miscarriage. Kirk always stated that Joyce never was pregnant.

All of these distasteful details become totally academic in light of future events. Kirk consulted his bishop, who suggested Kirk do his missionary work in London, England, the better to give Joyce the cold shoulder. Out of sight, out of mind. But neither Kirk nor the bishop counted on the passion and tenacity that heaved and puffed beneath Joyce's all too abundant bosom.

For three years Joyce pined away for her true love. She never forgave, but then again, she never forgot. Her love for Kirk burned brightly. At the same time, she fostered a deep and abiding hatred for the Mormon religion.

While all this loving and hating was going on, Joyce met Keith May and told him of her deep love for the reluctant Mormon missionary. Keith, 21, suggested that he might be an adequate substitute for Kirk, but the 27-year-old Joyce wouldn't hear of it. Besides, she planned on travelling to England to hunt for her old flame. Keith could come along and help convince Kirk of the error of his ways.

That's how Joyce and Keith ended up in England. Joyce had painstakingly planned the attack. She took the island by storm. If you mention her name in England today, years after her invasion, it is more readily recognizable than Henry VIII's second wife. Unlike Henry's unfortunate second, Joyce was prepared. She had a pair of replica .38 Colt pistols, a bottle of chloroform, a neat pair of handcuffs, a new pair of slippers, and the very quilt used as an accessory years earlier when she and Kirk had had their close encounter of an intimate kind back in Utah.

She also purchased a tape recorder complete with romantic music, a new bed and a new refrigerator. Whatever Joyce had in mind was going to be performed in a certain degree of comfort. She bought sheets for the new bed and had them monogrammed. Joyce didn't miss a

trick, if you'll pardon the expression. She purchased pyjamas for Kirk and a sexy see-through gown for herself. Then she rented a secluded little cottage in Devon. The stage was set.

With Keith's assistance, Joyce forced Kirk into a car outside the Mormon Church on Banstead Rd. in Epsom. At gunpoint, they hustled him to the cottage in Devon. Mormon officials quickly reported that one of their missionaries was missing. Although Kirk later professed that he was kidnapped, Joyce always maintained that he accompanied her willingly.

What happened in that cottage in Devon for three long days? When police heard the details, several remarked that they should be so lucky. A magistrate was so intrigued he failed to hear a lawyer's objections in court. The English public lined up at newspaper plants. They couldn't wait for the papers to hit the streets with the juicy details.

Two days after the mysterious prolonged weekend, Joyce McKinney and Keith May were arrested and charged with kidnapping and imprisonment. Spoilsport Kirk had run to the police and told them he had been kidnapped, handcuffed, and manacled to a bed. What's more, he had been sexually abused by the beautiful, blonde Joyce.

In November, 1977, Joyce and her companion, Keith May, faced the music at a preliminary hearing. It was the presiding magistrate's task to decide if enough evidence existed to warrant a trial.

Joyce told all in her own inimitable way. She reviewed how she dearly loved Kirk, had intercourse with him in Utah and had pursued him to England. She blamed the Mormons for turning her true love against her. She explained that Kirk had been the aggressor back in Provo. After all, she had been Miss Wyoming then, with credentials of 38-24-36. "I didn't have to beg for boys' services," she said. Not one person in the courtroom who had a clear view of Joyce doubted her for one moment.

According to Joyce, there was no kidnapping. On the trip from London to the Devon cottage, she and Kirk cuddled and kissed under a blanket. Why was she carrying a bottle of chloroform? "Simple," explained Joyce, "For my own protection, if the Mormons had come after me."

Kirk had quite a different version. He claimed he was taken at gunpoint from the church by Keith May, posing as a prospective convert. Once in the vehicle, Joyce put a blanket over his head. It was only removed when he was inside the cottage. Joyce told him that she still loved him and wanted nothing more in life than to marry him. He and Joyce stayed in the same room that night, but nothing of a physical nature took place.

Next morning, Keith May strapped him to the bed. Why didn't he leave during the night? According to Kirk, "I had thought about escape, but I really did not know where I was. I decided if I tried to co-operate and gain their confidence, I would be able to sort out a release."

Kirk told the court that Joyce was holding him for a novel ransom. He would have to give her another baby. Kirk went on, "That night she spent the night with me in bed. I kissed her and held her in my arms. But there was nothing else. I was trying to co-operate." Poor Kirk.

On the third night, he confessed, he was forced to have sex with Joyce. "She was wearing a negligee. She came at me as I lay on the bed. I said I would like my back rubbed. She proceeded to do that, but I could tell she wanted to have intercourse." Initially, Kirk, stout fellow that he was, refused.

Keith May came into the bedroom and, using chains, ropes and handcuffs, spread-eagled Kirk on the bed. He left the room. Joyce went to work on poor helpless Kirk and the deed was done.

Joyce saw things in quite a different light. She professed that Kirk knew all the time the guns used to urge him to the cottage were fakes. She had purchased them in a souvenir shop. As for their lovemaking at the cottage,

she said, "We made love several times at the cottage. If he didn't like it, why didn't he walk up to the people next door and say, 'Excuse me, there's a girl in the cottage next door and she kidnapped me. She's baking me a chocolate cake and making love with me?'"

Joyce answered her own tricky question. "Because nobody would have believed him. They'd think he was a fool." Joyce pointed out the obvious. She weighed 112 pounds; Kirk, 250 pounds. As she put it, "Come on, who's kidding whom?"

Joyce volunteered from the witness stand, "I think I should explain sexual bondage and Kirk's sexual hang-ups." The wheels of British justice paused, "Yes, yes, girl, explain!"

"Kirk had to be tied up to have an orgasm. I co-operated because I loved him and wanted to help him. Sexual bondage turns him on because he doesn't have to feel guilty. I would like to point out I acted out a sexual bondage scene directed by Mr. Anderson. You gradually remove the ropes until you can make love normally."

Joyce was a character, all right, and the English loved every minute of her recital. So did the Americans and Canadians and, for all I know, the Samoans. The story of the blonde beauty who tied up her missionary lover travelled around the world.

There was more. In the course of her recital, Joyce added immeasurably to the English language. The Duke of Windsor said something memorable about the woman he loved, but it was left to Joyce McKinney to put her love for her man in its proper perspective. Joyce said (Are you ready for this?), "I loved Kirk so much that I would have skiied down Mount Everest in the nude with a carnation up my nose."

The presiding magistrates cleared their collective throats and committed Joyce McKinney and Keith May to trial at London's famous Old Bailey. They were released on bail. After spending almost two months in jail, the two Americans had achieved celebrity status. They were wined

and dined. There was talk of a book. Someone discussed a movie. Joyce loved every minute of it. England couldn't wait for Joyce to take centre stage at the Old Bailey.

But alas, it was not to be. Shortly before they were scheduled to appear in court, the two accused, posing as deaf mutes, jumped bail and fled to the friendly shores of America. After much debate, it was decided that England would let sleeping dogs lie. The two bail jumpers would not be extradited.

Had Joyce learned her lesson? Well, not exactly. In 1986, she failed to show up for a court appearance in Salt Lake City. The charge was disturbing the peace and giving false identification to a police officer. Apparently, in 1984, Joyce had harassed an employee of the Salt Lake International Airport. Kirk Anderson complained to police.

Who can blame Joyce? After all, it had been nine years since she spent that pleasant weekend with Kirk in that romantic cottage in Devon.

THREE'S A CROWD

Alex Rhodes was a 25-year-old bank teller who neither drank, smoked nor swore. He stole a little.

Back in 1924, Alex was a sort of wimpy fellow who made a precarious living working as a teller in a Jersey City bank. In the classic mold of all bank employees who dip into the till, Alex started with dribs and drabs - $25 here, $100 there. But it did tend to mount up.

Alex's method was simple enough. He raided inactive accounts. When he dabbled in the stock market and lost, he soon found himself in the hole to the tune of $1000. That's when he decided to consolidate his debts. He found an inactive account with $15,000 on deposit, belonging to one Jack Box, a used car salesman whom Alex knew only slightly. Alex grabbed the $1000 and replaced the dribs and drabs.

Normally, naughty boys who steal from banks attempt to recoup their losses by further activity in the stock market, or even worse, they take to playing the ponies. Alex was different. He made it a point to become friendly with Jack Box. Unlike Alex, Jack was a well-built extrovert, who would slap you on the back and leave you coughing.

As opposites often do, the two men got along famously. When they became what Alex considered good buddies, he

pulled his great surprise. He told Jack Box that he had swiped $1000 out of his account at the bank. Displaying more gall than Heinz has pickles, he asked Jack for a loan of $1000 so that he could pay back the account. After all, explained Alex, Jack had $15,000 he wasn't even using. Surely, he could loan him $1000, which he swore he would repay. Otherwise, Alex faced exposure, ruin and oh, yes, jail.

Jack thought and thought. Then he agreed. He would get Alex out of his predicament under certain conditions. The conditions were a bit strange. Jack was married and the father of a small child. Despite these obvious encumbrances, he was seeing a 19-year-old beauty, Jeanne Taylor. Actually, he was more than seeing Jeanne, but we needn't get into details here and now. Folks, they were doing it all the time. Jack desperately wanted to marry Jeanne, who was madly in love with him, but his wife, who knew nothing of his year long affair with Jeanne, would never consent to a divorce.

It was a problem, but Jack had a plan. He could simply run away with Jeanne, but that was not only a messy solution, it had legal drawbacks. An adult male who transported a minor female across a state line could be prosecuted under the Mann Act. That nasty bit of legislation had sent many a red-blooded male to jail and, at the same time, ruined several young ladies' reputations.

Jack suggested that Alex elope with Jeanne. He would be best man at the wedding and accompany the young couple on their honeymoon. They would settle in California. Naturally, the happy couple would be married in name only. Each evening on the honeymoon, Jack would take Alex's place at Jeanne's side. Once in Los Angeles, they would rent a house as man and wife, while Jack would be their roomer. Here, too, in the evening, Jack would take over as the man of the house.

It would be no trouble for Jack to obtain a position as a used car salesman in L.A. Another thing Jack mentioned was the fact that Jeanne would be coming into an inherit-

ance of $400,000 when she attained the age of 21. This tidy sum was willed to her by her late mother and would go directly to her.

Now, then, Jack would give Alex $1000 to return to the bank, as well as pay all his expenses until he could find employment in L.A. The way Jack figured it, he would tell his wife he was going to L.A. on business and then start an annoyance campaign which would turn her against him, enabling him to obtain that elusive divorce. Then Alex and Jeanne would divorce. He and Jeanne would marry and live happily ever after.

That's exactly what happened. Almost. Jack explained the deal to his girlfriend. That winsome but simple lass went along with the scheme. Alex dated Jeanne and just as Jack Box had figured, her father believed Alex to be nothing more than a gold digger. He ordered Alex out of his house and warned him never to darken his elaborate doorstep again. Perfect, exclaimed Jack, a perfect excuse for eloping.

Alex and Jeanne ran away, married, and went on their honeymoon. The best man, Jack Box, accompanied the happy couple. Each evening he slept with the bride.

Everything was working out as planned. Alex, Jeanne and their roomer rented a comfortable bungalow in Glendale. Neighbors thought highly of the darling couple and their friend. Of course, they didn't know that each evening the roomer became the hubby.

There was one problem. Alex couldn't find gainful employment. As Jack was paying all the expenses, he was a little annoyed when he took off each morning for his job as a used car salesman while Alex slept in. When Alex took to nipping away at Jack's gin bottle, the latter gentleman thought things had gone far enough. He gingerly approached Alex about making a concerted effort to find a job. Alex swore he would give it an honest try.

Next morning, Alex was up bright and early. He arrived home high as a kite, with a cute little floozy on

his arm. Jack was furious and sent the fallen starlet packing. Then he told Alex off. Things were never the same after that.

It was time for Jack to make his wife hate him enough to suggest divorce. He wrote her a few nasty letters, but she wrote back that she missed him and couldn't wait until they were together again.

When Alex showed up one night loaded to the gills, with a cutie on each arm, that was the straw that broke the camel's back. Jack decided to take his chances with the Mann Act. Alex was told that the party was over. He and Jeanne should get a divorce immediately so that Jack could bigamously marry his true love.

Jack was fit to be tied when Alex informed him that he had no intention of obtaining a divorce. Why should he jump off the gravy train? As far as Alex was concerned, he had his expenses paid, as many starlets as Superman could handle, enough bubbly to stay sloshed on a daily basis, and a wife who was soon to come into $400,000. This was Shangri-La.

Jack Box lost his cool. Wimpy Alex had been transformed from meek bank teller to obnoxious freeloader. Jack grabbed a kitchen knife with the intention of cutting Alex's head off. After a noisy scuffle in the kitchen, Jeanne succeeded in separating the two men, but not before neighbors called police.

With the arrival of the police, Jeanne lost her nerve and spilled her guts. She told the whole story, from the moment Alex had lifted that $1000 back in Jersey. The Feds realized immediately that the marriage and entire scheme had been orchestrated to circumvent the Mann Act. All three participants were tossed in jail.

There were complications. The two men wouldn't volunteer a word. All the evidence came from the ruby red lips of Jeanne, who, by law, couldn't testify against her husband. Without her testimony, the case against Jack and Alex was decidedly weak.

Would you believe it, while lodged uncomfortably in jail,

Jeanne turned 21 and inherited that $400,000 — a healthy sum today; in 1925, a king's ransom. The inheritance enabled her to put up bail for herself.

In preparation for her release, Jeanne attempted to apply makeup. Unfortunately, she had no lipstick and used the color from a red paper poppy made by one of the inmates. She moistened the paper and reddened her lips. An irritation developed around her lips in a matter of hours. The red dye caused blood poisoning. Four days later, Jeanne Taylor died.

Them's the breaks, thought Alex. It wasn't his fault that he was the heir to Jeanne's fortune. He decided to tell all, spend a couple of years in jail and have the inheritance and a life of luxury waiting for him when he got out.

Jack Box stood trial. Alex was the principal witness. He revealed the whole scheme of the deceptive marriage, which enabled Jack to circumvent the Mann Act. In giving his testimony, Alex swore that his marriage to Jeanne had not been consummated. That was a mistake.

For starters, Alex and Jack were found guilty of violating the Mann Act. They received five years each in Leavenworth Prison.

There was more. Jeanne's relatives back home in Jersey City contested Alex's inheritance. Since he admitted that his marriage had not been consummated and the law stated that a marriage must be consummated to be legal, they felt he was not entitled to a red cent of Jeanne's money.

The courts thought so, too. All Jeanne's money went to her relatives.

SLAUGHTER IN NEW ORLEANS

Mark Essex was raised in a fine home by fine parents in the fine midwest town of Emporia, Kansas. From the time he joined the U.S. Navy in 1969, until January, 1973, something turned Mark Essex into a raging killer.

While in the navy, Mark successfully completed a three-month dental assistant's course. The 21-year-old black young man with the solid background let it be known that he intended one day to become a dentist.

But the navy held many surprises for Mark. He was unaccustomed to racial prejudice and was ill-equipped to cope with the petty indignities passed out by the white servicemen. Mark soon discovered that blacks were given the distasteful duties. The whites treated the black servicemen as inferiors.

In 1970, Mark couldn't stand the discrimination and abusive behavior any longer. He left the navy without leave and returned to Emporia. The young man who returned to his parents was a bitter individual. The world outside his sheltered midwest existence was not what he imagined. With a minister's help, his parents managed to talk Mark into voluntarily returning to the navy after he had brooded at home for a month.

Court-martialled, he was confined to the naval base for one month and sentenced to forfeit $90 pay each month

for the following two months. Mark's court-martial trial dwelt on two salient issues; namely, Mark's above average ability at his dental work and the amount of racial abuse he had absorbed in the service. However, the punishment devastated Mark and reinforced his now deep-rooted belief that all whites were the black man's natural enemy.

Discharged from the navy, Mark once more returned to his home town, where he stayed with his parents until 1972. He then took several trips to New York before moving on to New Orleans. While in New York, Mark picked up a .44 magnum carbine and a .38 calibre Colt revolver. In New Orleans, he took a vending machine repair course.

Mark was somewhat of a lone brooder until Nov. 16, 1972. That was the day a university demonstration in Baton Rouge culminated with two black students being shot by police. The Baton Rouge incident firmly committed Mark to a course of action from which there was no return. He wrote his parents, affirming his commitment to the cause of the black man in America. Mark even decorated the walls of his apartment with racial slogans.

On New Year's Eve of 1972, Mark secreted himself across the street from the New Orleans police department's Central Lockup and opened fire with his Ruger .44 magnum semi-automatic carbine. One shot struck a 19-year-old police cadet, Al Harrell, directly in the chest, killing him. Ironically, Harrell was one of the few black cadets attached to the New Orleans' police force. The same bullet exited Harrell's body and hit Lt. Horace Perez in the ankle. In a matter of minutes, scores of police were looking for the mysterious sniper, but the man had disappeared.

A few blocks away from the Central Lockup building, two policemen were checking out an alarm which had sounded in the offices of a factory building. Unknown to the police, Mark Essex lurked in one of the offices. A shot rang out, and Officer Edwin Hosli slumped to the floor. Two months later he would die of his wounds.

Thirty-five police officers surrounded the factory. Shots ricocheted off the walls, but once again, the sniper made good his escape. This time police found blood stains, indicating that their quarry had been wounded.

Police followed the sniper. It wasn't that difficult. He left a trail of bullets, as if inviting police to follow. The trail led to the First New St. Mark Baptist Church. However, not wanting to have another shootout that night, the police retreated from the area. Once more, the sniper had eluded capture.

A week passed. On Jan. 7, Mark walked into a grocery store managed by Joe Perniciaro and shot him in the chest. Mark ran from the store and commandeered a car idling at a stop sign. He then drove to a Howard Johnson's Hotel in downtown New Orleans.

Mark proceeded up an outside staircase to the eighteenth floor of the hotel before he could gain entrance. Lugging his rifle with him, he briskly walked by three black hotel employees. He reassured them with the comment, "Don't worry, I'm not going to hurt you black people. I want the whites."

Dr. Robert Steagall had the bad luck to cross Mark's path. Mark shot him in the chest and arm. Betty Steagall knelt to comfort her husband. As she did so, Mark shot her in the head. He then entered the Steagalls' room and set fire to the curtains.

Mark made his way down to the eleventh floor, where he met bellman Donald Roberts and office manager Frank Schneider. The two men took one look and ran for their lives. Bullets slammed into the walls. One struck Frank Schneider in the head, killing him instantly.

The sniper shot at anyone he met. General manager Walter Collins, accompanied by janitor Lucino Llovett, went looking for the sniper. They found him on the tenth floor. Collins was shot in the back.

Meanwhile, as the slaughter progressed, someone called police, who arrived along with the fire department. A ladder was raised outside the building. Lt. Tim Ursin was

climbing the ladder when Mark spotted him. A shot rang out and Ursin received a bullet in his left arm. The wound was severe enough to necessitate the amputation of the arm sometime later.

One can imagine the chaos the shooting caused in a large hotel. Guests screamed and ran for their lives. Occasionally, police would shoot at a moving object on an upper floor. The number of police mounted until well over 600 surrounded the building. Mark kept moving, setting fires in rooms as he spread havoc throughout the hotel. Firemen, attempting to battle the flames, feared for their lives; not only from the sniper but from the indiscriminate police gunfire.

Several men were wounded by the sniper. Patrolman Charles Arnold opened a window of a building directly across the street from the hotel. As he did so, a bullet smashed into his face. Robert Beamish, a hotel guest, was shot in the stomach. Officer Kenneth Solis was shot in the shoulder. When Sgt. Emanuel Palmisano came to Solis' aid, he was shot in the back. Patrolman Paul Persigo wasn't so lucky. He was shot dead by the sniper.

The strange scenario unfolding in New Orleans took on an unreal aura. Armed civilians joined the large crowd which stared up at the smoldering top floors of Howard Johnson's. Many shouted encouragement to the sniper.

Finally, the police advanced upward in the hotel, but not without paying a price. Deputy Superintendent Louis Sirgo was shot dead on the sixteenth floor. The sniper retreated to the roof. The first policeman to gain the roof was Officer Larry Arthur. He was shot in the abdomen, while the gunman shouted, "Free Africa! Come on up, pigs!"

Tear gas was fired to the rooftop without effect. To taunt police, Mark shouted, "I'm still here, pigs!"

A helicopter was brought in to stamp out the sniper. Unbelievably, Mark's fire drove off the first few passes. An armored helicopter carrying two Marine sharpshooters and three police officers was then used in an attempt to

bring down the desperate man. The sharpshooters poured bullets into the roof. Several volleys almost killed police officers who were hiding in stairwells and behind abutments. Nine policemen were wounded by their colleagues' fire.

Darkness descended on New Orleans. The armored helicopter, with its sharpshooters, made pass after pass at the lone sniper. A bullet wounded Mark, who then came out from cover and attacked the helicopter, firing from the hip. Bullets poured into Mark's body - from the helicopter, from the roof, from the stairwells.

In all, over 200 bullet holes were found in the unrecognizable mass that was once Mark Essex. In his wake, he left nine dead and ten wounded. Mark Essex's body was returned to Emporia, Kansas, where he was buried in an unmarked grave.

SAM
THE LADIES' MAN

Samuel Herbert Dougal had more gall than Elizabeth Taylor has diamonds. At the age of 20, philandering Sam joined the British Army. Three years later, he courted and eventually wed a pretty young thing we know only as Miss Griffiths.

You wouldn't call Sam the perfect husband. Although he stayed married for 13 years, Sam found time to sire two children out of wedlock.

In 1873, Sam and his wife were posted to, of all places, Halifax, N.S. He was promoted from corporal to sergeant in the Royal Engineers. Shortly after his arrival, Sam proceeded to sample everything in skirts this side of Peggy's Cove. Never one to let home fires wane, Sam had four children with his dear wife.

In 1885, Mrs. Dougal took violently ill. I mean bad. Within five days she was dead. Sam was sent home to England on five weeks compassionate leave. When he returned, he had a brand spanking new Mrs. Dougal. Rumor had it that she brought a substantial dowry to the union. This latest Mrs. Dougal had a far stronger constitution than her predecessor. Two weeks after landing on the shores of Nova Scotia, she took ill, but lasted a full 14 days before giving up the ghost.

Eventually, Sam returned to England, where he

received an honorable discharge and a small pension. Now footloose and fancy free, Sam proceeded to seduce ladies with the regularity of a rabbit in heat. He picked up one lady, who could at best be described as plain. This latest love had a pair of eyes set much too far apart. Besides, she had developed a condition now called allergies, but which, in those long past days, was referred to as a dripping nose. Sam tolerated the drip long enough to have two children by the lady. He then unceremoniously threw her out.

Our boy slipped over to Ireland, where he married a Dublin colleen, but, alas, this union disintegrated after only two years. Sam treated his wife so badly, she simply picked up and left.

While affairs of the heart occupied most of Sam's waking hours, he did find time to get into financial difficulty, which he attempted to rectify by passing a worthless cheque. This caper cost him 12 months in prison.

In 1898, at age 51, the old scoundrel emerged from prison. Sam took rooms at 37 Elgin Crescent in London, where his landlady introduced him to fellow roomer, Camille Cecile Holland. Now, folks, Camille was far different from any woman Sam had met in his checkered career. She was a good looking, genteel woman of 56 years, who looked far younger than her age. Her mother was a French woman who had lived near Calcutta, India, with her engineer husband. Camille had been brought up with the better things in life. She was a religious woman, who was extremely interested in music, literature and art.

Above all, Camille was well-fixed financially, with a healthy income from her capital investments. Still, life was passing her by. As a member of the over the hill gang, Camille was extremely susceptible to Sam's many charms. Even after he admitted being legally married to another, Sam's spell was strong enough that Camille divested herself of all moral restrictions and became Sam's woman in every sense of the word.

Four months after their first meeting, the love birds

took up digs about seven miles from the village of Saffron Walden. Their choice of a love nest was unusual. With Camille's money, they purchased Coldham Farm, which Sam immediately rechristened Moat Farm. With good reason, too. The rambling old house built on ancient foundations was surrounded by a moat, complete with drawbridge. The interior of the old building was redecorated. Camille had her furniture taken out of storage and sent to the farm. The happy couple moved in on April 27, 1899.

You would think scheming Sam now had everything his larcenous heart desired. But would he leave well enough alone? No, he would not.

Two weeks after Camille and Sam were comfortably ensconced at Moat Farm, Camille hired a sweet young thing to act as maidservant. That was a mistake. A week later, Sam attempted to break down the door to the new maid's bedroom. Her screams brought Camille on the run. Sam could only explain his actions by stating that he was attempting "to wind the clock." The maid left and Camille forgave.

Soon after, Camille was seen no more. Sam told anyone who cared that his wife had gone shopping in London. It proved to be a prolonged shopping spree. Camille was gone for four years.

Sam proceeded to fraudulently sell off Camille's assets by mail. He had no difficulty forging her name to the pertinent documents. In this way, he continued to live as a country gentleman. He now had the means to womanize to his heart's content. An array of ladies visited. Some were seen about the property wearing little more than a smile. Neighbors stared at the sight of nude ladies pedalling bicycles over the rough terrain of Moat Farm.

Naturally enough, rumors spread, if not like wildfire, at least like a well ventilated flame. After being seduced, one lady complained of Sam's ungentlemanly conduct. This had the effect of focusing attention on Sam and renewing the rumor that his old lady friend, Miss Camille Holland, had disappeared some four years previously.

The police called on Sam. They felt they were hot on the trail of a forger. Sam thought so too. The day after the annoying inquiries were made by the police, he closed out his bank accounts and travelled to London, where he attempted to cash some ten pound notes at the Bank of England. However, clerks had already been alerted to watch for the serial numbers of the notes. Sam was arrested on the spot.

Police searched Moat Farm. They found clothing and other personal effects which Camille would not have voluntarily left behind. But they didn't find Camille in the house. They dug up the garden without success. The moat was also examined without revealing any trace of the missing woman.

Someone in the area remembered that shortly after Sam took possession of the farm, he had hired laborers to fill in a drainage ditch leading from the farmhouse to a nearby pond. The large ditch became the focus of attention. Police sifted through an assortment of slime. After five weeks of the most disgusting task possible, what was left of Camille Holland was recovered.

In Chelmsford, England, on June 22, 1903, Sam Dougal stood trial for the murder of Camille Holland. He swore that Camille's death had been an accident. A gun had discharged accidentally, shooting dear Camille directly in the head. No one bought the story. Sam was found guilty and sentenced to death.

As the noose was placed over Sam's head, a member of the clergy, intent on having the poor sinner confess before his death, implored the doomed man, "Dougal, guilty or not guilty?"

At the split second that the trap door sprung open, Sam uttered what was probably his only truthful statement in years. "Guilty!" he yelled.

THE HITCH-HIKER

Charlotte and Mose McManus were understandably disappointed when their son Fred insisted on joining the U.S. Marines rather than attend Cornell University. But Fred was adamant. He didn't even wait around his Valley Stream, N.Y. home town to attend his high school graduation.

Because Fred wouldn't turn 18 until August, 1952, it was necessary for his parents to sign a release, allowing him to join the service. Reluctantly the McManuses signed and Fred was off to Paris Island for boot training.

Fred sailed through boot camp and, in fact, thrived on the tough marine training. Eventually he was stationed at Camp Lejeune, which enabled him to hitch-hike home whenever the opportunity presented itself.

The McManuses were proud of their tall, straight son in his marine uniform. Maybe they had been wrong; maybe life in the service suited their son best. There was one thing, though. Fred was a bit of a loner. He didn't go out with his fellow soldiers on a Saturday night, or make lasting friendships. Instead, he preferred to walk into the woods surrounding Camp Lejeune and practise shooting with his own .45 Colt automatic. Even on trips home, he carried his Colt and often practised shooting near the home of his aunt at Marion in upstate New York.

On one of these periodic visits, Fred met a wiry 16-year-old girl, Diane Weggeland. It started out as a simple date to take in a small town basketball game, but it ended up being much more. After the game, the two young people did not want to part. They poured out their innermost thoughts to each other. Diane told Fred of being shunted from foster home to foster home all her life, how she hated not having roots, how she wanted to be loved. Fred related how his parents only cared for themselves. He told Diane they stifled his life. Fred and Diane agreed they were two free spirits who had found each other.

In the wee hours of the morning, Diane and Fred parted with the firm promise that they would write to each other. A regular correspondence took place. Diane informed Fred that she was being forced to move to yet another foster home, this time to Sommerville, near Rochester.

On March 22, 1953, Fred visited Diane at her new home. The young people travelled to Rochester, where Fred checked into the YMCA. Fred called on Diane each of the next five evenings. They took the bus into Rochester and spent their time eating ice cream, drinking Cokes and listening to the juke box. While thus engaged, they talked. The more they talked, the more they were convinced that they were deeply in love.

Each night, Fred had Diane home before midnight, except for the last night of his leave. They missed the bus and Diane didn't get home until 1 a.m. Her foster mother was furious. She swore she would report this infraction of the rules to Diane's social worker and threatened to have Diane thrown out of her home.

Next morning, Diane phoned Fred at the Y before he started hitch-hiking back to camp. She was hysterical and implored Fred to meet her at the bus stop in Rochester. Fred waited. Diane showed up and begged him to stay with her forever. Only their love and understanding mattered. She couldn't and wouldn't tolerate living without his love. Fred explained that he couldn't take her back to

camp, but there was another way.

They would strike out for California. Fred produced his Colt .45 and proudly told Diane, "You can get anywhere with this." Diane agreed, but insisted they get married immediately. As she was only 16, this presented something of a problem. Together, they walked into the Rochester library to find a state which would permit the marriage of a minor. At the time, Minnesota had such a law.

Fred purchased a 50-cent wedding ring. Diane bought him a 50-cent rosary. Next in order of importance was transportation. Fred dropped Diane off at a cheap hotel to wait for him while he stole a car. He took a bus to the outskirts of Rochester and hitched two rides. He found he had no trouble getting lifts while in uniform. Fred was picked up twice, but decided that the drivers, who revealed that they were married men with children, needed their vehicles. The third Good Samaritan wasn't as fortunate.

William Braverman, a Hobart College student, stopped to give the soldier a lift. Fred pulled out his Colt and forced Braverman out of the vehicle. The student quickly handed over his wallet containing $8 and his wristwatch. When Fred put the car in gear, Braverman clutched the wheel. "Not my car!" he said. Those would be the last words ever uttered by William Braverman. Fred shot him directly in the heart. The body fell into the front seat. After hours of aimless driving, Fred partially buried his victim in a nearby gravel pit.

Fred picked up Diane in his shiny new car. That night they drove through New York, Pennsylvania and into Ohio. In Toledo, Fred pawned Braverman's watch for $7. Next day, in Keeneyville, Ill., the couple checked into a motel. To celebrate their new life together, they went out for Chinese food.

On the way back to the motel, Fred pulled up at a combination garage and store, which was also home to the Bloomberg family. George Bloomberg and his wife were in

their living room watching T.V. Fred walked in and shouted, "This is a stickup!" George started to say, "Now, look here, son," when Fred pulled the trigger of his Colt .45. George was dead before he hit the floor. Mrs. Bloomberg screamed. Fred fired, and the defenseless woman lay dead beside her husband.

Fred left the Bloomberg home without gaining a penny. Later, Diane cried when she learned what had happened. She smothered Fred with kisses to comfort him.

Sunday morning, bright and early, the pair drove to Dubuque, Iowa. Fred thought he would try hitch-hiking again to replenish their badly shrunken bankroll. He put on his marine uniform and was immediately picked up by Mr. and Mrs. Fred Wharton. He relieved them of their car and $12. Fred then drove to the stolen Braverman car, where Diane waited.

Using their new stolen vehicle, Fred and Diane drove into Minnesota, where they slept in the car. Early Monday morning, while Diane slept, Fred walked to a roadside restaurant and attempted to break open the cash register drawer. As he did so, waitress Harriet Horseman caught him in the act. Without hesitation, Fred shot her dead. The roar of the Colt brought 43-year-old Agnes Beaston, knife in hand, running out of the kitchen. Fred killed her with one well-aimed bullet to the heart. He scooped $40 out of the cash register and left. Diane was still asleep when he returned.

The young couple drove to Minneapolis and checked into a hotel. Next day, they attempted to get married at city hall, but were told they would have to wait three days. They moved on. Outside Dubuque, Iowa, a highway patrolman spotted the car. Officer Jack Moore approached the wanted car with caution. "Get out of your car with your hands up!" he commanded. It was over. Fred offered no resistance.

At the sheriff's office in Dubuque, Fred couldn't wait to reveal all the details of his killing rampage. "I want to make you guys job easier for you," he said.

Fred never did explain why he killed five of his fellow human beings. His senseless killing rampage had netted him the grand total of $67.

On Sept. 8, 1953, Fred stood trial for murder and was found guilty. Because the jury recommended mercy, he was sentenced to life imprisonment. On Sept. 6, 1973, almost 20 years to the day of his conviction, Fred McManus was paroled.

MURDER BY PRESCRIPTION

One of the most unusual and, at the same time, interesting individuals ever to stand accused of murder has to be Dr. Alice Wynekoop. For one thing, Alice was old enough to know better. She was 63 in 1933 when she pulled the trigger.

Frank and Alice Wynekoop were medical doctors, who lived in a large, rambling custom-built home at 3406 W. Monroe St. in Chicago. During their happy years, the Wynekoops had three children. Walter, the eldest Wynekoop, became a successful businessman. He married, moved to the suburbs, and doesn't enter our story. The second child, Earle, was his mother's favorite from birth. Earle was no good. We'll get back to him later. Catherine, the youngest child, following in her parents' footsteps, became a respected medical doctor.

Unfortunately, Frank Wynekoop died before his children reached adulthood. It fell to his wife Alice to raise the children. She was quite a lady. Alice continued to practise medicine from her well-equipped office in the basement of her spacious home. Not only did she raise her children, she also found time away from her busy practice to work diligently for several charities.

While Catherine and Walter grew up to be honest, hard-working individuals who eventually moved out of the

Monroe St. home, Earle was quite another kettle of fish. Earle was in his early twenties when he married 18-year-old Rheta Gardner of Indianapolis. Because Earle was unable to support himself, let alone a wife, Alice converted the third floor of her home into an apartment for the young couple. The mansion on Monroe had one other occupant, Enid Hennessey, a middle-aged schoolteacher who had roomed at the Wynekoops with her elderly father. When her father died, Enid stayed on.

Rheta was not happy. She had several fair to middling reasons. First of all, what young bride wants to live under the same roof with her mother-in-law? Then there was Earle's habit of spending a lot of time away from home. It was an open secret that he habitually played the field with other ladies. On top of all this, Rheta was a bit of a hypochondriac, forever complaining of a variety of aches and pains.

Things came to a head on the evening of Nov. 21, 1933. At about 10 p.m., police were called to the Wynekoop home. Enid Hennessey and Alice met them at the door. Dr. Alice said, "Something terrible has happened; come on downstairs and I will show you."

Once downstairs, police were faced with the eerie sight of beautiful young Rheta Wynekoop lying on an operating table. Her nude body was wrapped in a thick blanket. The dead girl's clothing lay in a bundle beside the table. When the blanket was removed, a bullet hole was discovered in the girl's breast. Under a cloth on the operating table, police found a .32 calibre Smith and Wesson revolver. The girl's face appeared to be slightly burned.

Dr. Wynekoop said something about money and drugs being missing from the house. She thought robbers might be responsible. No one took the doctor's theory very seriously.

Naturally enough, police were anxious to chat with the deceased woman's husband. Earle was pursuing his latest attempt at making a living. He was on a train headed for the Grand Canyon, supposedly to take photographs. Noti-

fied of his wife's untimely demise, the grieving husband returned, a shapely brunette draped over his arm. When asked the identity of the lady, Earle told reporters that his little address book held the names of 50 more just like her. Earle suggested that some moron must have killed Rheta. He admitted that his marriage was a failure and volunteered that his wife was mentally ill. Earle didn't impress anyone.

When it became obvious that Earle the cad could not have killed his wife, police directed their attention to the victim's frail mother-in-law, Alice Wynekoop. Under intensive questioning, Dr. Alice confessed. She stated that Rheta had always been concerned about her health. She disrobed each day to weigh herself. Early on the afternoon of her death, the doctor had walked in on Rheta, who was sitting nude on the operating table. She had just weighed herself and was complaining of a severe pain in her side.

Dr. Wynekoop suggested that since Rheta had already disrobed, it was a convenient time for her to be examined. The doctor thought that a few drops of chloroform might ease the discomfort. Rheta breathed deeply from a chloroform–soaked sponge. Dr. Wynekoop inquired if her patient was still experiencing discomfort. She received no reply. Rheta wasn't breathing. Dr. Wynekoop tried artificial respiration without success. Rheta was dead.

Alice Wynekoop claimed that she panicked. It was a known fact that Rheta and Earle were not getting along, and that there was a great deal of ill-feeling between Alice and her daughter-in-law. Who would believe the freak death? There was a loaded revolver in the room. Holding it about six inches from the nude body, the doctor fired into the lifeless corpse.

Chicago detectives simply didn't believe Dr. Wynekoop's story. The doctor was arrested and charged with murder. Due to the accused's poor health, the trial was delayed several times. When it finally took place, things didn't go at all well for the good doctor.

From the witness stand, Enid Hennessey related details of the events of that fateful day. She had returned to the Wynekoop home about six that evening. Alice put pork chops on the stove for dinner. The two friends discussed literature. There was a place setting at the table for Rheta. Alice explained that Rheta had gone downtown at about three that afternoon and had not returned. That seemed strange to Enid. Rheta's coat and hat were hanging in full view.

After dinner, Enid and Alice chatted in the library. When Enid complained of hyperacidity, Alice volunteered to go down to her office to fetch some pills. It was then that the doctor discovered the body of her daughter-in-law.

Hold the phone! Something's wrong. According to Alice's own confession, Rheta was dead early in the afternoon. Did Alice calmly await her friend's return, cook up pork chops, chat about books, knowing all the while that Rheta lay dead as a mackerel in the basement? For shame!

The prosecution had a few other damaging tidbits. A post mortem indicated that Rheta had died as a result of the bullet wound. The body was exhumed. The burning about the face was caused by powder burns, not chloroform. In fact, Rheta's body held no traces of chloroform.

The prosecution proved through the evidence of several witnesses that Dr. Alice always thought that Earle had entered a poor marriage. Rheta was not good enough for her boy. To add frosting to the cake, she had recently insured Rheta's life.

An Illinois jury deliberated 14 hours before bringing in a guilty verdict. Dr. Wynekoop was sentenced to life imprisonment and was incarcerated in the Women's Reformatory at Dwight, Ill. After serving over 15 years, she was paroled in 1949 at age 78. Dr. Alice Wynekoop died two years after her release from prison.

PRETTY BUT DEADLY

Jim Olive had been employed in the oil industry in Quito, Ecuador for 14 years when he was relieved of his duties and returned to the U.S. Maybe the culture shock to his small family could have been anticipated. Maybe not.

Jim's wife Naomi didn't take the relocation well. In Quito, she led an active social life, had several servants and a fine home which came with her husband's executive position. The Olives' only child, 14-year-old Marlene, had been adopted at birth and knew no life other than that of the privileged minority in Quito.

In 1973, the Olives settled into the suburban community of Terra Linda, Cal., located about 15 miles outside San Francisco. Jim immediately threw himself into the task of building up a consulting business. It was tough sledding getting established. Naomi felt the change in her status. The phone didn't ring. There were no company functions, and no charities to occupy her time.

She discovered that a shot of vodka helped her get through the mornings. Another shot smoothed out the afternoons. Within a month, Naomi was drinking continuously.

Pretty, plump Marlene found it difficult to make friends at Terra Linda High. The girls were cliquish. Many had steady boyfriends. The vast majority were deeply involved

in the drug scene. Marlene, who had never so much as attended an unchaperoned party in Quito, at first was appalled by the availability and use of drugs. She stayed at home, wrote poetry, watched T.V., was bored sick.

Within a year of arriving at Terra Linda, Marlene knew that she couldn't refuse marijuana every day and be accepted among her peers. She relented. Once started, Marlene took to the drug scene like a fish takes to water. Socially, everything was turning out just perfect.

With her acceptance came problems. Marlene had always been an excellent student. Now her grades suffered. Her poor scholastic record caused arguments at home, but Jim Olive was an easygoing man. His baby girl was having some difficulty adjusting. Everything would turn out fine in the end.

The chasm which developed between Marlene and Naomi was far more serious. Once started, it grew like a cancer. Naomi accused Marlene of running around with the wrong crowd. Their shouting matches usually culminated with Marlene accusing her mother of being an alcoholic mental case. Naomi retaliated by telling her daughter she was nothing more than the unwanted daughter of a whore.

The Olives' home life had deteriorated greatly by the time Marlene met Chuck Riley. Chuck was a real butterball. In the sixth grade he weighed over 300 pounds. His family, with medical help, had attempted to curtail his weight without success. In high school, Chuck suffered the humiliation of being different with the exterior good humor typical of many overweight individuals. Chuck had his own car, which gave him some prestige. But it was dope that gave him acceptance.

Chuck had a good supplier and became the local dealer to the high school. He made enough money to quit school. As far as his parents knew, he just hung around. They pestered him about getting a job, but all the while Chuck had a job. He was also his own best customer. As his intake of dope increased, he found his ravenous appetite

decreased. Chuck slimmed down to a svelte 200 pounds.

Then Chuck Riley met Marlene Olive at an acid party. He was an 18-year-old virgin. She was a 15-year-old who had already had several encounters with other boys. Chuck was smitten. Eventually, the two young people became lovers. They took dope together, they made love together and, when the mood struck them, they shoplifted together. One day they were caught shoplifting but, because of their ages and firm promises that it would never happen again, they were released with a reprimand.

The parents of both teenagers were devastated, but it was only Naomi who wouldn't let her daughter forget. She taunted Marlene. Life at 353 Hibiscus Way was intolerable. Marlene now referred to her mother as "that disease." As the months passed, Jim Olive did everything in his power to keep peace in the family. He considered his wife to be a nervous, ill woman, who deserved better from her only daughter. He chided Marlene for her inconsiderate behavior. Now, Marlene seethed with anger toward both parents. To her dope-dazed mind, the whole world was against her. All except Chuck.

It is difficult to pinpoint just when Marlene decided to kill her parents. At first, she told friends that she wished they were dead. Then she inquired if anyone knew someone who would do the job. No one took her seriously. Chuck knew better. Marlene was dead serious.

A series of events brought the already turbulent situation to the boiling point. Marlene and Chuck were once again caught shoplifting. Marlene became involved in a dope purchase that went wrong. Her father bailed her out. All the while, Chuck was falling deeper and deeper under Marlene's dominant influence.

The killing was planned. Marlene was out with her father. Chuck entered the house, picked up a hammer and quietly made his way to Naomi's bedroom. Naomi was asleep, a sleep from which she would never awaken. Chuck caved in her head with several blows of the hammer. The badly wounded woman still breathed. Chuck ran

to the kitchen and returned with a knife. He plunged it into her chest. Naomi Olive would breathe no more. In minutes, Marlene returned home with her father. Chuck shot him dead.

After the killings, Chuck and Marlene washed up the blood, which seemed to be everywhere. To calm their nerves, they took in a drive-in movie. The killings had been planned, but what to do next had never been given a thought.

It was Marlene who came up with the idea of burning her mother and father. Chuck purchased a two and a half gallon can of gasoline. The pair disrobed before transferring the bodies into Jim Olive's Vega. In this way, the bodies were moved without Marlene or Chuck getting blood on their clothing.

They drove into the countryside with their macabre cargo. Finally they came to an isolated area sometimes used by picnickers. The bodies were heaped onto a cement barbecue pit and sprinkled with gasoline before being ignited.

That night Chuck and Marlene had intercourse in her father's bed. Next morning, bright and early, Chuck visited the barbecue pit. Only bits and pieces of the corpses remained. Chuck threw branches and old boards into the pit and once more lit the fire.

The fire was so intense that it was reported to a local fire station. Firemen Vince Turrini and an assistant drove out to the still smoldering barbecue. Turrini hosed it down. He then raked the area, noting bone fragments in the debris. Some fools had roasted a deer, thought Turrini. It had happened before. He shook his head and drove away.

That Sunday, the Olives were missed at church services. A few business acquaintances made cursory inquiries. Nothing serious.

Instead of keeping her horrible deed a secret, Marlene confided in several friends. One even helped her clean the house again to get rid of the blood. For a full week,

although several teenagers knew the Olives had been murdered, no one told anyone in authority. Finally, a business acquaintance of the Olives contacted police.

When questioned, Marlene initially denied any knowledge of her parents' whereabouts. Then she started making up stories before finally telling the truth. A search of the barbecue pit uncovered tiny bits of bone, the largest of these being a two-inch human vertebrae.

Both young people were arrested and charged with murder. Chuck Riley, 19 at the time of the murders, was found guilty and sentenced to death. While he was on San Quentin's Death Row, capital punishment was abolished and Chuck's sentence was commuted to life imprisonment. He is presently confined in the medium security California Men's Colony at San Luis Obispo.

Marlene Olive, who was 16 at the time of the murders, underwent a closed-door juvenile hearing. California law left no choice but to turn her over to the Youth Authority for incarceration until she was 21. Marlene was sent to the Ventura School north of L.A. to serve her sentence. On Oct. 9, 1978, just two months before she was to be paroled, Marlene escaped and made her way to New York City. After being at liberty almost a year, she was picked up returned to California to complete her sentence.

Marlene Olive was released in 1979, a few days before her twenty-first birthday. Under California law, all records of her participation in the crime have been destroyed.

THE MONKEY TRIAL

Monkeys can make big news.

If you happened to wander into Dayton, Tennessee during the scorching summer of 1925, you would have come face to face with every conceivable species of monkey in existence. There were storefront signs of monkeys, monkey dolls, monkey badges, live monkeys. Why all the monkey business? Well, I'll tell you.

John Thomas Scopes was a quiet, unassuming 24-year-old biology teacher. He had no idea what a hornets' nest he was unleashing when he taught his pupils Darwin's Theory of Evolution. Indeed, what Scopes considered to be nothing more than performing his duties as a teacher precipitated one of the most widely publicized trials in U.S. history.

Children told their parents they were being taught that the biblical account of creation was not to be taken literally. In reality, animal life on earth had evolved through a long and gradual process of development from single cells. The simple farm folk around Dayton were appalled.

The area was inhabited by fanatical fundamentalists, who believed without question in the word for word interpretation of the scriptures. News of the schoolteacher who taught that humans had descended from monkeys spread

throughout the state.

In time, a member of the state legislature, John Washington Butler, introduced a bill making it unlawful for any teacher in the public schools of Tennessee to teach a theory denying the biblical account of man's origin. The bill specifically stated that public schools were not to teach that man had descended from a lower form of animal. On March 21, 1925, the Butler Bill became law.

Scopes continued to teach the theory of evolution. In so doing, he was now breaking the state law. He was duly arrested and charged with "undermining the peace and dignity of the State."

The incident which occurred in the sleepy little town took on national significance with the entry into the case of two of the most prominent men in the U.S. William Jennings Bryan, an ardent fundamentalist, was appointed special prosecutor. The fiery old orator had three times been the Democratic candidate for president of the U.S. He lost on all three occasions. Bryan saw the trial as a double opportunity - a chance to strike a blow against the Godless, and at the same time, garner favorable publicity which might catapult him into the White House.

With the aid of the American Civil Liberties Union, Scopes was able to counteract the prosecution's heavy gun with the famed Clarence Darrow, one of the most prominent defence attorneys in the U.S. Only a year before, Darrow had saved Leopold and Loeb from death in the electric chair for the thrill murder of 14-year-old Bobby Franks in Chicago.

The die was cast. It was as if fate had brought these two totally opposite men to do battle in a little town in Tennessee. Avowed atheist Darrow, defender of lost causes, was a sloppy, informal man, given to spinning down home yarns. Bryan was a fundamentalist through and through and had been in great demand as a speaker, lecturing on the literal interpretation of the Bible.

In essence the trial boiled down to science versus religion; some said enlightenment versus ignorance.

The Monkey Trial began on Friday, July 10, 1925. Reporters came from the far reaches of the U.S. and several foreign countries. A blanket of heat descended on Tennessee, making the poorly ventilated courtroom a virtual steambath. The symbol of the event, the monkey, was everywhere. Hucksters, medicine men and carnival side show barkers hawked their wares on Main St. Fundamentalists argued. Some fought with those who didn't share their opinion. In all, the community took on a festive air.

Inside, the two protagonists joined battle. Darrow pointed out that the defendant Scopes readily admitted teaching the theory of evolution. At no time did he disagree with the Bible. In fact, according to Darrow, many people believed in both Darwin's theory and the Bible. It was all a matter of interpretation.

Darrow's address to the court was thought by many to be the finest ever given by a defence lawyer in any court. He pointed out, "The Bible is not one book, but is made up of 66 books written over a period of about one thousand years, some of them very early and some comparatively late. It is a book primarily of religion and morals. It is not a book of science. Under it there is nothing prescribed that would tell you how to build a railroad or a steamboat or to make anything that would advance civilization." He went on, illustrating that at the time the Bible was written, there were many universally believed scientific theories which were later proved to be incorrect with the advancement of knowledge.

Bryan, who addressed the jury for 79 minutes, claimed that teaching children evolution was robbing them of their faith in God.

In a surprise move, Darrow had his adversary, Bryan, take the witness stand as an expert witness on the Bible. Bryan admitted that he believed in the King James version of the Bible word for word. Then, for 90 long minutes, Darrow posed embarrassing questions to the squirming Bryan. "Where did Cain's wife come from if, as the Bible states, the earth was inhabited only by his brother

Abel and his mother and father, Adam and Eve?" Darrow also had Bryan admit it may have taken longer than six 24 hour days to make the earth.

The wily old defender had Bryan state that he firmly believed "God punished the serpent by condemning snakes forever after to crawl upon their bellies." Bryan was stymied when asked, "Have you any idea how the snake went before that time?" All in all, his time spent on the witness stand was a humiliating experience for William Jennings Bryan.

In eight days the trial drew to a close. It took only nine minutes for the forgotten man in the case, John Scopes, to be found guilty. He was fined $100, the minimum penalty under the statute. An appeal was launched on a technicality. The Supreme Court of Tennessee reversed the judgment of the jury, but ruled that the law itself was constitutional.

Clarence Darrow emerged as the unofficial victor and went on to defend other unpopular causes.

The trial and the personal humiliation he had endured took their toll on William Jennings Bryan. He died in his sleep of heart failure while still in Dayton six days after the trial.

In 1960, John Scopes was presented with the key to the town of Dayton by the mayor. They celebrated the thirty-fifth anniversary of the trial on Scopes Trial Day.

An excellent movie, Inherit the Wind, based on the Monkey Trial, was made in 1960. In it, Spencer Tracy played Clarence Darrow, Frederick March played Bryan, and Dick York played John Scopes.

In 1967, the Butler Act, which had caused all the excitement in Dayton 42 years earlier, was repealed.

John Scopes outlived all the principals connected with the controversial Monkey Trial. He died of cancer on Oct. 21, 1970.

181 DAYS OF HELL

Donald Alexander Hay lived about 100 feet down the road from the Drover family at 1601 Barnet Hwy. in Port Moody, B.C. Little 12-year-old Abby Drover often dropped in and played with the Hay children. The fact is, almost every day Abby passed the Hay house on her way to school. Nothing unusual about that, until March 10, 1976, the day Abby disappeared.

The morning started out as always. Abby left her home in good cheer, carrying her schoolbooks. Then nothing. The little girl simply vanished.

Abby's mother, Ruth Drover, reported her daughter's absence to the Port Moody police. A massive search was undertaken. Mrs. Drover contacted her divorced husband, Cecil, who had remarried and was living in Calgary. He returned to Port Moody to assist in the search for his missing daughter. Neighbor Don Hay took part in the search, as did other neighbors. Sometimes Hay accompanied Abby's sister looking for the missing girl.

Don Hay was different from the scores of concerned parents who took part in the hunt for Abby Drover. You see, Hay was the only one who knew exactly what fate had befallen the missing girl. Others talked of murder, but not Hay. He knew better.

Hay, a former mental patient, had sometime earlier

believed himself to be in love with his own 15-year-old stepdaughter. Somewhere in his twisted mind he devised a scheme whereby he would enslave his stepdaughter. Hay built a cement block cell below his garage. The cell measured seven feet by seven feet and was approximately seven feet high. The man with the strange urges equipped it with a bed, wash basin and portable toilet. He brought electricity into the cubicle, which was illuminated by a lone 60 watt bulb. Then he waited. By March 10, 1976, Don Hay was ready to strike.

It was Abby Drover's bad luck to be passing the Hay house on the day he decided on impulse to capture a female victim. It was not difficult. The promise of a drive to school, and before she could comprehend what was happening, Abby Drover was confined in the underground, windowless dungeon.

From the garage above, it was impossible to see the shaft leading to the cubicle. Hay, a self-employed builder of campers, had concealed the opening with a workbench.

Days passed. The search for Abby wound down. Those acquainted with Abby knew she would never leave home voluntarily. Surely she had become a murder victim.

Down in her cell, Abby was thrown a few candy bars for nourishment, sometimes a can of soup mixed with warm tap water, on occasion a bag of chips. Abby lost weight, but she didn't starve.

At first, Hay spent a lot of time with his captive. When he wanted her for sex, he chained the helpless girl to the cement wall. When drunk, he further abused the child. Abby called on all her resources to maintain her sanity. The madman had given her a tiny transistor radio. Abby attempted to keep track of the days by marking her hands with a pen. She also read and reread her school-books, the books she had been carrying the day she was thrust into the cell. From time to time Hay told Abby he was going to let her go but, in her own words, as time passed, "I finally didn't believe him."

Days turned into weeks. The tiny cell was filthy and

the stench became unbearable. The portable toilet was often left unattended for days. Empty tin cans littered the floor.

Six months after Abby was abducted, Hay's common-law wife called police. She believed her husband had locked himself in their garage and was attempting suicide. Constable Paul Adams and Bob Reed of the Port Moody Police responded to the call. They checked out the garage, but found nothing amiss. Don Hay was nowhere to be seen. As they drove away, they received a radio message requesting their return. Mrs. Hay had called again.

This time Adams spotted a man climbing up a ladder in the shaft under the workbench. He pulled the man into the garage. Adams was amazed to hear a faint whining. "I looked down the shaft," he said, "and here was this frail little thing coming up." The mystery of Abby Drover's disappearance was solved. She had been in her personal prison for 181 days. She had missed the spring and summer of 1976.

Abby had 177 ink marks on her hands, indicating the number of days she had been held captive. Under the circumstances, she proved to be remarkably accurate, missing only four days throughout her ordeal. Taken to hospital, Abby's only physical problem was her inability to walk without difficulty. Being confined in such a small space for such a lengthy period of time, the muscles of her legs did not respond normally, but her ability to walk properly soon returned.

Donald Alexander Hay was taken into custody. He was charged with kidnapping and with three sex offenses, including rape and gross indecency. Later, the Crown accepted Hay's guilty plea to kidnapping and having sexual intercourse with a girl under 14 years of age. To spare Abby a court appearance, all other charges were dropped.

Hay was sentenced to life imprisonment on the kidnapping charge and eight years imprisonment on the sex offence.

A QUESTION OF LAW

Everyone in the murder business agrees that Merrie England, for some unknown reason, produces unique murderers.

Years from now, peaceful law abiding citizens like you and me will still be pondering the mystery of necrophiliac Reg Christie, who developed the atrocious habit of planting prostitutes in the walls of his squalid flat. Who can forget Dr. Crippen, that meek little man who disposed of his wife in the cellar of their home and then had the unmitigated gall to sail away with his mistress?

Unusual and intriguing all, but none of these pose the moral dilemma which dominated the legal and religious communities as did the crime of Christopher Craig and Derek Bentley.

Christopher Craig's parents were respected citizens who provided their children with a good, middle class home. In 1952, Mr. Craig was employed as a bank cashier. His hobby of gun collecting had a great and unfortunate effect on his two sons. At early ages, the two boys became fascinated with guns. The eldest, Neville, had been sentenced to 12 years imprisonment just two days before Chris set out on the mission which would change his life forever.

Derek Bentley, 19, was not the brightest lad in the

world. Earlier that year he had been rejected by the army as being "mentally deficient." The two boys hopped a bus near their south London homes and travelled to Croydon. Both were well-armed. Bentley carried a knife and a knuckle duster. Craig carried a .45 calibre Colt. He had meticulously cut down the barrel so that the weapon fit into his pocket. A second pocket held an extra clip of ammunition. The two boys intended to rob the Barlow and Parker Warehouse of Tamworth Rd. of whatever they could find.

The locks securing the building proved to be a problem. They wouldn't budge. Craig and Bentley made their way to the roof, figuring there would be a door leading to the interior of the building. They were right, but discovered that it too was locked and barred.

Unknown to the two boys, their inability to gain entrance to the building was to be the least of their worries. Their real problems had started ten minutes earlier. In her home directly across from the warehouse, Mrs. Edith Ware was putting her nine-year-old daughter to bed when the little girl spotted two men passing their house. They seemed to be avoiding street lamps. When they jumped a fence surrounding the warehouse, Mrs. Ware called police.

Within minutes, two patrol cars arrived at the scene. Constables quickly surrounded the warehouse. The would-be robbers were on the roof with nowhere to go. They immediately noticed the police movements and looked for cover. There were four low glass skylights in the centre of the roof, totally inadequate for concealment purposes. The only other possible hiding place appeared to be an elevator shaft. Craig and Bentley took cover.

Unarmed police officers were now on the roof. Det. Const. William Fairfax, who would later receive the George Cross for his action, inched closer to the shaft, shouting, "I am a police officer. Come out from behind the stack."

Craig heard and replied, "If you want us, well, come

and get us (expletive deleted)!" Undaunted, Fairfax rushed the pair. Bentley stepped forward and was immediately grabbed by Fairfax. With a sudden twist, he struggled free, at the same time shouting, "Let him have it, Chris!"

Shots were fired. One shot wounded Fairfax in the shoulder. One whizzed over his head. Craig was only six feet from Fairfax when he fired. Although wounded, Fairfax once more clutched Bentley and dragged him behind protruding roof lights.

Craig made his way to the other side of the roof and fired at anything that moved. Meanwhile, Fairfax searched Bentley and relieved him of his dagger and knuckle dusters. By this time, Craig had made his way to a position on top of the elevator shaft. Once more, Fairfax called out, "Drop your gun!" Craig replied, "Come and get it," and fired several more shots.

Backup police officers were now at the scene. The warehouse was completely surrounded. The manager of the warehouse was located and provided the officers with keys to the interior of the building. They entered and dashed up the stairs. First man out on the roof was police constable Sidney Miles. Craig shot him directly between the eyes as he came through the door. Miles fell dead.

Craig shouted again, "Come on, you brave coppers, think of your wives. I am Craig. You just got my brother 12 years. Come on, I'm only 16!"

Police officers Norman Harrison and James MacDonald, together with Fairfax, retreated into the building, using Bentley as a shield. As they moved, Bentley called out, "They're taking me down, Chris!" The three officers went into the building. Fairfax was given a gun and once more appeared on the roof. This time he warned Craig, "Drop your gun, I also have a gun." To prove the statement, he fired in Craig's direction.

Suddenly, Craig hollered, "It's empty!" referring to his own gun. He then threw himself off the roof. The fall most certainly would have been fatal had he fallen unob-

structed from the roof to the ground over 30 feet below. However, as luck would have it, Craig's body struck the corner of a greenhouse and bounced off, thereby saving his life. As he lay on the ground, he told police, "I wish I was dead. I hope I have killed the bloody lot." Christopher Craig had a broken back, broken arm and internal chest injuries.

As he recovered from his wounds, Craig showed no remorse for what he had done. In fact, he displayed his disdain for authority by stating, "If I hadn't cut a bit off the barrel of my gun, I would probably have killed a lot more policemen. That night I was out to kill, because I had so much hate inside me for what they did to my brother. I shot the policeman in the head with my .45."

Craig and Bentley stood trial for the murder of Officer Miles. Both were found guilty and convicted, but their sentences were to be far different. Craig, who had fired the shots which killed the officer, was only 16 at the time of the killing and was detained at Her Majesty's pleasure. This was the only possible sentence in England for a boy of 16 convicted of murder. Bentley, who was 19, received the full wrath of the law. Despite not firing a shot, and being in custody at least 10 minutes before the fatal shots were fired, Bentley was sentenced to death.

The fact that Bentley had shouted, "Give it to him, Chris!" weighed heavily against him. There was no doubt whatever that he knew Craig had a gun and intended to use it.

Bentley appealed the conviction, stating that the joint operation of robbing the warehouse had terminated when he was taken into custody by Fairfax. He claimed he was not responsible for Craig's subsequent actions.

The death sentence stood. Never in the history of England had such a hue and cry ensued to save a life from the gallows. On Jan. 28, 1953, despite rallies and petitions, Derek Bentley was executed.

DEATH IN THE CARDS

I have taken bridge lessons twice in my life. Never, I hasten to add, because I had any great desire to become an expert, but only because, at the time, under threat of having my fingernails pulled out from each digit, my wife insisted that I learn how to play that infernal card game. On both occasions, I quit early on in my education. I couldn't stand the shouting.

It is enlightening to discover that bridge has precipitated more than mere shouting - would you believe bloody murder?

Myrtle Adkins, a winsome young lady who originally hailed from Arkansas, bumped into John Bennett on a train. It is from such chance encounters that lives are sometimes altered. Terminated, even.

The First World War was raging in Europe, but that altercation had little effect on the two young people who, after the train jostling, became inseparable. On Nov. 11, 1918, they were joined in holy wedlock in Memphis, Tenn.

The Bennetts, who resided in Kansas City, had a happy marriage for 11 long years. John made a fine living representing a perfume manufacturer. All was fragrance and light until Sept. 29, 1929.

The day started off pleasantly enough. The Bennetts played a round of golf with dear friends Charles and

Mayme Hoffman. Later, the group retired to the Bennetts' apartment. They had supper and planned on attending the movies. However, their plans changed when the men complained that it had been a tiring day and felt they should stay at home.

Someone suggested contract bridge - the Bennetts and the Hoffmans at half a cent a point. Everyone thought a lighthearted game was a capital suggestion, and soon the foursome were engaged in, for want of a better word, combat.

Initially, the Bennetts appeared to have Lady Luck on their side. However, that fickle lady soon favored the Hoffmans. As the Hoffmans' luck changed, so did the attitude of the Bennetts toward each other. Occasionally, John imparted to Myrtle such endearments as idiot, stupid, and in moments of utter exasperation, dunce.

It is with reluctance that I am compelled to inflict upon non-bridge playing readers that portion of the game which is germane to our story. If you don't play the game, merely skip over the next two paragraphs and you won't miss a thing.

John Bennett was dealing. He opened the bidding with one spade. Charles Hoffman followed with two diamonds. Myrtle Bennett ventured four spades. Mayme Hoffman passed. John Bennett passed as well. Charles Hoffman doubled and everyone passed, which concluded the bidding and the play began.

Myrtle Bennett placed her hand on the table. Being dummy, she retired to the kitchen to prepare munchies. When she returned to the table, she found that her husband had been set two. He claimed she overbid and was furious.

Welcome back, bridge abstainers. When Myrtle returned to the table after preparing a snack, her husband was enraged at the way she had bid the last hand. Myrtle didn't take criticism well. She told John, "You're a bum bridge player."

It is my understanding that in some circles such criti-

cism is akin to casting aspersions on one's parentage. John replied. Actually, he did a little more. He hauled off and slapped Myrtle across the face. Apparently he thought this token of expression far too slight to salve his injured feelings. He repeated the slap not once, but twice.

Myrtle was humiliated. Besides, her jaw hurt. She wept. Mayme Hoffman comforted her friend. Charles Hoffman tallied up the score. After all, fun's fun. They were ahead.

With the score accurately calculated and with Myrtle still weeping, Charles admonished John for putting the slug on his wife. Such things were rarely, if ever, done among their set. John Bennett responded to this friendly advice by ordering the Hoffmans out of his home. Mayme and Charles didn't have to be told twice. Mayme put on her coat. Charles was about to follow her when Myrtle Bennett, who had slipped away for a moment, returned brandishing a revolver.

Charles Hoffman could only stammer, "My God, Myrtle! What are you going to do?" An answer wasn't really necessary. Even if it had been forthcoming, it would have been drowned out by the roar of the revolver. Myrtle shot twice, at a bedroom door and lintel. Then, improving with practice, she poured two slugs into John.

It would be less than candid of me not to point out that the fourth and fatal shot entered John Bennett's back. Shots in the back are most annoying. They tend to disprove the theory that the puller of the trigger was acting purely in self-defence.

It has been reported that on the very day after the shooting, Mrs. Bennett said, "Nobody knows but me and my God why I did it." I suppose it is safe to say that since Oral Roberts was not at that time on a first name basis with the Almighty, by the process of elimination, we could only find out the whys and wherefores from Myrtle Bennett herself.

Myrtle was arrested and charged with murder. In due course, she was brought to trial. The defence's lot was not made any easier when it was learned that thoughtful John

had taken out an insurance policy leaving Myrtle richer by $30,000 should he depart this mortal coil by accident.

Defence counsel claimed that the whole thing was an unfortunate accident. According to Myrtle, her husband was leaving on a trip bright and early the next morning. She had fetched the weapon to give to John when she stumbled over a chair, accidentally discharging the gun twice. In the instant between the second and third shots, John lunged at Myrtle, attempting to disarm her. During the ensuing struggle, dear John was ventilated twice, once in the back.

It is rather pleasant to relate that the Bridge Table Murder, as it came to be known, had a happy ending for everyone except John. The Missouri jury believed Myrtle Bennett's story. Many students of the crime also feel that any man who would slap his wife in front of company deserves to be shot, accidentally, of course.

Myrtle Bennett was found not guilty, collected the $30,000 and quietly disappeared. There is no record of anyone ever criticizing her bridge playing again.

MURDER OF A COP

Someone hated Bill McIntyre enough to kill him, but no one knows the identity of the killer.

The obvious suspects, those individuals who found themselves facing criminal charges as a result of Bill McIntyre's relentless determination, have been exonerated of involvement in his murder. You see, Bill McIntyre was an undercover police officer with the Ontario Provincial Police. He wasn't killed in a shootout. He wasn't murdered while undercover. He was shot to death in his own luxurious apartment at 1300 Marlborough Court in Oakville, Ont.

When his family moved from Winona to Oakville, Bill was enrolled in school. In 1969, he graduated from White Oaks Secondary School. After graduation he immediately applied for a position with the OPP, but was rejected as being too young. In 1972, he reapplied, was accepted and stationed in Goderich.

Over the years, working out of Goderich, Exeter and Mount Forest, Bill McIntyre took part in many undercover operations. He often worked in conjunction with other police forces. His colleagues, as well as his superiors, speak highly of him. In fact, his tireless efforts won him several commendations. By 1981, he was employed in Hamilton under the direction of the Special

Services Branch of the OPP. A year later, he sold a home he owned near Exeter and purchased the condominium in Oakville.

During his 11 years on the force, Bill had become a highly qualified officer. He graduated from the Ontario Police College in Aylmer in 1973. A year later, he completed a marine course, followed by a criminal investigation course, and a physical surveillance course. Finally, in the fall of 1983, Bill successfully completed an analysis and intelligence course. In 1983, Bill McIntyre, career police officer, was promoted to the rank of corporal and assigned as a team leader in the physical surveillance section of the OPP. Six months later, he was found dead on the floor of his condominium.

On Thursday, April 19, 1984, Bill and a colleague were working as a surveillance team in Toronto. Later that day, they visited Grant Brown Motors to look at cars. Bill was interested in a Trans Am. They checked in at OPP Headquarters on Harbour St., after which they joined other officers for a beer at a bar in Burlington. The exact times of Bill's activities that Thursday are well documented.

Subsequent investigation revealed that while Bill was in the bar in Burlington, his neighbors in the condo in Oakville heard strange noises emanating from his apartment. Three neighbors, questioned separately, were later to tell police they heard doors slamming and thought they heard two males shouting at each other. Unfortunately, the actual conversation could not be heard.

The next day, Friday, Bill McIntyre worked as usual. In hindsight, some officers who came in contact with him thought he acted strangely. At a meeting in Bowmanville, Bill left his colleagues in an office and made phone calls in private. In the past, he had always called members of his team in front of the other officers.

That evening at 7 p.m., Bill showed up for a dinner date with his longtime friend, Bill Truax. McIntyre and Truax had known each other since both attended grade

three in Oakville. A half hour later, the two men were digging into the prime rib special at the Executive Tavern in Burlington. After the meal, the friends parted. Bill McIntyre had less than a day to live.

Bill had promised to help Acting Sergeant Nelson Kincaid move some furniture the next day, Saturday. He didn't show up, nor did he answer his pager. Kincaid phoned McIntyre around 2 p.m., but received no response.

The day wore on. Two other officers attempted to contact McIntyre, but no one answered their knock on the apartment door. When McIntyre failed to arrive at a scheduled meeting in Bowmanville, Sgt. Kincaid became concerned. McIntyre was not the type of officer who would fail to show up for an appointment without notifying his superiors. Something had to be wrong.

Kincaid phoned Cpl. Ken Allen and advised him of the ominous situation. Allen was ordered to pick the lock of the McIntyre apartment. Together with Acting Cpl. Dave Crane, he proceeded to 1300 Marlborough Court. McIntyre's two vehicles were in the underground parking lot. The officers listened at the apartment door. They could hear McIntyre's pager beeping inside.

When the officers gained entrance to the unit, they found McIntyre's body on the floor in the hallway leading to the bedroom. An autopsy performed at the Centre of Forensic Sciences in Toronto indicated that Bill McIntyre had been killed as a result of a single wound to the head from a .22 calibre bullet.

Naturally enough, when an undercover police officer is murdered, it is most logical to look for the culprit among those he had helped apprehend. Investigators checked McIntyre's previous cases. Although they came up with several suspects, all their investigative efforts indicated that none of these individuals were involved in Bill's death.

Investigative probes into Bill's work life indicated that he was an exceptional police officer. Some described him as a workaholic. His personal life was surprisingly private.

Officers who had worked with him for months didn't really get to know him. Many never realized how very little Bill McIntyre related to them of his family or his private life.

Who had been in Bill's apartment that Thursday? Evidently, there was more than one individual present. Why were they there? Why did they shout and slam doors? There was no evidence of forced entry.

The door to McIntyre's apartment could only be locked with a key from the outside. Since Bill McIntyre's keys were found intact in the apartment, it is logical to assume that Bill had given the key to his killer, who was cool enough to shoot Bill and calmly lock the door behind him as he left the condo.

Police assure me that they found "physical evidence in the apartment that could help identify the killer if and when he is apprehended." However, it is one thing to conjecture about the whys and hows and quite another to trace the killer.

Here matters stood for almost a year, until a woman, whose identity would serve no useful purpose here, came forward with her story. She was visiting her father, who lived in the same condominium complex as Bill, on the day Bill McIntyre was murdered. That morning she was out walking the dog at approximately 10:00 a.m. She noticed a man looking up, talking to someone on a fifth floor balcony. The woman looked up and later was able to identify Bill McIntyre as the man on the balcony. He was wearing jeans and no top, the same way he was dressed when his body was found that evening.

As the woman walked by, the man on the street stopped talking. Inside the condo, her father nonchalantly glanced out the window. He too saw the man talking upward toward the balcony.

What were the two men saying to each other? The woman can't be sure, but she thought she heard the man say, "What are you going to do today?" The reply might have been, "I don't know, maybe nothing."

The woman, who may have been the last person, other than his killer, to see Bill McIntyre alive, was alarmed when she learned that the man on the balcony had been murdered. When she discovered he was a police officer, she and her husband thought the killing might be a gangland slaying. What would prevent the killer or killers from coming after her if she came forward? As a result, she remained silent for almost a year before revealing what she had witnessed on the day of the murder.

The woman's memory was less than perfect after such a lengthy period of time. However, under hypnosis, she gave the following description. The man on the sidewalk that day was a white male, wearing a white shirt, blue jeans, white running shoes and beige jacket. He was holding a motorcycle helmet in his hand. The man, who was approximately 5 ft. 9 ins. tall, was in his twenties or early thirties. He was clean shaven, had a light complexion and straight blonde hair.

It is now over five years since Bill McIntyre was gunned down in his own apartment. Despite the best efforts of investigating officers, many of them McIntyre's own colleagues, his killer has never been apprehended.

FAITH IN MURDER

Let's face it, there have been many distasteful murder schemes put into action by men and women intent on becoming rich the easy way. Why these individuals didn't pursue the art of hitting a baseball has always puzzled me.

Faith healing was Dr. Morris Bolber's game. It seems back in the late twenties the faith healing vocation, unassisted by television, was not the lucrative business it has become as practised by Oral, Jimmy, Jerry, et al.

We must immediately apologize to the medical profession for calling Dr. Bolber a doctor. He was no such thing. He was a liar, con man, faker and murderer. That's what he was. But he did call himself Doctor.

Now, then, Morris lived and healed in the brotherly love city of Philadelphia; more specifically in the Italian district. It was 1931 and times were tough all over. The Great Depression hit the healing game hard, and if it weren't for his sideline, Morris would have been hard pressed to make ends meet. His clientele consisted in the main of ladies who complained bitterly of their husbands' penchant for wandering far from the home fires. What's the point in kidding you - they slept around with other women.

Morris had a smidgen of success in curing these gentle-

men, by providing their wives with a mixture of ginger ale and saltpeter to administer to the wandering man of the house. Look, it wasn't the practise of medicine as envisioned by Hippocrates, but it kept the wolf from Morris' door — just.

It was in February, 1932, when the 30-year-old wife of Anthony Giacobbe strolled into Morris' fly-specked office, complaining that her husband was going broke in the pursuit of the devil rum and wild, wild women. Morris was reaching for the saltpeter when Mrs. Giacobbe mentioned that not only were they having trouble paying the rent, they were also hard pressed to keep up their insurance.

Morris' ears perked up. "What's this insurance?" he asked. Mrs. Giacobbe explained that her husband carried $10,000 insurance on his life. Like Ford, Morris had a better idea. He prescribed an aphrodisiac strong enough to set the already virile Tony scratching and a-kicking for the two weeks until Mrs. Giacobbe's next visit.

Morris put his brain into action. Around the corner from his office toiled an acquaintance, one Paul Petrillo, who was actively, if not profitably, employed in the garment industry. He owned a nearly bankrupt tailor shop. Sometimes, sleazy Morris would provide equally sleazy Paul with the names of neglected ladies in return for new threads.

Now, Morris had bigger things in mind. Mrs. Giacobbe would be the first. Paul, who despite his lack of morals wasn't a bad looking guy, would seduce and have Mrs. Giacobbe fall in love with him. They would then poison Mr. Giacobbe and split the proceeds. Mrs. Giacobbe would, of course, receive her fair share.

That's the way it happened. Paul, posing as a book salesman, made the acquaintance of Mrs. Giacobbe. Two weeks later, Mrs. G. kept her appointment with Morris. The stuff the healer had given her hadn't done the job. If anything, her Tony was pursuing the ladies more than ever before. But there was a bright side. Mrs. G. had a

lover who knew how to treat a lady. She was now madly in love with a tailor named Paul Petrillo. In fact, Mrs. G., the hussy, would marry Paul if only she were free.

That's all our Morris wanted to hear. He told Paul the pigeons were ready for plucking. A few days later, Paul gingerly approached Mrs. Giacobbe with the novel suggestion that they murder her husband. "What a wonderful idea!," exclaimed Mrs. Giacobbe.

A few nights later, when Tony staggered home dead drunk, Mrs. Giacobbe helped Paul undress her unconscious husband and place his nude form beside an open window. The mercury fell to an even zero. Tony developed pneumonia. A doctor was called; he took one look and prescribed medicine.

Mrs. Giacobbe hustled the bottle of medicine over to Paul, who in turn passed it along to Morris. Sleazy Morris substituted a lethal herb, conium, which is sometimes simply called hemlock. After all, if it was good enough for Socrates, it should suffice for Tony Giacobbe. It did.

The funeral was a tear-jerker. The insurance company paid off. By previous arrangement, Mrs. Giacobbe kept five big ones for herself, while Paul and Morris split the remaining five.

A few months later, when Mrs. Giacobbe complained to Morris that Paul's amorous ways had decidedly cooled since her tragedy, Morris could only offer condolences. Boys would be boys and there was nothing he could do about it.

Morris realized he was on to a good thing. He and Paul looked around and came up with another prospect, a roofer named Lorenzo, who was just dying to have an accident. Morris put in a new wrinkle. He arranged to have the victim insured.

The unholy duo solicited the aid of Paul's cousin, Herman Petrillo. What can we tell you about Herman, other than that he would do anything for money. Herman's function was to pose as Lorenzo the roofer and purchase an insurance policy for $10,000 with a double indemnity

clause in case he succumbed as the result of an accident.

The wheels spun into motion. Paul seduced Mrs. Lorenzo. She would accept his proposal of marriage if only she were rid of her philandering roofer. That could be arranged. Herman, posing as Lorenzo, called the Prudential Insurance Co. to acquire a piece of the rock. The very next day, a salesman came around to the Lorenzo residence when the real Lorenzo was out on a roofing job. Herman, with Mrs. Lorenzo's assistance, took on Lorenzo's identity, and was successful in acquiring $10,000 insurance. Herman was examined by Prudential's doctor and in due course the policy was issued.

Busy Herman then made the acquaintance of the real Lorenzo. Under the pretense of selling dirty pictures, Herman met his mark on a Philadelphia rooftop. A sneaky push, and Lorenzo's roofing career abruptly ended seven storeys below.

Several months later, the group disposed of a Mr. Fierenza, who almost cried out to be a victim. His hobby was fishing. Within a year, Fierenza was fished out of the Schuylkill River. The take was $25,000.

In 1933, Morris Bolber, Herman and Paul Petrillo were living high off the hog when they decided to expand. To facilitate their plans, they took on a fourth partner, who was herself in the faith healing racket. Her name was Carino Favato. Yes, Carino could provide more ladies, whose husbands had a distinct aversion to home fires. She, too, was a dispenser of saltpeter.

It is almost unbelievable to report that between 1932 and 1937, the gang did a flourishing business. Morris and/or Carino would dig up a disgruntled wife. Paul would have the susceptible lady fall in love with him and agree to her husband's death. Herman would pose as the victim and obtain insurance. Soon after, the victim would die, either accidentally or by illness induced by poison.

The gang received one bad scare before the end. One day, Herman recognized the examining doctor as one who had examined him only a year earlier, when he had posed

as another individual. The doctor thought he knew Herman, but Herman said that was impossible. He had never been insured before. The doctor agreed he must be mistaken.

A loose tongue was the gang's downfall. A gentleman named Harrison was serving time in a Philly slammer. For want of something better to do, he had invented a cleaning fluid. Upon his release, he was told that a chap named Herman Petrillo had the funds to market such a product.

When approached, Herman showed no interest in the cleaning business, but upon learning that Harrison was an ex-con, he confided in him that he was in dire need of fresh victims to murder. Harrison listened and went directly to the police. Herman was picked up. When his picture appeared in the newspaper, who saw it but that Prudential doctor who had examined him under two different names. The doctor cried foul and ran to the police.

Herman was interrogated and thought it decidedly unfair that he was bearing the brunt of all the heat. He squealed and the gang was rounded up. Each member professed innocence and blamed the entire matter on the other members. The exact number of their victims has never been established. However, it is estimated that the diabolical scheme was responsible for the death of 30 individuals.

All stood trial. A few of the participating wives received prison sentences. Carino Favato was sentenced to life imprisonment, as was Morris Bolber. He died of natural causes while still serving his sentence. Paul and Herman Petrillo didn't fare as well. Both were executed for their crimes.

THE PERFECT FAMILY

Harry and Mary Jane De La Roche were justifiably proud of their home and the lifestyle they had carved out for themselves. This was middle class America. The way it should be.

Harry and Mary Jane lived in the New York City suburban town of Montvale, New Jersey. Most of Montvale's 8000 citizens were interested in the high school football team and Little League baseball. With three sons, Harry Jr., 18, Ronnie, 15, and the always smiling Eric, 12, the De La Roches were no exception. Encouraged by their father, the boys took part in sports. Ronnie was an exceptional athlete. All three were introduced to guns at an early age by their father. They practised at a rifle range located a short distance from their comfortable home.

In 1976, when 6 ft. 3 in. Harry Jr. graduated from high school, the family was thrilled to learn that he had been accepted by The Citadel, a liberal arts military college in Charleston, South Carolina.

Harry Jr. was the first to leave the De La Roche nest. His parents wished him well. Harry Sr., a Ford Motor Co. employee, had always emphasized the need of a good education. His son would be an officer some day. The strict discipline which Harry had stressed in his relationship

61

with all three sons, would stand young Harry in good stead now that he had chosen a career in the military. Even his familiarity with guns would be an asset.

Photographs of Harry Jr. in his snappy cadet uniform were sent home during those first few months. The family couldn't wait until November, when Harry would be coming home for Thanksgiving. Many of the De La Roches' friends in town shared the family's pride in Harry.

Finally, November rolled around. Harry didn't talk much about his life at The Citadel, but his parents let him know how very pleased they were with him. Unknown to the De La Roches, Harry had made up his mind not to return to The Citadel. He knew the news would be devastating to his parents, particularly his father. Harry decided that he wouldn't break the news to them until after Thanksgiving dinner.

The meal was a culinary and social success. The boys' grandparents joined in the celebration. The three De La Roche boys wolfed down turkey and all the trimmings. Harry was in a turmoil. He couldn't get up the courage to break the news to his family of his decision to leave The Citadel. The gnawing thought that sooner or later his mother and father had to be told preyed on his mind. He thought of little else.

While Harry Jr. struggled with his dilemma, his brother Ronnie also faced potential problems. Ronnie was actively using drugs. He kept a stash under his bed and was delighted to show it to his older brother. Harry admonished Ronnie, warning him that if their father ever found out about his involvement with drugs, there would be hell to pay.

And so the middle class American family had flaws, invisible to the outsider, but flaws nevertheless. The oldest son, a disgruntled student, fearful of being a failure in his ambitious father's eyes. The middle son involved with drugs. Above all, gun enthusiast Harry Sr. had the ever present instruments of death in his home.

Three days after Thanksgiving, Harry Jr. drove his

1970 Falcon downtown and blurted to Patrolman Carl
Olsen, "Quick, come to my house! I have just found my
parents and younger brother dead and my middle brother
missing." It was 4 a.m. Olsen rushed to the De La Roche
home and took in a scene of wanton carnage. One bed
held the bloody body of Mary Jane De La Roche. Harry
Sr. lay dead in another bed. Eric's body was on the floor.
All had been shot.

Other officers were quickly at the scene. Harry Jr. was
questioned. He related that he had come home and
discovered the three murdered members of his family and
his younger brother Ronnie missing.

Meanwhile, police swarmed over the De La Roche
home. Around noon the next day, two officers made their
way up stairs leading to the attic, where they opened a
metal locker. Stuffed inside, under Christmas decorations,
was the body of Ronnie De La Roche. Like his parents
and brother, he had been shot to death.

Shortly after the body was discovered, detectives found
the murder weapon, a .22 calibre pistol. It was wrapped
in a blood soaked rag and had been placed in a basement
drawer. In Harry Jr.'s room, police found a Citadel t-shirt
and a pair of long underwear. Both were bloodstained.
Harry Jr. was subjected to a lie detector test, which
indicated that he was not telling the truth concerning the
murders.

That same day, Harry confessed. It was a cold-blooded
confession, describing in detail how in a few minutes he
had annihilated his entire family. He revealed that he had
removed his clothes except for the t-shirt and long
underwear. He desperately thought of his dilemma. He
simply would not return to a life he hated in Charleston,
S.C. Yet, he couldn't tell his parents of his decision. He
approached his parents' room several times, but each time
returned to his own room without saying a word.

Finally, he made his way to their room and said, "I
can't go back." At the same time, he closed his eyes and
pulled the trigger of the .22 calibre pistol he clutched in

his hand. He then turned the weapon from his father to his mother. Operating in a frenzy, he entered Ronnie's room and turned on the lights. According to Harry, Ronnie opened his eyes and was shot dead.

In his twin bed, Eric stirred. He too was shot. But Eric wasn't dead. When Harry returned to his own room, he heard noises coming from his brothers' bedroom. He went back to find Eric attempting to speak and get out of bed. Harry put his hand over his brother's eyes and said, "Eric, go to sleep, go to sleep. It's just a dream." Eric, if he heard at all, paid no heed. He managed to get up. Harry pistol-whipped him until he was dead.

In an attempt to divert blame from himself to Ronnie, he lugged Ronnie's body up to the attic and hid it in the locker. Noticing blood on Ronnie's bed, he had the presence of mind to realize that he would have to account for it. He transferred his father's body to Ronnie's bed. Harry then hid the gun, placed his two pieces of bloody clothing in his drawer, took a shower and raced downtown to tell officer Olsen that someone had killed Eric and his parents and that Ronnie was missing.

Harry De La Roche was charged with four counts of first degree murder. He later recanted his confession, claiming that his brother Ronnie had been caught with drugs by their father. Ronnie had killed the family. Harry, in turn, had killed Ronnie. Harry's story was not believed.

On Jan. 26, 1978, after deliberating six and a half hours, the New Jersey jury reached a verdict. They found Harry De La Roche guilty on the four murder charges. He was sentenced to four terms of life imprisonment to run concurrently. Because the sentences are not to run consecutively, Harry will be eligible for parole in 13 years. He is presently serving that sentence at Rahway State Prison.

WHO KILLED DOTTIE?

It's seldom that a child's pink plastic piggy bank becomes one of the main pieces of evidence in a sensational murder trial. But that's exactly what happened when Arnfin Thompson arrived home from work on the evening of June 15, 1965, and found his wife's body on the back lawn of their home.

Thirty-two-year-old Arnfin was a bookkeeper at the Carpenter Brick Co. in South Windsor, Conn. He commuted each day from his rural home in Barkhamstead, a distance of some 30 miles. His wife, Dorothy, 30, was a rather nervous, quiet woman, who had been born and raised in the adjoining town of New Hartford. After graduating from high school, she was employed at the Riverside Trust Co.

Dotty, as she was called by everyone, also played the organ down at the Lutheran Church. She continued working until her daughter Christa was born on Christmas Eve, 1962. Folks around the village thought the now two and a half-year-old child to be the spitting image of her dad.

Despite the outward appearance of peace and tranquility associated with the Thompson family, there was tension brewing within the four walls of their small but comfortable home. One of the causes of the tension was the

fourth member of the household, Arnfin's mother, Agnes.

Agnes, whose husband had died when her two sons were infants, marched to her own drummer. She had raised her sons, Arnfin and Ted, without outside assistance. It had been a hard life for a woman physically strong but mentally disturbed. Agnes was extremely religious and was a dyed-in-the-wool fundamentalist.

She did more than speak to her God; she told members of her family that she could see God with her in the same room. Agnes blamed her severe headaches on the devil, whom she claimed was inside her head. When she took a butcher knife to her legs to let the devil out of her body, she was confined to the Connecticut Valley Hospital in Middletown, an institution for the mentally ill.

Now Agnes was home on probation to ascertain if she could cope in an unsupervised environment. To accommodate his mother, Arnfin, with the help of neighbor Tobey Solberg and his son Harry, a high school student, had converted the upper floor of the Thompson home into a separate apartment. Agnes had her own kitchen and bathroom.

Initially, Agnes appeared to be much more stable than when she had entered the mental institution ten months earlier. However, her health gradually deteriorated, until once again she complained of demons in her head. Friends of the Thompsons felt that Dottie lived in fear of her mother-in-law and her weird religious visions.

Who knows if Dottie was aware that her husband was seeing another woman? It started after Christa was born. Arnfin took on some extra part-time accounting jobs. To get the work done, he farmed out the simpler procedures to Jean Griffin. Soon, Arnfin was seeing Jean on the sly. If Dottie didn't know, she must have suspected something. After all, in rural Connecticut, a married man who stays out two or three times a week without a plausible explanation automatically becomes a hanky panky suspect.

On the night of June 14, 1962, Arnfin stayed out with Jean until 11 p.m. Next morning, Dottie told him to come

home right after work that day. She was preparing a roast.

To comprehend the sight that greeted Arnfin when he entered his home, it is necessary to understand the layout of the Thompson dwelling. Sliding doors opened from the dining area to an unfinished back porch. The floor of the porch was in place and Arnfin was planning to enclose it with a railing. The porch floor was level with the dining area, but the lawn sloped dramatically, so that the porch was eight feet off the ground. A second storey overhang provided the porch with a roof.

Arnfin walked into his home that night about 6:10 p.m. He entered through the front door, walked through the hall and into the kitchen. The kitchen was spattered with blood; on the floor, on the walls and on the counter. Arnfin grabbed the phone and called Dottie's mother, Annie Burdick. Mother and daughter were very close. They called each other several times a day. Mrs. Burdick could give no clue as to where her daughter might be. When Arnfin described the condition of the house, she burst into tears.

Arnfin put down the phone and noticed a trail of blood leading out to the porch. The glass doors were open. He walked out and peered over the porch edge. There, on the lawn, lay the bludgeoned body of his wife. Arnfin ran out the front door and around the house. He touched Dottie's cold body. There was no doubt that she was dead. Arnfin screamed out his daughter's name, but received no response. He raced to the home of his nearest neighbors, Bob and Carole Stadler, and blurted out the news to them.

Bob returned to the Thompson house with Arnfin. He went directly to the body and quickly ascertained that Dottie was beyond help. Arnfin entered the house and again screamed for Christa. At the same time, Bob Stadler came in the front door. Just then, Agnes appeared at the top of the stairs with Christa in her arms. She

inquired, "Is she dead yet?" She then closed the door to her apartment.

Meanwhile, Carole Stadler had called police. They arrived a short time later and investigated the murder scene. In the kitchen, aside from the large quantity of blood on the walls, floor, counter, telephone, refrigerator and stove, police found two bloody forks on the floor. Later, it was ascertained that these forks had been used to stab Dottie in the neck. The dead woman's skull had been horribly smashed. She had been attacked with a blunt instrument. The killer had then tied an electric toaster cord around her neck. Dottie's clothes were not in disarray, indicating that she had not been sexually attacked.

Six feet from the body, police found the toaster. There was a bloody rock nearby. No doubt it too had been used as a weapon. An aluminum stepladder was directly under the porch ledge. In the kitchen, an ironing board was set up. The iron was still on when police arrived.

A spike had been driven into the edge of the porch. A piece of the toaster cord was attached to the spike. This matched the toaster cord around Dottie's neck. Medical examination of the body indicated that Dottie had died as the result of three vicious blows to the head with a blunt instrument.

In reconstructing the crime, investigating officers theorized that Dottie had been ironing when the assailant attacked her with the kitchen forks. She fought for her life until the attacker hit her with a blunt instrument. Lying on her kitchen floor, Dottie may have shown some sign of life. In a frenzy, the killer grabbed the toaster and wound the cord around his victim's neck. Dottie was dragged out to the porch. The killer wound the cord around the spike and pushed Dottie over the edge. The cord broke and Dottie's lifeless body plunged to the ground, toaster and all.

Dottie's purse was left intact. In fact, nothing had been removed from the home except Christa's pink plastic

piggy bank. Had someone killed Dorothy Thompson for the contents of a child's piggy bank?

When questioned, Agnes related that, from her upstairs window, she had seen a man lowering something over the edge of the porch, but couldn't make out what it was or who he was. Before she looked out the window, she had heard two loud knocks, but did not bother to investigate. She had been in her upstairs apartment all day, and had only opened the door when Christa visited her before she heard the knocks. Agnes was agitated and almost incoherent. As a result, she was returned to the mental hospital that same night.

The day after Dottie's death, police found the murder weapon in some woods behind the Thompson home. A bloody sledgehammer had been used to inflict the fatal blows to Dottie Thompson's skull.

On the Saturday following the crime, Arnfin Thompson received a letter printed in capital letters. He immediately turned it over to the police. The unsigned letter read:

"I KILLED YOUR WIFE. SHE WORKED WITH ME AT THE BANK. I TOLD HER IF I COULDN'T HAVE HER NO ONE WOULD. SHE DIDN'T BELIEVE ME. IT TOOK A LONG TIME BUT I SUCCEEDED IN WHAT I PLANNED. SOON I WILL KILL THE BABY SO NO SIGN OF HER WILL REMAIN IN MY MIND. I STABBED HER WITH A MEAT FORK. I DRAGGED HER THROUGH THE HOUSE WITH AN ELECTRIC CORD. I USED A HAMMER TO POUND IN THE SPIKE TO HANG HER. SHE FELL TO THE GROUND. I BASHED HER HEAD IN SEVERAL TIMES WITH A LARGE ROCK. I USED A NEIGHBOR'S CAR, A DARK BLUE 58 FORD HARDTOP. I WANTED TO TAKE HER WITH ME FROM HERE BUT SHE WOULDN'T GO. MY CAR WAS TOO OLD AND RAN VERY POORLY SO I STOLE SOMEONE'S ON THE WAY TO HER HOUSE. PRETTY SMOOTH, EXCEPT SHE WOULDN'T GO WITH ME. I'LL KILL

THE BABY SOME DAY SOON. I'LL KILL THE BABY
TOO, AND MY WIFE."

That's where matters stood. Who killed Dottie Thompson? Was it the main suspect, her insane mother-in-law
Agnes, who had been home all day? Was it her unfaithful
husband? Was it a neighbor or friend? Was it a transient
who might never be found? Who wrote the letter to the
dead woman's husband? Who took a child's piggy bank
from the scene of the crime, yet left untouched a purse
containing much more money?

A strained relationship existed between Dottie and her
mentally disturbed mother-in-law Agnes. As a result,
Agnes became the logical suspect. After all, she had been
in the house at the time of the murder. However, she
professed innocence, but did admit to having heard
strange noises and to having seen an unidentifiable figure
on the porch.

To complicate matters, a police officer reported seeing a
black 1959 Ford in the vicinity of the Thompson home on
the evening of the murder. A neighbor, who recognized
the driver, also saw the car, but failed to come forward
until much later.

The printed confession received by Arnfin was not written by Agnes Thompson. Agnes, who had been returned
to the Connecticut Valley Hospital immediately after the
murder, was now questioned thoroughly by detectives.
She grew agitated and would not coherently discuss the
murder.

Police came away from the interview astonished at the
strength of the 115-pound woman. Her small physique had
bothered them, as Dottie's killer had to be relatively
strong to move the body. They also concluded that the
murder had been committed by someone who was not in a
hurry to get away from the house. Of course, Agnes had
only to go a few steps to her apartment.

Agnes' words to Bob Stadler when the body was first
found — "Is she dead yet?" — implied knowledge of the
killing. Questioned several times, Agnes gave answers

which were tantamount to a confession of sorts. She would say, "Yeah, I did it with a sledgehammer." In the very next sentence, she would deny having had anything to do with the crime. Still, bit by bit, in her incoherent way, she related how she killed her daughter-in-law.

That fall, a coroner's inquest found "reasonable cause to believe that Agnes Thompson was criminally responsible for the death of Dorothy Thompson." A warrant was issued for her arrest and delivered to the Connecticut Valley Hospital. No one believed that Agnes would ever be released but if she was, she would be charged with murder as soon as she stepped out of the institution.

That, for all intents and purposes, should have closed the investigation into Dorothy Thompson's murder forever, but such was not to be the case.

On Dec. 31, 1965, almost six months after the murder, Cora Clark was walking along a little-used path with her five grandchildren. One of the children found the long missing piggy bank behind a crumbling stone wall. The bark was discovered about 10 feet off the road, at a location about two and a half miles from the Thompson home. The piggy bank had been cut open near the slot and was empty when picked up by the children.

How did the piggy bank get there when Agnes had not left home until she was taken to hospital by police? Detectives realized that the piggy bank's discovery was not consistent with Agnes' guilt, but felt that this lone piece of evidence was not enough to reopen the case.

Remember the neighbor who recognized the driver of the black '59 Ford, seen in the area on the night of the crime? This reluctant witness now came forward and reported that the driver was Harry Solberg.

Harry was picked up and confessed to killing Dorothy Thompson. According to Harry, he walked in on Dottie while she was ironing. In answer to direct questions, Harry had the disconcerting habit of saying, "I must have..." He would then give details which were already public knowledge.

However, Harry was driving his father's '59 Ford on the night of the murder. He was recognized, and although he professed not to remember minute details, he did confess that he had committed the murder. He also confessed that he wrote the anonymous letter to divert suspicion from himself. Handwriting experts confirmed that the letter was in fact written by Harry.

In regard to the piggy bank, Harry claimed that he threw it into the trunk of his car, where it remained for a few days. "I cut it open and took the change out and threw it away." To the question, "How did you kill her?" Harry replied, "I guess I stabbed her and beat her."

"Did you strangle her?"

"Yes, with an electric cord."

On Sept. 22, 1966, Harry Solberg stood trial for the murder of Dorothy Thompson. He was an unlikely killer, without an apparent motive. He had been married only five months before the murder took place, and was still attending school. On the day of the murder, he arrived home from school around 12:30 p.m. Arnfin Thompson had recently given him some assistance with an economics report.

Harry drove over to the Thompson house to pick up some papers he had left there. When he knocked on the door and received no reply, he walked in. Accordingly to a psychiatrist who later testified on his behalf, he could remember no more until he left the house.

At times, Harry would change his story. He claimed that he walked into the house after the murder had taken place. When he saw the bloody kitchen and Dottie's body, he immediately left, fearful of becoming involved.

After a three week trial, the jury reported that they were hopelessly deadlocked. Harry stood trial a second time. The prosecution felt that the jury might once more fail to agree. After all, one could not entirely dismiss Agnes' confession. There existed the very real possibility that Harry had walked into the death house right after the murder, as he sometimes claimed.

Dramatically, the prosecution reduced the charges against Harry from murder to "threatening." This charge was related to threats made in the letter Harry had written to the victim's husband.

Harry Solberg gratefully pleaded guilty to this relatively minor charge and was sentenced to from one to ten years imprisonment. After serving eight months, he was paroled. Most students of the Thompson crime feel that Harry Solberg was innocent of murder. Not too bright Harry could have walked into the Thompson home, and in a state of panic, fled with the piggy bank. He later got rid of the bank and stupidly wrote a letter he felt would divert suspicion. His confession could have been given in the hope of receiving a lighter sentence if convicted.

In response to my inquiries, the Connecticut Valley Hospital in Middletown would only reveal that Agnes Thompson was admitted to their institution in 1965. In deference to her privacy, they will not reveal details of her present whereabouts.

DESIRE TO KILL

Nasty people who commit murder usually have a motive. Greed, sex and revenge rank right up there as popular reasons for speeding someone along to the great hereafter. When standard reasons for the most despicable of all crimes are not readily available, murderers invent them.

It seems to me that many killers have either fallen out of their cribs onto their craniums or have been hit on the head by abusive fathers. Some juries consider injuries thus inflicted as justification for murder.

Then there are the cruel, motiveless murderers who kill for the sheer pleasure of the exercise. Such a killer lived in Abertillery, Monmouthshire, Wales back in 1921.

Nine-year-old Freda Burnell was sent out to purchase birdseed for her parents at a local corner store. It was a clear Saturday morning in February. The errand was routine. Yet Freda never returned. Her parents' concern turned to extreme apprehension when she failed to show up by dusk.

The hardy miners in and around Abertillery formed a large search party. They presented an eerie sight as they turned on their miners' headlamps at nightfall. Next morning, a man found Freda's body down a much travelled lane. The child's hands and feet were tied and she

had been strangled to death with her scarf.

As word of the vicious murder swept through the area, the miners who had doggedly searched throughout that night desperately wanted the killer. There was a real fear that if the murderer was apprehended, he might very well be lynched unless spirited out of the district.

Scotland Yard was immediately asked to assist local police in the investigation. Freda's last known movements were traced. She had made her way to the corner store, where she apparently purchased the birdseed. Fourteen-year-old Harold Jones, who had served Freda, remembered the little girl well. He told Scotland Yard inspectors that Freda put the birdseed in a black shopping bag she had brought with her for that purpose.

Harold told a straightforward story and initially no suspicion was attached to him. However, when detectives found particles of chaff adhering to the dead girl's clothes, they reassessed Harold's possible involvement. It was conceivable that the dead girl had been carried to the lane in a sack and dumped there. A nearby shed, belonging to Harold's employer, was used as a storeroom for bags of chaff. A handkerchief belonging to Freda's sister was found in the shed.

Police theorized that Freda had been attacked in the shed, tied up, placed in a burlap bag and carried to the lane shortly before she was found. The lane was well-travelled and the body had not been lying there earlier on that Sunday morning.

Medical examination of the body revealed that the child had been struck on the forehead before being strangled with the scarf. An attempt had been made to sexually attack the victim, but this was not believed to be the prime motive for the crime.

Mainly because he was the last person known to have seen the victim alive, Harold Jones became a suspect. He had access to the shed and knew the streets well, but the boy told a believable story and certainly did not fit what police believed to be the profile of the killer of Freda

Burnell. Harold was a music lover and an accomplished organ player for his tender years. He was extremely intelligent and an avid reader. Despite prolonged questioning, Harold would conclude each session with the definite statement, "I am not guilty."

An inquest into the death revealed that enough evidence of an incriminating nature existed to charge young Harold Jones with murder. He was arrested and placed in jail.

The senseless murder of nine-year-old Freda Burnell overshadowed all other news in Wales. The tough as nails miners, who made their living in the pits, worked hard and played hard. They took the loss of the little girl to heart, yet they found it difficult to believe one of their own could be the killer. The unofficial verdict among the populace was split for and against Harold Jones.

Meanwhile, a procession of humanity two miles long, consisting of 50,000 citizens, attended Freda Burnell's funeral.

That June at Monmouth, Harold Jones stood trial for murder. There was precious little hard evidence against the boy. He told his simple story and maintained his innocence throughout. At the conclusion of the four-day trial, he was found not guilty.

Harold Jones returned to Abertillery as a hero. Large crowds lined the streets to welcome home their vindicated native son. Harold even made a heart-rending speech, holding no one to blame for the ordeal he had just endured.

Two weeks after Harold's triumphant return, 11-year-old Florence Little disappeared. The Littles were neighbors of the Jones family. Once more the eerie glow from the miners' hat lamps could be observed crisscrossing the hills around Abertillery. For three days and nights the search went on without success. Finally, it was decided to conduct a house to house search. Storage rooms were inspected, boarded up closets were opened. House after

house was searched until the search party reached the Jones home.

An officer made his way up a small hole in the ceiling to the attic. The search for Florence Little was over. She lay in the attic with her throat cut. Someone had struck her a severe blow to the temple. From the evidence found in the attic, it was apparent that the killer had pulled Florence up through the hole with a rope.

When Harold's father, stunned at the discovery of a body in his own home, asked his son if he had anything to do with the death, Harold looked him in the eye and said, "I never did it, Dad."

Questioned by Scotland Yard, Harold Jones confessed to killing Florence Little. He had attached a rope to the child and pulled the body up to the attic. Harold also confessed to the earlier murder of Freda Burnell.

This time around, Harold pleaded guilty to murder. During his short trial, he answered the question on everyone's mind. Why? Why had this seemingly normal boy turned murderer and, in a matter of months, snuffed out the lives of two innocent children? In Harold's own chilling words, "The reason for so doing was a desire to kill."

Because of his age, Harold Jones escaped the gallows. He was ordered "detained during His Majesty's pleasure."

FORBIDDEN LOVE

Leave it to the French. Wouldn't you just know it? The country that gave us mistresses and choice vintage wines was unable to tolerate the breakdown of the rigid teacher/pupil relationship which has existed in France since Voltaire was a boy.

Let's face it, 16-year-old Christian Rossi wasn't your average fuzzy-faced teenager. In fact, he had a full black beard, stood tall and had broad shoulders. Both his parents were university professors, who claimed to be dyed in the wool Communists. Not only did Christian have Communist leanings, he was also active in the protest movement. It was at a student protest meeting in Marseilles that he first met Gabrielle Russier.

Just as Christian didn't have the bearing of a 16-year-old kid, neither did Gabrielle look or behave like a 31-year-old divorced mother of two young children. Gabrielle stood no more than five feet and weighed under 100 pounds. She was a teacher at the Lycee Saint-Exupery in Marseilles. Her pupils loved the diminutive teacher, and with good reason.

The average teacher at Saint-Exupery stood aloof from their pupils. Not Gabrielle. She not only dressed as her pupils did, she became their good friend as well. Many evenings, she invited students to her flat. Over wine and

cheese, they discussed literature and politics. Gabrielle often took her students' side in political matters and, like them, displayed definite left wing tendencies. Above all, she seemed to be their ally in their ever increasing struggle with authority.

Who knows how it started? Student and teacher fell in love. Gabrielle's and Christian's first date was harmless enough. They took in a movie. To illustrate the strict moral code of the school, Christian insisted that Gabrielle telephone his parents for their consent. Gabrielle agreed and readily obtained the Rossis' permission.

Within a few weeks, Gabrielle and Christian were lovers in every sense of the word. A month after their first meeting, the odd couple vacationed together in Italy. Christian's family were still in the dark. He told them he was vacationing with a male friend.

That summer of 1968, Christian was sent to stay with family friends in Germany. He was there only a few days, when who should show up but Gabrielle in her bright Citroen. The sticker on the bumper, "Make Love Not War," should have served as a warning of what was to follow. Gabrielle, posing as Christian's cousin, spirited her lover back to her home in Marseilles.

Gabrielle attempted to keep things on a certain level. Her affair with young Christian had been private, but she changed that when she visited the Rossis and asked permission to have their son live with her. The Rossis were furious.

Well, the Camembert hit the fan. Gabrielle, tears flowing from her eyes, fled from the Rossi home. If the family thought their troubles were over, they were far from correct. Their son disappeared for days at a time. When he returned, there were violent arguments. He professed undying love for his Gabrielle.

As for Gabrielle, she suffered from what amounted to a nervous breakdown. It got so she was unable to function. She took sick leave from her teaching position in October, 1968.

In an attempt to break up the affair once and for all, the Rossis sent their son to a private school in the Pyrenees. Gabrielle soon showed up. The couple were discovered making love in her car.

In the academic world, Gabrielle Russier was highly regarded. When the department of education found out about her impetuous love affair with a 16-year-old pupil, they offered her a position at the University of Rennes, hundreds of miles from Marseilles. Gabrielle refused the substantial promotion. When Christian heard of this latest development, he left his school in the Pyrenees, made his way to Marseilles and into Gabrielle's waiting arms.

Gabrielle hid her lover at the home of friends. In so doing, she broke the law for the first time. In France, it is illegal to "remove a minor from the place where he had been put by those in authority over him." The offence is punishable by 10 years imprisonment.

The Rossis brought Gabrielle to court in an attempt to locate their son. When an examining magistrate asked where she was hiding Christian, Gabrielle replied, "Find out for yourself, it's your job." When warned that such responses would not be tolerated by the French court, she replied, "All right, then, arrest me." Voila. They did. Gabrielle was placed in jail and refused bail.

They say everyone loves a lover, especially the French. When the newspapers featured the tiny, well-educated teacher in jail, all because she was in love with one of her students, there was a public clamor for her release. But the authorities were adamant. Gabrielle was to stay put until Christian was located. The scheme worked well enough. Christian gave himself up and was immediately detained in a home for delinquent adolescents at the urging of his parents. Meanwhile, Gabrielle was released from jail.

Christian's parents, who had the best interests of their son at heart, proceeded to make some wrong decisions. They had their son confined to a psychiatric clinic, where he was given massive doses of tranquilizers. Kept in

isolation and continually drugged, Christian became nothing more than a zombie.

Is true love to be denied? Not on your life. In desperation, Christian escaped and fled to Gabrielle's apartment. His parents had him picked up and returned to the institution. Continual escapes brought an official warning.

The lovers were brought to the Palace of Justice and told that they must separate for good. When the warning fell on deaf ears, Christian was seized and returned to the psychiatric clinic, where he was incarcerated in a padded cell. Once more, he was heavily tranquilized. After two months of this treatment, he broke down and swore never to see Gabrielle again.

As soon as he gained his freedom, he rushed to Gabrielle's flat. Later, he fled. This time the authorities picked up Gabrielle and placed her in jail. Again, they let it be known that if Christian turned himself in, Gabrielle would be released. The cat and mouse game worked once more. Christian gave himself up and Gabrielle was released to await her trial on the original charge of removing a minor.

Three weeks later, on July 10, 1969, Gabrielle's trial commenced. Over and above her innocence or guilt, another factor dominated the proceedings. The public prosecutor was well aware that a general amnesty was to be granted to all those awaiting sentences of 12 months or less. Should Gabrielle receive such a sentence, she would have no official police record. However, anything over 12 months would incur an official police record and enable the Department of Education to prevent her from teaching in any French school for the rest of her life.

After hearing all the facts, the presiding judge gave the accused a 12 months suspended sentence and a one hundred dollar fine. Gabrielle was overjoyed, but her elation didn't last. Before she left the courtroom, the prosecutor, in an extremely unusual step in France, entered an appeal.

Gabrielle was devastated. She would have to endure

another trial and possibly jail. Her career was in jeopardy. Now weighing somewhat less than 90 pounds, she was a broken woman. The French public was divided. Was this woman breaking up a family by stealing away the Rossis' young son or was the pair truly in love and not to be denied each other, regardless of age or tradition?

A second trial was never held. Alone in her flat, Gabrielle Russier stuffed the cracks around her windows and doors with old newspapers and rolled up towels. She then swallowed a box of sleeping tablets, turned on the gas and ended her life.

The love affair was over.

DISCREET
BUT DEADLY

It takes a lot to stir up the news wise populace of Washington, D.C. The citizens of the capitol of the good old U.S.A. have seen and heard it all from the demise of Abe to the shenanigans of Nixon.

A simple murder is often relegated to the interior of the newspapers. That's why it's so surprising that a rather pedestrian murder, if any murder can be called that, captured the imagination of Washingtonians to the extent that they actually thirsted for details both titillating and gruesome.

One might believe that back in 1901, moral values were held in higher esteem than they are today. Nothing could be further from the truth. Discretion was the order of the day. Ladies in long black dresses didn't kiss and tell. They strayed from the straight and narrow, but kept it all a deep, dark secret.

James Ayres was a dashing, virile youth of 21 years, who attended Columbia University's School of Dentistry. When not drilling, he worked part time at the U.S. Census Office. Now, James was not your average, run of the mill student. He came complete with impeccable credentials. His daddy was one of the leading Republicans back in Port Austin, Mich. As a result, James occasionally dated Congressman Weeks' daughter from back home.

Sometimes, he kept company with ladies who had far more earthy qualifications. He loved to dance and he loved to partake of the demon rum.

Tall, handsome James lived at the Kenmore Hotel, which has long since come under the demolitioner's ball. The Kenmore was chock full of what James liked best - ladies. Big ones and little ones lived there. James took out Congressman Weeks' daughter, but he also had a thing with Agnes Marcy, a dance student, who naturally enough loved to dance the night away.

On the evening of May 14, James was in an exceptionally good mood. He had just received the results of his exams and he had passed with flying colors. It was to be James' last night at the Kenmore. He planned on moving to quieter premises the next day. In honor of his last night, several male friends took James out for a night on the town. An acquaintance saw him return to the Kenmore around midnight.

A lady with the singsong name of Mary Minas occupied a room next to our James. That night she was entertaining several girlfriends in a friendly game of cards, an extremely popular pastime at the turn of the century. She, too, heard James enter his room just as her card game was breaking up. Mary went to bed, only to be awakened two hours later by the loud report of three shots. Mary sat bolt upright. When questioned later, she said, "I heard him call for help and then he groaned and cried most piteously for five or ten minutes." Mary was one cool cat. She went back to sleep.

Next morning, she went down to breakfast rather surprised that somebody or other hadn't been found in the hall or staircase. She had breakfast with her friend, Mrs. Lola Bonine. Over toast and bacon, she mentioned the gunshots and the moaning. Lola wasn't as cool as Mary. She suggested they tell someone.

At that precise moment, waiter Daniel Woodhouse was passing by with a pair of four minute eggs. The girls suggested that Daniel go up and give James' door a

knock. Daniel did just that. When he received no reply, he peeked through the keyhole. There was well ventilated James, lying in his own blood on the floor. Daniel did something which Mary had felt unnecessary to do the night before. He raised the alarm.

Washington's finest dashed to James' room. Lying on the floor beside James was a Harrison and Richardson .32 calibre revolver. The barrel of the weapon was blood smeared. A woman's bloody handprint was noted on the windowsill. The handprint was not as incriminating as it would be today, since fingerprinting was not yet in use as an investigative tool.

Detectives questioned inhabitants of the Kenmore and discovered that others had heard poor James' plaintive plea for help. They did nothing. One woman in a neighboring building had heard the shots and had seen a woman in a nightrobe leave James' room via the fire escape. Thus encouraged, detectives canvassed the building immediately adjoining the Kenmore.

They came up with Thomas Baker, a government employee with the Department of Fisheries. He told police that the shots had awakened him. He looked out his window. "While watching, I saw a form come from a window on the fourth floor and descend the fire escape leading to the second floor. The woman was in her nightrobe and stocking feet. She used her left hand on the rail of the fire escape and held up her gown with her right hand. When she reached the veranda on the second floor, she re-entered the building."

The second floor was occupied exclusively by women. Police questioned them all. They were delightful ladies who wouldn't hurt a fly, but if the police promised to discreetly handle the information they gave, they would individually tell all. When their information was correlated, it was confirmed that randy James had bedded down with the vast majority of the occupants of the second floor.

Days passed, and the good citizens of the capitol had

fun attempting to pick a killer from the roster of the Kenmore's second floor. As the investigation heated up, Congressman Weeks produced a hate letter he had received from an anonymous source. The letter stated that his daughter was running around like crazy with a real ladies' man named James Ayres. The congressman hadn't taken the letter seriously until he was advised of James' untimely demise. The police also received a postcard, advising them that Mary Minas was the culprit. The missive was signed, "The Chambermaid."

All the chambermaids at the Kenmore were questioned. One of these young ladies, Eliza Gardiner, confessed that she had sent the postcard, falsely accusing Mary Minas. Now that the fat was in the fire, Eliza admitted that it was actually Mrs. Lola Bonine whom she had seen with James in his room on several occasions.

Lola was considered the most unlikely suspect. Why, you might ask. Well, the 34-year-old Lola was a mite older than the other second storey girls. Besides, she was the mother of two boys and the wife of a travelling salesman, who returned to Washington only on weekends.

Detectives called on Lola. Hubby was at her side when she admitted being in James' room when he was punctured. Lola told a heart-rending tale. James had invited her to his room as she had some bromo quinine tablets he wanted to clear up his nasty cold. Lola, obviously a night owl, picked an ungodly hour to perform her act of mercy. Lola travelled light. She slipped on a robe, but never bothered with anything else. When she walked into James' room, she couldn't help but note that James wore only an undershirt. He pointed a pistol at her and said, "Now, will you do what I want you to do?"

· According to Lola, instead of answering, she ran toward the window. She then tripped, bumped into James and the gun went off - would you believe three times? At the conclusion of her confession, Lola dramatically dropped to her knees and swore to her husband that every word was true. He believed her. The police didn't.

On Nov. 19, 1901, Lola Bonine stood trial for the murder of James Ayres. Eight years earlier, Miss Lizzie Borden was accused of chopping up her mummie and daddy. By the time she stood trial, public sympathy was on her side for no good reason other than well-bred ladies simply do not commit such despicable acts.

The same thing happened to Lola. Between May and November, public opinion crystallized in her favor. She was perceived as a woman wronged by a lecherous student. Despite the overwhelming evidence against her, the jury took only five hours to find her not guilty.

UNLUCKY WIN

What started out as exceptional good fortune for Freda and Bazil Thorne of Sydney, Australia, quickly turned into a veritable nightmare.

In June, 1960, Bazil won the first prize of £75,000 in Australia's Opera House Lottery. The prize, equivalent to $200,000 Canadian, had not had time to effect a change in the Thornes' lifestyle when their eight-year-old Graeme was kidnapped.

The little boy left home for school on the morning of July 7 to walk the two blocks from his home to where Mrs. Phyllis Smith, a family friend, normally picked him up and drove him to school. On this particular day, when Graeme didn't show up, Mrs. Smith called Freda.

Because of their recent windfall, Freda Thorne immediately anticipated the worst. She called police. A sergeant was at her home taking notes at 9:30 that same morning. While the police officer was still in her home, the phone rang. Freda answered. A man's voice said, "I have got your son, Mrs. Thorne. I want £25,000 in cash before 5 o'clock this afternoon."

Freda almost fainted. She passed the phone to Sgt. O'Shea. The man on the other end of the line continued, "You have plenty of time before five. And I'm not fooling. If I don't get the money, I'll feed him to the sharks."

O'Shea asked, "How am I going to contact you?" The man replied, "I will contact you later." Then he hung up. The sergeant noted that the caller had a slight foreign accent, which he could not identify.

Minutes later, the entire law enforcement facilities of Australia were directed to the task of apprehending the kidnapper. The police had no experience in dealing with such a crime. It was the first kidnapping case ever to take place in Australia.

Twelve hours later, the kidnapper called again. A detective picked up the receiver. "Is that you, Mr. Thorne?"

"Yes," said the detective.

"Have you got the money?"

"Yes."

"Put it into two paper bags."

"Wait a minute," stalled the detective, "I want to take your instructions down. I don't want to make a mistake." The kidnapper hung up.

Encouraged by the telephone call, police figured the kidnapper would contact them again. In the meantime, they asked the Thornes to think back for any unusual incident which might possibly be connected to the kidnapping. Mrs. Thorne remembered that about three weeks earlier a stranger had called at her home looking for a Mr. Bognor. She told the man she didn't know anyone by that name, but suggested that Mrs. Lord, who lived in an upstairs flat, might know the man.

When police questioned Mrs. Lord, she too remembered the stranger. He had knocked at her door and asked for a Mr. Bailey. Neither woman could remember anything distinctive about the man's appearance, but they did recall that he spoke with a slight foreign accent.

The hunt was on for the missing child. The main topic of conversation across the entire country was the kidnapping of little Graeme Thorne. This was a crime Australians had difficulty comprehending. They were understandably appalled.

On July 11, a police officer found some of Graeme's

belongings in an area known as French's Forest. A school bag, cap and a plastic raincoat were identified by the boy's parents. The Thornes, tired and pale, appealed to the kidnapper on television. A command post was set up in the Sydney suburb of Bondi, where the Thornes lived. Thousands of phone calls and letters were received by the police.

Of the multitude of tips received, one proved to be valuable. An electrician and his fiancée reported having seen a parked car blocking a footpath which Graeme had to take in order to meet with Mrs. Smith on the morning of his abduction. The electrician, a car buff, described the vehicle as a 1955 iridescent blue Customline Ford. A man had been standing beside the car.

There were 5000 1955 Customline Fords in the state of New South Wales. Of these, 189 were iridescent blue. Police checked out every vehicle and actually interviewed the kidnapper, who satisfactorily accounted for his time on the morning Graeme was kidnapped.

On Aug. 16, 40 days after his disappearance, Graeme Thorne's body was found by children in bushes in the Sydney suburb of Seaforth. The body was wrapped in a rug. The little boy's feet were tied and a scarf had been wrapped around his throat. Death was attributed to "a blow to the skull and asphyxiation."

The physical material found with the body came under microscopic study. Each piece revealed a part of the puzzle which was to be instrumental in apprehending the murderer. Lab men studying the rug discovered tiny particles of pink sand imbedded in the fiber. There was no such sand in the area where the body was found. The boy's clothing was also sprinkled with tiny particles of the same pink sand. After being analyzed, these particles were identified as pink mortar, commonly used on garage floors. Police deduced that Graeme's body had been in a garage before being transported to French's Forest.

Also imbedded in the rug were minute traces of plant material. Botanists informed police that these specimens

came from two types of cypress trees, one common and the other extremely rare. These two cypress trees no doubt were growing close to each other, a very uncommon phenomenon. Adhering to the rug as well were two distinct types of hair. One had come from a blonde female, the other from a Pekinese dog.

From the information they had received concerning the car, along with the physical evidence garnered at the scene of the crime, police had something concrete to work on. Teams of detectives scoured Sydney. They were looking for a house with a garage, the floor of which would be pink mortar. Outside might be parked a 1955 iridescent blue Customline Ford. Near the garage, there might be a common cypress tree as well as a rare specimen. Inside would dwell a man with a trace of an accent. His wife might be a blonde and the family pet could be a Pekinese dog.

It took weeks, but, finally, with the help of a local postman, detectives located the house at 28 Moore St. There it was; the pink mortar floor in the garage, the two cypress trees outside. Strangely, the occupants of the house didn't fit the clues. There was a reason. The present residents explained that they had only recently moved into the house. The date of their move was July 7, the very day Graeme disappeared. They informed police that the previous owner had spoken with a slight accent. His wife was a blonde and they had three children and a Pekinese dog. The previous owner's name was Stephen Leslie Bradley.

Bradley had already been interviewed as the owner of a 1955 blue Ford, but he had been questioned at his place of employment. He had been absent from work on the day of Graeme's disappearance, but he had an explanation. Bradley stated that he was home helping movers. At the time, his story was checked out and verified. His alibi was now scrutinized much more thoroughly.

The moving company's records indicated that they had arrived at the Bradley home at 11 a.m., hours after the

abduction. Further investigation revealed that Bradley was a Hungarian, which accounted for his slight but obvious accent.

Detectives raced to Bradley's new residence in Manley. They were one day too late. The family had moved again, this time to England. They had sailed from Freemantle that very morning on the liner *Himalaya*. The ship had a scheduled stopover in Colombo, Ceylon. It was there that Bradley was picked up, charged with murder and returned to Australia to stand trial.

Bradley confessed, but swore that his victim had suffocated by accident. His story didn't sit well with the jury. Graeme's hands had not been tied, which would have enabled him to remove the scarf from around his neck. The boy had also received a blow to the head severe enough to fracture his skull.

Moving company workmen told police that Bradley had helped them move his possessions on the day of the kidnapping. He had kept the garage door locked while they worked. Detectives believed that Graeme Thorne's body was lying on the pink mortar floor in the locked garage that morning.

An old roll of film found by police in the Bradleys' garbage was developed and presented as evidence. There was a photo of a picnic, which clearly depicted the Bradley family sitting on a rug - the very rug used to wrap the body of Graeme Thorne.

Stephen Leslie Bradley, whose real name was Stefan Lazlo Baranyay, was found guilty of murder and sentenced to life imprisonment.

THE LAST DUEL

This is the story of a man who stood trial for murder in Ontario and returned to the very same courtroom years later as a judge.

In the 1830s, Perth, Ont. was quite unlike other frontier towns of Canada. Perth had been settled around 1816 through land grants. It became home to members of disbanded regiments who had fought in the Napoleonic wars. At the same time, dirt poor Scottish and Irish immigrants arrived in the area and were consigned to the bottom rung of the social ladder. For the following 15 years, the town developed a class structure which was just as stringent as the one they had left back home.

Robert Lyon was probably the most eligible single young man in town. Tall, handsome, athletic Robert, 19, was the son of a wealthy, socially prominent family. He was studying law, as was his friend Henry Lelievre, the son of a French frigate captain.

Another of Lyon's close friends was John Wilson. Today, we would say John came from the wrong side of the tracks. In reality, his parents were honest, hard-working farmers, who had made many sacrifices to enable their son to study law.

The scenario, which was to find a place in the history of our country, began innocently enough.

In 1833, Lyon and Wilson were dispatched by their respective law firms to Ottawa, then called Bytown, on business. The two law students met often, had a few drinks and, like young men everywhere, talked about the girls back home. They knew many girls in common. Wilson had once squired Elizabeth Hughes, who had recently arrived in Perth from England to teach school. Elizabeth was alone in the world, having lost her father to a bout of cholera on the way over. She was a good-looking girl and had several of the town boys doing flip flops over her affections.

Lyon had no way of knowing that Wilson no longer cared for Elizabeth. He had fallen hard for another Perth girl, pretty Joanne Lees. Lyon himself had no sincere interest in Elizabeth, as he was engaged to still another Perth belle, Caroline Thom.

Now, if you follow all this, fine. If not, it is enough to know that as these two young law students from such different backgrounds chatted over drinks, neither was particularly concerned with the affections of Elizabeth Hughes.

Lyon decided to have a bit of fun at Wilson's expense. He told Wilson that Elizabeth was in the habit of "allowing men to indulge in unbecoming freedoms." He told Wilson that their mutual friend, Henry Lelievre, "had sat alongside her with his arms about her in a position which no woman of spirit would permit."

Folks, back in 1833, those were fighting words. However, they didn't have the desired effect because Wilson had shifted his affections to Miss Lees.

John Wilson then did a rather silly thing. He sat down and wrote a letter to Elizabeth's guardian, a Mr. Acland. He quoted Lyon word for word. Later, Wilson revealed that he wrote the letter to finally end his relationship with Elizabeth. Acland was a blabbermouth. He spread the word that Robert Lyon had made "a dishonorable remark about an unprotected female."

Lyon returned from Bytown to find half of Perth giving

him the cold shoulder. What a cad to have said such things about a defenceless woman. Even his betrothed, Caroline, wouldn't have anything to do with him. Lyon checked with Lelievre, who was furious at Wilson for writing such a letter. Lyon went looking for John Wilson.

Robert Lyon and John Wilson met in front of Perth's courthouse on June 6 that summer of 1833. Lyon didn't waste time with formalities. Did Wilson write that letter? Wilson readily admitted that he had, but before he could offer any explanation, Lyon hauled off and punched him in the face. Lyon then turned, shouting over his shoulder, "You're a damn lying scoundrel, Sir, and I'll treat you as such every time I meet you."

Wilson realized that to do nothing about the insult would be tantamount to ostracism in Perth. He issued a duelling challenge to Lyon, firmly believing that Lyon would accept his explanation of why he had written the letter. Initially, Lyon did show an inclination to seek a peaceful solution but, under the urging of Lelievre, became convinced the dispute could only be solved on the field of honor. Lyon was a crack shot, while Wilson had probably only held a gun in his hands once or twice in his life.

The time and place for the duel was set. It was drizzling rain at 6 p.m. on June 13, 1833, when the assembled entourage walked about one mile outside Perth to a plowed field. The locale was carefully chosen to be outside the jurisdiction of the local sheriff, whom both men knew well. Lyon's second was Henry Lelievre. Wilson was seconded by Simon Robertson. Official medical representation for the event was Dr. William Hamilton.

At the count of five, both men fired. Wilson missed. Lyon's bullet barely creased Wilson's skull. Both men were unhurt. Wilson was to state later that at this point he was surprised to be alive. It was the custom of the time that double misses called for apologies all around and that was that. However, Lyon and Lelievre wouldn't hear of calling off the duel in midstream, so to speak.

The duelists reloaded. As Wilson stood waiting for the signal, he noted that a plowed furrow connected him to his adversary in a perfectly straight line. He used it as a point of reference to aim. Wilson shifted his weight slightly, turned his head away and fired on signal. Lyon fell to the ground. The fluke shot had pierced his lungs. He was taken to a nearby home, where he died within minutes. Wilson stood unharmed, amazed at his accuracy and thankful to be alive.

Henry Lelievre left Perth immediately after the shooting and is variously reported to have spent the rest of his life in the U.S. or Australia.

Wilson and Robertson turned themselves in to the authorities. Wilson was charged with murder, while Robertson was charged with being an accessory.

The two men stood trial in Brockville. Both took the witness stand in their own defence and made impassioned pleas, stressing that at no time did they have any malice toward Lyon. They also pointed out that during the events leading up to the duel, they had made repeated attempts to have the whole thing called off. The jury found both defendants not guilty.

John Wilson attempted to pick up the remnants of his life after his acquittal. He tried to renew his relationship with Joanne Lees, but her parents would not let their daughter have anything to do with someone who had been dragged through such a scandal. Wilson moved to London, but kept in contact with Elizabeth Hughes. Following a script which would be unbelievable if written in Hollywood, he returned to Perth two years later and married her.

Wilson went on to have a distinguished legal and political career. In 1847, he became a member of parliament, succeeding William Draper, who had been the prosecuting attorney at his murder trial 14 years previously. In 1863, Wilson was appointed a judge of the Supreme Court of Ontario. Ironically, the first case he presided over was in the very same Brockville courthouse where he had stood

accused of murder 30 years earlier.

John Wilson's public life was successful, but not so his private life. It is said that the former Elizabeth Hughes was an inconsiderate nagging wife. John Wilson died in London in 1869. Elizabeth outlived her husband by many years. She died in 1904 in Toronto at age 93.

If you are ever visiting Perth, you might enjoy a walk through the local park. It has the fitting name of Last Duel Park to commemorate the last duel ever fought in Canada.

SCHEMING FEMALE

Judith Morton was devious and utterly without morals. She was also very beautiful. We have to go back over 150 years to rural England to examine exactly what made Judith tick, but I think you will agree the trip is well worth the effort.

There were many men in the charming Judith's life, but for the time being we need only concern ourselves with three - Charles Harpur, Robert Masters, and Richard Penson. All three were the sons of farmers living in Westmorland County. Judith's parents were also farmers and were by far the most prosperous in the area.

The three young men, who knew each other well, had one thing in common. They were hopelessly in love with gorgeous Judith. Now Judith was not your average farmer's daughter. She was well aware of her many attributes and knew how to keep Charles, Robert and Richard hovering over her as a moths to a candle.

Richard, although lacking in material wealth, felt certain that one day Judith would be his wife. He firmly believed that she didn't take her other two suitors all that seriously. That's why he was devastated when he asked the 17-year-old beauty for her hand in marriage and received the equivalent of today's "No way" as an answer. Judith explained that the man whose bed she

would someday share would have to be a man of substance.

Richard was so distraught that he left Westmorland County for London, where he immediately began studies leading to the honorable profession of attorney at law. Studious Richard achieved his goal. Five years later, he returned to Westmorland a full-fledged lawyer. He would show Judith. If he didn't have wealth yet, it would only be a matter of time.

Richard found the now 22-year-old Judith more beautiful and charming than ever. Her father had recently died, which left her a comfortable fortune to augment her many physical attractions. Alas, she broke the bad news to him. She was in love with someone else. That someone was Robert Masters, who Richard knew very well and didn't much like. Downcast and dejected and in general fed up, Richard returned to London, where he obtained employment with the law firm to which he had been articled.

Shortly after Richard returned to London, he read in the newspaper that Robert Masters had been murdered. The other angle of Judith's private triangle, Charles Harpur, was deeply involved. Evidently, Harpur had travelled to America, made a small fortune and, like Richard, had returned to seek Judith as his bride. By the time he arrived in Westmorland, Judith was engaged to marry Robert Masters. Evidently, the two men had a heated argument in front of witnesses. Blows were exchanged. A few days later, Masters' body was found in a clearing in nearby Gilgraith Forest. He had been shot directly through the heart. His gold watch and money were missing.

Initially, it was thought that a transient had done poor Masters in for his valuables, but this theory was soon dismissed. A farmer, James Blundell, told authorities that he had been walking through Gilgraith Forest when he heard a pistol shot. He then saw a young man dashing out of the woods, pistol in hand. The moon was full. Blundell

recognized Charles Harpur, whom he knew well. In a flash, Harpur dashed into thick brush. Next day, Robert Masters' body was found near that very spot. Based on Blundell's story, Harpur was arrested and taken into custody.

In London, Richard Penson shook his head. True, Harpur had always been a rival for Judith's affections, but nevertheless he liked the man and was upset to learn that he was in such serious trouble.

Two days later, who should walk into Richard's law office but the beautiful Judith Morton. Nothing had changed. Richard loved her more than ever. But Judith was there for a reason. First, she detailed all the known facts to Richard and asked if Harpur had a chance of acquittal. Richard sadly related that he didn't have a snowball's chance in Hades of gaining an acquittal. It was then that Judith revealed, "I killed Robert Masters. That's what I have really come to tell you."

Judith went on to explain that Harpur had arrived home from America. She was engaged to Masters, but had always been in love with Harpur. Quick as a bunny, she broke off her engagement to Masters and became engaged to Harpur. Masters didn't take the jilting well. He swore that unless she changed her mind, he would show Harpur the love letters she had written to him three years earlier when she was an active 19-year-old. The letters were real sizzlers.

Judith appealed to Masters' honor and begged him to return the sexually incriminating letters. Masters agreed, under one condition. He would have one last opportunity to convince her of the error of her ways. Judith and Masters arranged to meet in Gilgraith Forest. They met and argued. Masters mocked Judith and read aloud one of the juicier portions of her letters. In desperation, she grabbed for the incriminating letter. There was a struggle. Her hand closed on a pistol she had been carrying for protection. A shot was fired. Masters lay dead at her feet.

For a short while, Judith could only stare at her former lover. Then the instinct of self-preservation took over. She snatched Robert's gold watch and money from his body. As she did so, she heard a voice and looked up to see Charles Harpur standing there. Harpur had called at the Morton home and was told that Judith was taking a walk towards Gilgraith Forest. Unaware of her meeting with Masters, he had gone looking for her. Harpur swore to Judith that he wouldn't tell a soul what he had witnessed. Now, even though he faced execution for the murder of Robert Masters, he had told no one that Judith was the killer.

Judith implored Richard to save Harpur's life. There was an added startling turn of events. Harpur, despite his loyalty to Judith, now felt that even if he escaped the hangman's noose, he could never marry her. Plain and simple, he was no longer in love. Judith, who was a quick thinker on her feet, asked, "Do you still love me, Richard?" When she received an affirmative reply, Judith went on to say that if Richard could somehow save Harpur and keep her out of the entire mess, she would be very receptive to becoming his wife.

Richard had been enthralled with Judith since childhood. Now she was within his reach. He agreed to attempt to obtain an acquittal using every legal tactic available. Judith then came up with a tricky piece of footwork, "Let's frame James Blundell." For starters, she gave Masters' gold watch to Richard.

In due course, Harpur was tried for murder. The main prosecution witness, James Blundell, had a rough time. Defence counsel produced one Thomas Aldous, the owner of a supposedly reputable pawnbroker's establishment in London. He swore that the murdered man's watch had been pawned by none other than the chief prosecution witness, James Blundell. Harpur was acquitted and the protesting was Blundell charged with murder. Shortly after the trial, the bogus pawnbroker, Aldous, was paid off by Richard for his trouble.

Richard and Judith had agreed to skip to America right after the trial. Richard realized that the phony scenario he had concocted would not stand up for long. He and Judith had arranged to meet at a hotel in London. When Richard arrived, there was a note waiting for him. "Thanks a million for what you have done. I am confident that with your astuteness you will see that no harm comes to poor Blundell. I will write you in a few days. Judith."

Upon investigation, Richard found out that both Judith and Harpur had disappeared. Meanwhile, James Blundell had retained a reputable Liverpool law firm to handle his case. They quickly proved that their client was at his home at the exact time he was supposed to have pawned the dead man's watch in London. When it was established that pawnbroker Aldous was a phony, authorities quickly issued a warrant for the arrest of Richard Penson and Charles Harpur.

There appeared to be little hope of apprehending the fugitives. It was assumed that Harpur had returned to America. It was also discovered that Richard had booked passage for himself and Judith from Liverpool to Boston. In those long ago days there was no way to contact a ship at sea. Once in America, fugitives from England were free forever from facing the consequences of their foul deeds back home. The murder was listed as unsolved.

What really happened to our three main characters? Richard, crushed at Judith's deceitful ways, changed his name and lived in hiding in London. A year after the trial, a loyal friend back in Westmorland County forwarded him a letter sent by Judith from America. It read, "You were a poor fool, Richard. My husband and I are now safe and sound in the land of liberty, far beyond all possible pursuit. Charles Harpur is my second husband. I was married to him the day after Robert Masters, my first husband, was killed. Judith."

Judith loved to rub salt in the wounds. Richard now realized that Harpur had killed Masters at Judith's urging.

Richard hit the bottle hard after that and ended his days in a London workhouse. When he died, authorities found a clipping from an American newspaper on his body:

"Mr. Charles Harpur, thinking his friend, Mr. William Harrison of Philadelphia, was seeing too much of his wife Judith, challenged him to a duel. The duel proved fatal to Mr. Harpur. Mrs. Harpur married Mr. Harrison on Friday, exactly 18 days after her husband's death."

That Judith was up to her old tricks. Although rumors abound, the remaining years of her life are not documented.

DEADLOCKED JURY

Unfortunately, there are no statistics on the greatest number of times one man has stood trial for a single murder. Quite possibly, John Paris of Truro, Nova Scotia holds the record.

It happened on a pleasant summer day in 1921. Little Sadie McAuley was nine years old that August 2 when she and her friend, 11-year-old Hattie Levigne, left her Clarence St. home in Saint John, N.B. to pick raspberries. Hattie's dad had told her there were lots of plump berries just waiting to be picked near Riverside Park.

Away the two little friends went, carrying empty jars. They located the berry bushes, and were soon joined by a man who helped Sadie with her picking. The stranger claimed that there were plenty of berries over a fence down the hill a bit. Sadie accompanied the man.

After she was out of Hattie's view, Hattie called to her friend, but received no reply. She saw some local men working on the road nearby and told one of them she couldn't find Sadie. No one paid much attention. Hattie went down the hill, called to her friend one last time, then went home and told her mother. A few of the Levigne kids searched for Sadie during the afternoon. When they couldn't find the missing child, Sadie's mother called police.

Police officers and volunteers combed the area for Sadie. Next day, the search intensified without concrete results. Police questioned the men working on nearby Douglas Ave. They remembered seeing a rather suspicious looking man hanging around the previous day. He was wearing khaki pants, but the men could add little more. A week passed. Still no sign of Sadie.

On Aug. 9, James Kimball, 13, went picking berries at Riverside Park. He found that he couldn't quite reach some choice berries high up on the tall canes. James climbed onto a large rock and reached out. Suddenly the rock slipped over. James lost his balance and tumbled to the ground. He stared transfixed at what he had uncovered when the rock moved. There was no doubting it; he had stumbled upon the body of Sadie McAuley.

Soon the hillside was swarming with Saint John's finest. It seemed impossible that they had walked through the area several times without discovering the body. Upon closer examination it was revealed that someone had lifted a large rock out of the ground and placed the little girl's body in the resulting cavity. The killer had covered the body with small stones before placing the large rock on top of the heap. The body had been efficiently and completely concealed. An autopsy indicated that Sadie had been raped and choked to death.

The murder of the little girl, considered one of the most revolting in the history of New Brunswick, angered the populace. A $500 reward was offered by the city of Saint John for information leading to the conviction of the guilty party. This amount, not an inconsiderable sum in 1921, was later doubled to $1000.

Hattie Levigne told police that the man who had helped them pick berries had worn khaki pants, a brown coat, had long black hair and a very dark complexion. She was certain she would know the man if she saw him again.

The hunt was on. Who was the extremely dark man who raped a nine-year-old child in broad daylight and disappeared? The search for the wanted man was the

most extensive ever conducted in New Brunswick. Several men were arrested, only to be released later when their innocence was proven beyond a doubt.

A month after the murder, Bun Humphrey, an unsavory character and well-known vagrant around Saint John, went to the police with an amazing story. He knew who had killed Sadie McAuley. According to Humphrey, he had rowed John Paris, a native of Truro, N.S., across the Saint John River around 11 a.m. on Aug. 2. They landed near Riverside Park. The following morning, Humphrey declared that he had again met Paris, who once more asked to be rowed across the river to a point near Riverside Park. During this trip, Paris told Humphrey that he had murdered Sadie and wanted some help with burying the body. Humphrey claimed that he would have no part of the proposition.

Because Humphrey's character left a lot to be desired, the police hesitated to act. However, when one John Mac-Donald came forward and told police that Humphrey had related the same story to him earlier, they had to take Humphrey's tale seriously. MacDonald added that he had also seen a very dark man, whom he took to be a mulatto, hanging around Riverside Park on Aug. 2.

Saint John police travelled to Truro, arrested Paris and brought him back to St. John, where he was charged with murder. Who was this man police claimed was a rapist and killer? John Paris was a 28-year-old native of Truro and a member of the substantial black community residing in the Nova Scotia town at the time. Although he couldn't read or write, he was an intelligent, good-looking man who made his living as a laborer. He often travelled to other Maritime towns to obtain work. At the time of the murder, he had an apartment in Saint John at 181 Water St.

John Paris was in big trouble. On Sept. 28, 1921, he stood trial for the murder of Sadie McAuley. Very quickly, the Crown established through witnesses that Paris had been in Saint John on the day of the murder.

Alfred Byers was visiting his sister, Bertha Croft, that day and claims he chatted with Paris. Mrs. Croft's apartment was in the same building as Paris'. She too claimed she saw the accused man. Bill Sweet stated that he talked to Paris in Saint John on Aug. 2. Ernest Campbell testified that he saw Paris on Aug. 3 in the city. Most important of all, Bun Humphrey vehemently stated that he was asked by Paris to assist in the covering up of the crime. If Humphrey and the rest were to be believed, Paris was definitely guilty.

There was one fly in the prosecution's case. Hattie Levigne said, "No, he isn't the man in the park picking berries with Sadie and me."

Paris' defense was simple enough. He maintained he was not in Saint John at the time of the murder. Humphrey was lying in order to claim the $1000 reward and the rest were mistaken about the dates. Defence counsel produced several witnesses from Truro, who swore that Paris was in Truro at the critical time and could not possibly be the murderer.

Stanley Nicholas stated that Paris was in his garage on Aug. 2. Several garage employees verified their boss' testimony. Other Truro natives claimed they either saw or had conversations with Paris on Aug. 2 in Truro. Still others gave strong evidence that Paris left Saint John on July 23 and returned on Aug. 4, two days after the murder. To solidify their case, the defence produced the chief of police of Truro, John W. Fraser. He testified that while investigating a theft on Aug. 2, he had stopped and chatted with John Paris.

There the evidence stood. One group of witnesses were wrong and the other correct. Swaying in the balance was the life of John Paris. The jury retired to deliberate, but reappeared, hopelessly deadlocked. The 12 member jury was in favor of conviction by a vote of seven to five. They were dismissed and a second trial was ordered.

On Nov. 22, 1921, Paris stood accused of murder once more. The same witnesses were paraded to the stand. If

ever the adversary system was placed under a microscope,
this was the time. The trial took on the aspect of an
athletic event - Saint John, N.B. versus Truro, N.S. The
centre of attraction, John Paris, gave evidence for a full
10 hours without once losing his composure or giving con-
flicting evidence.

The Truro team had increased its roster to include
several more citizens who had spoken to Paris in Truro on
the crucial day. One witness, James McNaught of the
Eastern Hat and Cap Co., testified that Paris had signed
a receipt with an X on Aug. 2. Evidently, on that day
Paris had been paid 90 cents by the hat company and
McNaught had Paris sign a receipt for the money.

Prosecution attorneys attempted to find holes in the
defence's claims. For example, when one witness, Norman
Green, swore he saw Paris walking on the streets of
Truro by the light of the full moon, the prosecution attorney quickly produced an almanac which indicated the
moon had not risen until the wee hours of the following
morning.

In summing up, the Crown conceded that Paris left
Saint John on July 23, but theorized that he returned on
Aug. 1, went back to Truro on the night of Aug.
3, and returned to Saint John on Aug. 4. To accept this
theory, the jury had to dismiss all the witnesses who
swore they saw Paris in the Nova Scotia town on Aug. 2.

The jury returned a guilty verdict. Paris was sentenced
to hang on March 30, 1922. An appeal was launched on
the technicality that for a few minutes during the trial
Paris had not been in the courtroom. An appellate court
felt this was enough to invalidate the trial.

On April 25, 1922, Paris stood trial for the third time.
Still more witnesses were produced from Truro. Saint
John countered with new witnesses as well. After close to
10 hours deliberation, the jury returned hopelessly deadlocked at seven to five for conviction.

Trial number four commenced on July 4, 1922. All the
same witnesses were called. All gave the same evidence,

with one exception. Hattie Levigne now said she thought John Paris might be the man who helped her and Sadie pick berries. After 46 hours of deliberation, the jury returned deadlocked at ten for conviction and two for acquittal.

Trial number five, which may very well be a record for one man standing trial for one murder, began on Sept. 26, 1922. Once more, Hattie Levigne stated, "In my judgment and belief, that is the man." Her words seemed to fall on deaf ears. Indeed, all of the testimony, some of it repeated for the fifth time, had become too well known. The testimony had lost all semblance of the dramatic. The jury faced the same dilemma as the previous four juries - who to believe. Like their predecessors, they simply didn't know. They returned from the jury room deadlocked nine for acquittal, three for conviction.

Two weeks after the fifth trial, Attorney General J. P. Byrne indicated that there would be no further action against Paris. In total, the five juries had voted 39 to 21 for conviction. The Crown insisted on the right to a sixth trial if it saw fit. Paris was made to post a $1000 bond guaranteeing his appearance should the charge against him ever be revived. It never was.

After posting bond, John Paris walked out of the court-room a free man. The murder of Sadie McAuley has never been solved.

THE BREAKING POINT

When is enough enough?

Jane Stafford of Nova Scotia reached her breaking point on March 11, 1982, when she took a shotgun and blew her husband's head off. Years of abuse were behind that blast. With one squeeze of the trigger, Jane crystallized the dilemma of thousands of abused women across Canada.

In the U.S., Francine Hughes reached her breaking point and, in so doing, dramatically brought the plight of abused women to the attention of the American public.

Francine had already dropped out of school when she met Mickey Hughes. The scenario has been repeated thousands of times in small town America. Boy meets girl. Wedding bells. Children, prosperity and happiness. Some call it the American Dream. But something went wrong. That something was Mickey Hughes.

Francine and Mickey were married on Nov. 4, 1963 in Dansville, Michigan, population 500. She was 16, he was 18.

It started out gradually. A month after the wedding, Mickey complained that Francine's clothing was provocative. Voices were raised. Mickey destroyed what he felt were the offending garments. Later, he apologized. It was the first of many apologies which Francine would hear for the next 13 years. Over those years, Mickey would be

employed only sporadically.

The Hughes family was poor, often relying on family and friends to assist them through dry unemployment spells. They moved often when unable to meet the monthly rent.

Francine Hughes soon learned that the flamboyant, rather handsome boy she had married had strange personal standards. Any attempt to improve her appearance with an item of inexpensive clothing sent Mickey into a rage. According to him, cosmetics were only for whores. At first, if Francine glanced at a male stranger, Mickey would reprimand her sternly. As time went on, the reprimands gradually developed into punches to her face. It got so Francine was living in fear - fear that her cooking wasn't up to Mickey's standards, that her clothing was too provocative, that a glance at a stranger would bring a punch to the face. Always, there would be tearful apologies.

Interspersed with Francine's nightmarish existence were short periods of tranquility when Mickey would behave with a semblance of normality. These short periods didn't last. After severe beatings, Francine would leave and travel the short distance to her family's home in Jackson. Protestations of love always lured her back to Mickey's side.

Six months after their wedding, Francine became pregnant. In the next six years, she had four children; Christy, Jimmy, Dana and Nicky. The children became accustomed to hearing their parents quarrel and fight. Sometimes Mickey ordered them from the room. At other times, completely out of control, he humiliated Francine and administered severe beatings to her in front of the children.

Francine and her children were literally destitute. Because of Mickey's lack of employment and his penchant for beer, money in the Hughes' household was non-existent. The Hughes family went hungry. In order to obtain welfare, Francine divorced Mickey. In this one bold, inde-

pendent move, she solved one problem, but not the other. The need for food and shelter were partially alleviated, but Mickey called the divorce documents nothing more than pieces of paper. As far as he was concerned, he was still married. The beatings grew in intensity.

Sometimes the beatings drew the attention of other people. Occasionally, Mickey's own family called the police. A few times, Mickey couldn't control himself and took a swing at a police officer. On these occasions he was arrested and taken away. Always, he came back. The beatings continued.

After 10 years of living in her personal hell, conditions grew worse. Often Francine would flee the house, only to have Mickey pursue her outside. Sometimes he ran after her with a knife. Most of the time, Francine's body was bruised and her eyes black. The thought of running away obsessed her.

Francine loved her children and couldn't leave them. After a beating, Mickey was quick to remind her that if she ran away he would track her down and kill her. He claimed he didn't care if he lived or died. Francine believed every word.

To temporarily escape her horrendous domestic life and to satisfy a deep thirst for knowledge, Francine returned to school. Mickey objected strenuously, but there was little he could do about it.

On March 9, 1977, Francine returned home from school at mid-day. Mickey was already drunk. Nothing Francine said or did satisfied the man. As his rage grew, he ordered the children out of the house. Then he demanded that Francine quit school. To emphasize his point, he proceeded to destroy her notebooks and textbooks page by page. He forced Francine to take the torn books outside and burn them in a trashcan.

Mickey proceeded to punch Francine in the face and choke her with his bare hands until she was almost unconscious. In a daze, Francine cleaned up the torn pages, many of which held weeks of her hard work, and

threw them in the trashcan. She lit the paper and watched as the flames consumed her broken dreams. When she returned indoors, Mickey hit her once more. This time, as he held her on the floor, he poured beer over her head.

Francine washed and changed her clothes. As she did so, she told her eldest daughter, Christy, to flee to her grandparents' house and call the police. Twenty minutes later, the police arrived. They lectured Mickey and left. The visit meant little more to Francine than a momentary respite. She had gone through this scenario many times before.

Francine warmed T.V. dinners for her children, who had not eaten all that day. The children sat at the table. Mickey, with one swipe, sent all the food tumbling to the floor. As he yelled at the children to leave the room, he forced Francine to her knees and pushed her head into the mess on the floor. He then ordered her to clean it up.

After treating his wife worse than an animal, Mickey was far from through. He demanded that Francine prepare a meal for him. After he ate alone in his bedroom, he forced his wife to have sex. Satiated, Mickey fell asleep.

Francine Hughes sat down with her four children. According to her evidence later given in court, she decided to leave and never return to the house, which held so many bitter memories. "I decided there wouldn't be anything to come back to. I was going to burn everything," she said.

Francine directed her children outside into their car. In what she later described as a daze, she retrieved a can of gasoline from the garage and sprinkled it on the floor surrounding her snoring husband. A match set the house on fire. Francine watched the flames as she and her children sped away. She drove directly to the Ingham County Jail and, with the help of her eldest daughter Christy, told the police what she had done. Mickey Hughes would torment her no longer.

Francine was arrested and charged with murder. If found guilty, she would be sentenced to life imprisonment. Her court-appointed lawyer was in a dilemma. He was convinced that Mickey Hughes would have eventually killed Francine had she not killed him first. However, he still could not plead self-defence for his client. Like Jane Stafford's husband Billy in Nova Scotia, Mickey was asleep at the time he was killed. A self-defence plea is only effective if death is inflicted at the time the defendant is being attacked.

On Oct. 17, 1977, Francine Hughes stood trial for her ex-husband's murder. Defence counsel pleaded temporary insanity, claiming that Francine had been in a dazed state when she struck the fatal match. The prosecution maintained that Francine knew what she was doing and had committed a premeditated crime by murdering Mickey Hughes while he slept.

The trial concluded on Nov. 4, the fourteenth anniversary of Francine and Mickey's wedding. The verdict - not guilty by reason of temporary insanity.

Francine Hughes was set free and became the focal point of abused women throughout the United States. In 1986, a television drama called *The Burning Bed*, in which Farrah Fawcett portrayed the tormented Francine Hughes, received one of the highest ratings of any American television broadcast that year.

Since her widely-publicized trial, Francine has done everything in her power to live a normal life. She works and lives with her children in Michigan.

THE OREGON TRAIL

Back at the turn of the century, when good men and women were heading west to clear land, plant crops and all that sort of thing, they sometimes took time off from their labors to murder each other.

Norman Williams was a virile toiler of the soil, who hailed from Shelby County, Iowa. Norm never had time for marriage. He was far too busy tending the crops and playing the field. No question about it, Norm was a ladies' man through and through.

Now, it so happened that adjoining Norm's spread was the Nesbitt farm. Stud that he was, 50-year-old Norm couldn't help but notice that young Alma Nesbitt had grown up to be a beautiful young lady. As a fruit farmer looks at a plum, Norm figured that, at 20 years of age, Alma was ripe for picking.

Alma's mother, Louisa Nesbitt, had other ideas. There was no way the old rascal was going to lay his hands on her one and only daughter. That's the way things stood when Norm gave up. What the heck, he wasn't going to pine away for Alma when the adventurous west beckoned with its wild, wild women and all.

Norm took off for Oregon. He settled in the Hood River Valley on one hundred acres of virgin land. Norm did well in a minor way as a farmer. He built a house of sorts and

worked like a dog, but there was one thing missing from his life. There were no wild women. Norm longed for female company, in particular that tasty little morsel he had left back home.

Our boy started a letter campaign. He wrote to Alma, he wrote to Mrs. Nesbitt. They had misinterpreted his honorable intentions. It took Norm five years, but in the end he convinced the Nesbitts that he wasn't such a bad guy after all.

Alma, now a firm 25, headed west. Her letters to her mother were newsy and cheerful. She had filed a homesteader's claim and been granted 160 acres right next to Norm Williams' farm. Things looked so good, Mrs. Nesbitt joined her daughter. She, too, was suitably impressed and wrote to her son George back in Iowa that, while life was hard, she was pleased with the concern Norm Williams showed for her and Alma. George got the impression that Norm and Alma might one day be husband and wife.

Matters then took a diametrically opposite turn. On March 8, 1900, George received a letter from his mother. She and Alma were returning to Iowa. The letter was written from a rooming house in Portland. Then, nothing. No mail. No Alma and no Mama.

George wrote Norm and received a vague reply, hinting that Alma had run off with another man. George didn't know what to do. He really expected his mother and sister to show up any day. When months passed, he sent off letters to anyone in Oregon who might shed light on the disappearance. No one was overly concerned.

After four years of frustration, George took the bull by the horns, so to speak, and made the tedious trip from Iowa to Oregon. Tenacious George located Norm's farm. It was deserted. Not one to be easily discouraged, George looked around the spread for signs that the earth had been disturbed. When he found such a spot in the henhouse, he commenced digging. Six feet down, he discovered an old, stained sack. Adhering to the sack were

several hairs. Charcoal ashes were also extracted from the hole.

That was good enough for George. He hightailed it over to Waco County's district attorney Frank Menefee and told his story much as we have related it here. George Nesbitt was convinced that his mother and sister had been murdered and their bodies burned. All he had to back up his allegations was an old sack, a few hairs and some ashes. But that was sufficient for Menefee to call in Sheriff F. C. Sexton to investigate.

Sexton dug up the Williams' henhouse. Other than some ashes, he found absolutely nothing. He then decided to pick up the missing women's trail. He travelled to Portland and located the rooming house from which Mrs. Nesbitt had written the letter to George.

The owner of the rooming house remembered the mother and daughter team. He even recalled that on the night the Nesbitt's left his house, they had had an argument with a man. He had heard the muffled conversation through walls, and was able to make out the word "property", but little else.

Norm Williams was easily located working at a sawmill in Bellingham, Washington, some 300 miles away. He proved to be a loveable old codger. When faced with the gunnysack, he almost laughed. Sure, the stains could be blood - animal blood. Same with the hairs. What was more common on a farm? As for the ashes, Norm had a ready explanation. The henhouse was built on the site of an old outhouse. Before building, Norm had filled in the area with the remains of a trash fire.

No one was more distressed about Alma's disappearance than Norm. He remembered well her last visit to his farm when she told him she was leaving to marry a younger man. She asked him for a lift to the Hood River railroad station, so she and her mother could catch the train back to Portland. Norm added that he had hired a rig at the Fashion Livery Stables to take the pair into Hood River. The Sheriff checked out this story and, sure enough, the

livery stable had a record of the four-year-old transaction.

Norm's past was thoroughly investigated. Detectives found out that Norm and Alma had married two months after she arrived from Iowa. What's more, Norm had another wife in Dufar, Ore., whom he had deserted without benefit of divorce.

Now hot to trot, detectives kept probing. They discovered that no outhouse had existed where George had dug up the stained sack. Norm had built the henhouse after the Nesbitts disappeared. They also found a laborer who remembered a strange incident which had occurred four years earlier. Norm had him pile stumps and trees on top of a huge mound of gunny sacks containing oats. The man was amazed when Norm set the whole kit and kaboodle on fire. It was the hottest, most intense blaze the man had ever witnessed.

Investigators were sure that the rooming house proprietor had heard Norm and the Nesbitts arguing over property, especially when they discovered that Alma's property was valued much higher than Norm's. From homestead records on file in Portland, it was learned that Norm had shown up with a document dated after Alma's disappearance, signed by her, deeding her 160 acres to him. The document proved to be a forgery.

The plot was thickening and the noose was getting closer to Norm's neck. One must remember that in 1904 forensic science was not what it is today. However, using the most modern methods at their disposal, doctors were able to state definitely that the stains on the gunnysack were human blood. What's more, the hair was human hair which had been pulled from the heads of persons still alive. Under a microscope, roots were observed clinging to the hairs. After death, hair comes away without roots.

District Attorney Menefee knew he had a strong circumstantial case, but it would help if he had a body. The earth on the Williams' farm was put through a sieve, but not as much as one human toenail was found. Norm was guilty of bigamy, Norm was guilty of forgery, and there

was no doubt about it — Norm was guilty of murder, bodies or no bodies. Menefee decided to go to trial.

Defence attorneys called no witnesses, but based their entire case on the premise that no jury would convict a man solely on the evidence of an old stained gunnysack, a few hairs and some ashes. They were wrong.

Norman Williams was hanged on the gallows for the murder of Alma Nesbitt. No bodies were ever found, and Norm never confessed.

MYSTERY BOY

Everyone loves a good mystery. Was Anastasia executed with the rest of her family? Whatever became of the crew of the *Mary Celeste*? Not as well known as these mysteries, but nevertheless just as puzzling, is the tale of Kaspar Hauser.

In May, 1828, a police officer in Nurenberg, Germany, picked up a youth off the streets of the city. The boy was different in many ways. He stammered, but didn't appear to have the ability to talk. When questioned by the officer, the youth cowered, as if associating speech with some sort of abuse. The boy's hair and body were filthy and his clothing was homemade shapeless rags. His feet were encased in crude, cracked shoes made of wood and leather.

The skinny lad was taken to a police station. He was stripped of his clothing and made to bathe. Sewn into the lining of his jacket, police found a note dated 16 years previously. It read, "I am a poor girl and cannot look after my child. His name is Kaspar Hauser. He has already been baptized. His father is dead. He was a soldier. When he is 16 years old, I beg of you to send him to Nurenberg to the Sixth Cavalry Regiment. His father used to belong to it."

The unsigned letter was examined and proved to be

fraudulent. The ink on the letter was of a type currently in use and the writing had not faded, as it surely would have after 16 years.

A doctor examined the boy, who was now known as Kaspar Hauser, and confirmed that he was about 16 years old. He also stated that Kaspar had never been taught to speak. There was some doubt if he had walked a great deal, if at all. He stumbled forward in the manner of an unsure infant taking his first steps. The soles of his feet were soft, like a baby's. He whimpered and had little control of his fingers.

The strange youth, who appeared as if from nowhere in the middle of a city, caused a sensation. Who was he? Where did he come from? How did he get to Nurenberg? The answers to these questions proved most frustrating, because the subject of all this conjecture, Kaspar himself, could shed no light on his origin.

Kaspar was placed under special care. Gradually, he developed a vocabulary. It was obvious that he was a bright boy with a good memory. As he was taught to speak, he readily told authorities as much as he knew about his previous life. He had lived in a dark place underground. A man had brought him food twice a day, but never spoke to him. When he was younger, the man sometimes whittled crude wooden toys for him. He had not been physically beaten, but had lived in filth, being able to wash only at intervals of time which he had no way of measuring.

Kaspar told authorities that one day he was released from his underground confinement and left to walk through the woods. He had great difficulty walking, and after a short time fell to the ground exhausted. His keeper found him and helped him to a road, where an enclosed carriage waited. Kaspar was made to enter the carriage, and was driven for some time before the door was swung open and he was unceremoniously thrown onto the streets of Nurenberg into a world about which he knew absolutely nothing.

The public, as well as the police, was fascinated by the strange tale of Kaspar Hauser. The chief of police initiated a massive investigation into Kaspar's past. In the course of these inquiries, a fisherman produced a bottle which he had found two years earlier. Inside the bottle was a note. The writer of the note, Hares Sprauka, claimed he was a prisoner in an underground cavern near Lauffenburg on the Rhine. The letter was of no particular significance until the fisherman discovered that by rearranging the letters of Hares Sprauka he could spell Kaspar Hauser.

The letter couldn't have been written by Kaspar because he couldn't write. Shortly after the note was turned in by the fisherman, an attempt was made to murder Kaspar. Someone broke into his room while he slept and stabbed him in the left breast. However, Kaspar survived the attack.

Four years passed, during which time Kaspar received an education. He obtained employment as a clerk in a law office. Learned professors attempted to discover his true identity through research. Several theories resulted from their efforts, the most prominent of which concerned the Crown Prince of Baden, who had died in infancy in 1812, the supposed year of Kaspar's birth. The Crown Prince's mother, the Grand Duchess Stephanie, later suspected that there had been foul play. The baby died during a storm one night and was hastily buried without the body being viewed by his mother. Grand Duchess Stephanie was told that her child had died of a contagious disease.

Some time after the death, a servant told of seeing a lady sneak into the Palace of Karlsruhe with a bundle, which appeared to be an infant. She was later seen sneaking past two snoring nurses and out of the palace with another bundle. It was the servant's opinion that a dead baby had been substituted for the Crown Prince. The succession to the throne was then shifted to the child of one Countess von Hochberg.

When the grieving mother attempted to investigate the

rumor and interrogate the servant, she found she was too late. The servant had died. There matters rested for 20 years. Now, researchers wondered if Kaspar Hauser could be the kidnapped infant and if he had been kidnapped by accomplices of Countess von Hochberg.

There was little hope of finding out the truth after 20 years. However, they decided to inform the Grand Duchess Stephanie of the possibility that her earlier suspicions had been well-founded. Her son could be alive. He might be Kaspar Hauser.

A letter was sent to the Grand Duchess, outlining Kaspar's story and the professors' research in detail. The Grand Duchess Stephanie was immediately convinced that her son, once thought to be dead, was alive and well. She made arrangements to travel the 30 miles from Nurenberg to Anspach, where Kaspar was working as a law clerk.

While the Grand Duchess was en route to what she believed would be a glorious reunion with her long lost son, tragedy struck. Kaspar received an anonymous note informing him that the sender could clear up once and for all the mystery of his birth. The writer suggested a meeting in a nearby park.

Kaspar walked to the public park, where he was stabbed to death. In his pocket, investigators found the note which had enticed him to his death. Moments after his murder, the Grand Duchess Stephanie arrived in the Bavarian town, only to be informed that the young man whom she believed to be her son was dead. Kaspar's murder was never solved.

Plays have been enacted and books have been written based on the story of Kaspar Hauser, but the mystery remains. You see, no one really knows the answer to the question - Who was Kaspar Hauser?

THE BUTCHER OF HAMBURG

This little tale of terror concerns Fritz Haarmann, a man who was unique in that he had three distinct motives for murder. He received sexual gratification from the act, simply enjoyed killing and also murdered for cold, hard cash.

Fritz was born in Hanover, Germany in 1879. His father was a stoker on the German railway but quit working when Fritz's mother received an inheritance sufficient to support the family of six children, the youngest of whom was our Fritz.

The three Haarmann daughters all took up the profitable but precarious occupation of prostitution. One son, Wilhelm, was institutionalized as a teenager when he attacked a 12-year-old girl. Lest you think that I am leading you to believe that all the Haarmann brood were bad seeds, let me hasten to add that one son led an average, reputable life. And then there was Fritz.

He was an odd kid. No sooner was he able to walk than it was observed that he preferred to play with dolls. Sometimes he dressed in his sisters' clothing. You get the idea.

As he grew into his teens, Fritz developed into a rather good-looking chubby lad. At 16, he attended a military academy. One day he took a sort of fit while on parade.

Some records indicate his fainting spell was the result of sunstroke. After this incident, Fritz left the academy.

At 17, Fritz was accused of indecent acts against children and was sent to the Provincial Asylum at Hildesheim. Six months later, he escaped and spent two years wandering around Switzerland, before returning to Hanover and joining the army. Fritz stayed in the army until 1903. Upon being discharged, he practised every vice imaginable. He stole, committed indecent acts and spent more time in prison than outside. When World War I broke out, Fritz was confined to prison and sat out the entire war. He was released in 1918 into a Germany in turmoil.

In Hanover, Fritz found a city fraught with swindlers, thieves and cutthroats, all intent on exploiting a poorly clothed and hungry populace. The centre of the illicit activity was the Head Railroad Station and the Schieber Market across the street. Here, for a price, one could purchase literally anything from the thousands of little stalls where hawkers merchandised their wares. Among the sellers and buyers were the destitute, the prostitutes, the sneak thieves, the perverts and the fugitives from justice. Hanover truly attracted the dregs.

Fritz took one look and felt right at home. Within six months he had established himself in two professions. He prospered as a butcher and also acted as a police informer to the grossly undermanned Hanover police force. Fritz Haarmann had found his niche. He managed to undercut his competitors' meat prices, making him very popular with his customers. His semi-official police work earned him the nickname of Detective Haarmann.

To the outside world, Fritz even appeared to be performing charitable acts. He was known to befriend homeless boys. On many occasions, he would take a homeless waif and, with the promise of a meal and a mattress, lead the hapless youngster to the warmth of his rooms. The boys never left the butcher's quarters alive.

It is impossible to relate exactly what happened to all

of Fritz's victims. It will suffice here to follow the fate of one as representative of all.

Seventeen-year-old Friedel Rothe ran away from home and headed directly for Schieber Market. Two days later, his mother received a brief postcard from him. The Rothes were certain that if they could find their son, they could bring him home. All would be forgiven. A friend of Friedel's told the Rothes that their son had visited a male friend at 27 Cellarstrasse. That's how the Rothes ended up knocking at Fritz Haarmann's door.

With police at their side, the Rothes were shocked to find Haarmann performing an abnormal sex act with a young boy. A rather casual search of his rooms uncovered no evidence of the missing Friedel Rothe. We know the search was perfunctory because, four years later, at his trial for murder, Fritz remarked, "At the time when the policemen arrested me, the head of the boy Friedel was hidden under a newspaper behind the oven. Later on I threw it into the canal."

In the meantime, Fritz was sent to prison for nine months for indecency. Upon his release, he moved and continued his murderous ways in his new location.

In 1919, he met Hans Grans, a well-built young man with the face of an angel. Fritz and Hans became close friends. Now, with a confederate, it was even easier for Fritz to entice young boys to his quarters for a good time. Certainly, Grans knew of his companion's murderous ways. Later, Fritz would accuse Grans of being his willing accomplice in all the murders.

From 1919 to 1923, Fritz, with Grans as an accomplice, brought young boys to his rooms. Here, they were killed. Every stitch of the victims' clothing was sold on the black market, with the exception of certain items young Grans fancied. These he kept for his own use.

Around this time, rumors spread about the district that human flesh was being sold on the open market. Suspicion fell on Fritz Haarmann, mainly because of his association with young boys and also because his meat prices were

always the lowest. No one did much about the suspicions. That's all they were - suspicions, nothing more.

How did Fritz kill with impunity over a lengthy period of time? Several conditions existed which favored his nefarious deeds. The disruption of post-war Germany lent itself to a laissez-faire attitude toward criminal activity. The police were desperately understaffed. Finally, there was Fritz's occupation. What was more natural than a bloody apron or a bloody knife in a butcher's premises? Fritz acted quite openly. In hindsight, neighbors remembered him carrying buckets of bloody water through the halls. No one thought much about it. After all, he was a butcher.

On May 17, 1924, youngsters playing on the banks of the Leine River found a human skull. Twelve days later, another skull was found further down the river. In July, boys playing along the river bank found a sack of human bones and a skull. News of the gruesome finds spread like wildfire. There was a killer on the loose. Maybe those rumors about someone selling human flesh were authentic after all.

Citizens gathered by the score to stare at the waters of the Leine River. Police searched the murky depths. They were not disappointed. On the first day they recovered 500 human bones. Doctors agreed that the bones had come from 22 different bodies, all young boys.

Fritz was immediately suspected. Police imported detectives who were not known to the suspect. When Fritz and a young boy were observed arguing on the street, the detectives intervened. Fritz claimed the young man had travelled on a train without a ticket. The youngster charged Fritz with an indecent act. Police seized the opportunity to haul both off to jail while they searched Fritz's rooms.

Blood smeared pieces of clothing were found and were readily traced to many of the missing boys. One wall of Fritz's room was caked with human blood.

Under extensive questioning, Fritz confessed to "30 or

40" murders. He couldn't remember the exact number. His trial for mass murder brought forth sensational evidence of cannibalism and the butchering of humans. Evidence pointing to the sale of human flesh was suppressed. The German government thought that the conviction of a mass murderer was sufficient.

Hans Grans was found guilty of murder and sentenced to life imprisonment. Fritz Haarmann, one of the most prolific and despicable mass murderers of all time, was found guilty of the murder of 24 young boys. He received the death sentence. In 1925, he was decapitated by a swordsman.

LOVE TRIANGLE

Sometimes there isn't any justice. Take the case of Petty Officer Roger B. Eastlake and his girlfriend, Sara Knox, for example.

In 1921, Roger was the doting father of two small children, Roger, Jr., 8, and Margaret, 6. The career U.S. Navy man was also a loving husband to his winsome wife, Margaret.

I'll let you in on a little secret. Appearances are often deceiving. All was not kosher with the Eastlakes. For years Roger had been seeing one Sara Knox on the side. Roger and Sara were doing it whenever and wherever the opportunity arose. It arose often.

The lovers committed the unforgivable faux pas of writing each other letters that would one day be described by a judge as "unprintable." The letters depicted in detail the unique lengths to which they would go in order to entertain each other.

The Eastlakes resided in Washington, D.C. and maintained a cottage in Colonial Beach. It was here that the infidelity hit the fan. Toward the end of December, the weather gets a bit brisk along the mouth of the Potomac. Most of the cottages were boarded up for the season, but not the Eastlakes'. Their cottage, which was several blocks from the beach, was being used by the family.

Now, it should be noted that Margaret had found out about her husband's numerous and prolonged dalliances. She didn't take it well. She wrote Sara several letters, accusing her of being something less than a lady. Actually, she called Sara a tramp. Sara replied to these letters by denying that she was anything other than a respectable graduate nurse from John Hopkins Hospital. She claimed she had never shared a bed with Roger Eastlake, which, between you and me, was nothing more than a barefaced lie.

Margaret Eastlake was furious, but it was Sara who decided to do something about the untenable situation. On the rather blustery day of Sept. 29, Sara moseyed on over to Colonial Beach and checked into the Azeele Hotel. She travelled light, arriving with only two overnight bags. One held a quick change of clothing, the other a hatchet.

That evening, after darkness fell, Sara made her way to a shack near the Eastlake cottage. For company, she brought along the hatchet. Let's leave Sara and the hatchet together with their thoughts in the shack for the time being. Here's what happened inside the Eastlake cottage.

Little six-year-old Margaret got out of bed and started to cry. Her brother Roger woke up. It was 5 a.m. The sobbing Margaret told Roger that a man wearing a raincoat who looked just like Papa had pushed her aside and run from the house. Roger, Jr., put his sister back in bed. He then dressed with the intention of going into the parlor. Unfortunately, the door wouldn't budge. And with good reason, too. Unknown to young Roger, on the other side of the door lay the body of his mother.

Roger absently looked out a window and observed Sara Knox running through his back yard. Puzzled, he sat down on his sister's bed. In a few moments, his attention was once more drawn to the scene outside his window. There, leading a group of neighbors, was Sara, headed straight for his house. That's all Roger could relate about the most eventful night of his life. He and his sister were

taken to a neighbor's home to be spared the ensuing turmoil.

According to Sara, here's what happened. She had secreted herself in the shack in order to spy on her lover's wife. She never in her wildest dreams thought that murder most foul would take place that night. She was awakened from her not too restful sleep by the noise of a dark man fleeing from the Eastlake cottage across the yard, over a fence and into the night. On tippytoes, she had entered the cottage and found the chopped up Margaret Eastlake.

Doctors later were to state that Margaret had received 29 individual blows to the head with a hatchet or axe. While this total is impressive, it is 11 short of the number Miss Lizzie Borden allegedly inflicted upon her mother's cranium almost three decades earlier. This may be the reason Lizzie's attack is so much better known than Miss Knox's.

Sara fetched neighbors, who in turn called Dr. William Carruthers. The good doctor located Roger and informed him that his wife had been murdered. Roger wasted no time getting to the cottage. The petty officer surveyed the situation and then told police to do their duty.

"What in the world do you mean?" asked the startled police.

"Arrest Sara Knox," replied gallant Roger.

Before taking Roger's advice, detectives asked Dr. Carruthers for an opinion. He stated that, from the location of the wounds and other physical evidence, it appeared to him two individuals had been involved. He estimated that the murder had taken place between 2 a.m. and 4 a.m., some hours before Miss Knox had discovered the body. That was enough for the police. They arrested both Sara and Roger.

Roger, the cad, was tried first. He testified that he awoke as usual on the morning of the murder. He ate a substantial breakfast, after which he strolled down to the beach. Come to think of it, he had heard a scream, but

assumed it came from a neighbor's cottage. Roger boarded
a navy launch at 5:40 a.m.

Roger's personal theory was simple enough. He had
broken off his prolonged affair with Sara. Crazed with
jealousy, she had killed his wife.

Roger's alibi, if it can be called that, didn't sit well with
the prosecuting attorney. Let's face it, Doc Carruthers
figured the time of death was between 2 and 4 a.m.
Roger would have had to sleep through the butchering of
his wife, eat breakfast, and wander about the house, being
careful not to walk or even glance toward the open door
leading from the kitchen to the parlor, in order not to
have noticed his wife's body. Like Mr. Magoo, our Roger
missed all the noise and excitement and then strolled out
of his house.

Juries are a strange lot. They must have believed
Roger's dubious tale was possible. They found him not
guilty.

That Roger was a fast worker. He met a young lady in
January, became engaged in February and was married in
March. The 90 days from introduction to altar beat the
starting date of Sara Knox's trial for the murder of
Roger's wife number one.

At Sara's trial, Roger testified in the strongest possible
terms against his former lover. According to the prosecuting attorney, Sara waited in the shack until the dead of
night, when she slunk into the Eastlake home and killed
her lover's wife. The jury believed that's exactly how it
happened. Sara Knox was found guilty and sentenced to
20 years imprisonment.

What really happened that night in the Eastlake cottage? Most students of the old crime, as well as detectives
who covered the case, felt that both Roger and Sara
planned the murder. Sara arrived in Colonial Beach and
made her way to the shack beside the Eastlake's cottage,
where she waited until Roger showed up.

Remember Dr. Carruthers' opinion? Two people had
delivered the deadly blows. Together, Roger and Sara had

killed Margaret. The man who little Margaret thought "looked like Papa" was indeed Papa. When Dr. Carruthers stated that two people had killed Margaret Eastlake, Roger decided to bail out of the scheme. He left Sara high and dry. His gamble paid off.

As I said earlier, sometimes there isn't any justice.

HAYSTACK HANKY PANKY

They do more than butcher cattle down on the farm. Sometimes they butcher each other.

Come along with me now to Butler County, Ohio, close by the Indiana state line and meet Marie and Morris Abbott. Salt of the earth were Marie and Morris. Prosperous farmers. Well-liked, too.

That's why everyone was so shocked when Morris was found deader than a mackerel on the Baltimore and Ohio Railroad tracks on the morning of June 1, 1948. Marie had called around the night before looking for Morris when he didn't return home from gossiping with the boys over at Buell Lake. Mr. Buell said Morris had spent some time chatting and eating ice cream at his resort, but left for home in his pickup at 10:30 p.m.

No question about where Morris ended up. He was right there on those tracks with his head a terrible mess. The rest of Morris was in perfect shape. His truck was parked near the tracks. Initially, it looked as if Morris had left his truck and walked onto the tracks and into the train.

An autopsy proved just how deceiving appearances can be. Morris had been bludgeoned to death with an axe or shovel. Eleven trains had passed over Morris that night without disturbing his body. Time of death was estimated

to be shortly after 10:30 the previous evening.

Who would want to kill Morris and place his body on the B and O Line? That was the question placed squarely on the shoulders of Sheriff Charles B. Walke. Now Charlie didn't handle a murder case every day, or even every year, but he took to the murder business like a duck takes to water. For starters, Charlie noted that the bed of the victim's pickup truck was scrubbed clean. Charlie, who may have been part bloodhound, could smell gasoline from the bed of the truck. He figured that Morris might have been killed elsewhere and transported to the tracks in his own truck. If that was the case, the killer had to leave the scene by foot.

Big city cops could take lessons from Charlie. He poked around. Sure enough, he found that stalks of grain in a nearby field were bent. Charlie followed the bent stalks through the field as far as he could. The trail couldn't be followed through a meadow, but Charlie picked it up again in a plowed field on the other side of the meadow. Smudged tracks led Charlie to a lane, which led right up to Morris' back yard.

Ah, thought Charlie. The murderer had waited for his victim in his own vehicle. He killed Morris, placed the body in Morris' pickup, drove to the tracks, placed the body on the tracks, and walked back to Morris' yard to drive away in his own vehicle.

Charlie's theory was given credence when one of his deputies found freshly overturned earth in Morris' back yard, about 500 feet from the Abbotts' spacious home. Under the earth was a patch of blood.

Charlie dreaded interrogating Marie, who was understandably beside herself with grief. Marie was a fine cut of a woman. Despite her 40 plus years, she had a voluptuous figure to go with her pleasant good looks. She could only tell Charlie that she had driven to nearby Hamilton at 7:30 p.m. the previous night to attend a recital at the YMCA, arriving home at 11:00 p.m. When Morris failed to return home, she called around and then called police. She

hadn't seen anyone drive out of her yard, which wasn't unusual. The road was some distance from the house and the line of vision was obstructed by trees.

Charlie thanked Marie and headed over to Buell Lake. Mr. Buell gave Charlie the names of the two men who had left his establishment with Morris at 10:30 p.m. These men swore that they had all gone their separate once outside Buell's door. However, they gave Charlie an earful. Seems there was a rumor going around about Marie Abbott and the Abbotts' former hired hand, Scotty Gordon. Scotty hadn't worked for the Abbotts since the previous spring, but, thought Charlie, where there's smoke there's sometimes fire.

Charlie drove to the Derickson farm in Oxford County to speak to Scotty. He found that Scotty had travelled to Indianapolis to take in that city's famed auto race. When he returned by bus, Charlie was there to meet him.

Scotty admitted that he and Marie had fallen in love and had been intimate for the past two years. Morris found out about their meetings in the hot but convenient haymow and the situation had become tense. When Marie refused to seek a divorce, Scotty broke off the affair and went to work for the Dericksons. It had all been very civilized. As a matter of fact, Morris had highly recommended Scotty to Mr. Derickson as an honest, conscientious worker.

To account for his time in Indianapolis, Scotty gave Charlie the name of a friend with whom he had stayed for two nights and the name of the hotel where he had spent the third night. A phone check verified Scotty's story. Still, the whole kit and kaboodle didn't sit well with bloodhound Charlie. Why would anyone incur the expense of a hotel if he could stay with a friend? One way to find was to ask Scotty's friend.

It took under two hours to cover the 85 miles to Indianapolis. Scotty's friend informed Charlie that he had invited Scotty to stay with him on Monday night, the

third night of his visit, but Scotty had insisted on moving to a hotel.

That's it. Charlie figured that Scotty could have driven to the Abbott farm, killed Morris and returned to the hotel in the wee hours of the morning without being observed. He could never have done that had he remained with his friend. The move to the hotel had been to establish an alibi.

But how did Scotty do his travelling? He had arrived in Indianapolis by bus and returned home by bus. Charlie checked the car rental agencies in town. Sure enough, Scotty had rented a small truck at 6:30 p.m. on the evening of the murder and had returned it at 3:00 the next morning. Records indicated that it had travelled 180 miles.

As they say in dance circles, the jig was up. Faced with the incriminating evidence, Scotty confessed. He claimed that he had rented the truck and driven to the Abbott farm to plead with Morris to give his wife a divorce. The two men talked in the yard. Morris was furious and lunged at Scotty. In desperation, Scotty picked up an axe and swung with all his might. In a frenzy, he rained blows to his fallen victim's head.

Scotty also admitted his liaisons with Marie. They had been meeting at hotels, motels and the ever-handy haymow for years. After the attack on Morris, Scotty told Marie what he had done. She immediately became hysterical.

Well, Charlie wasn't born yesterday. He knew very well that it was illogical to believe that Scotty had waited until it required a round trip of 190 miles to talk to a man about divorcing his wife. No, thought Charlie, the trip to Indianapolis had been solely to provide an alibi.

Then there was the weeping Marie to contend with. She had been calling friends at 11 p.m. looking for her husband. He had left Buell Lake around 10:30 p.m., placing him at home shortly after that time, which was the estimated time of death. When Marie was making those

desperate calls, she knew very well Morris was already dead.

Marie Abbott and Scotty Gordon were arrested and stood trial for murder on July 20, 1948. Scotty's lawyers conceded that their client had killed Morris Abbott, but attempted to prove that the deed wasn't premeditated. Scotty Gordon was found guilty and sentenced to life imprisonment.

Marie's attorneys admitted to Marie's horizontal hay-mow activities, but claimed she was innocent of murder. Marie Abbott was found guilty of second degree murder. She was sentenced to 20 years imprisonment.

DIRTY MONEY

There have been robberies and then again, there have been robberies. This is the story of the grandaddy of them all.

The mastermind behind the largest robbery ever successfully pulled off was the owner of a photography shop, Photo La Valliere, in Nice, France. Albert Spaggiari, a Vietnam veteran, had tried his hand at real estate with something less than outstanding success. By 1972, Albert was well ensconced in the photographic business and, for all intents and purposes, appeared to be a successful small businessman. There was just one thing different about Albert. He wanted to rob the most prestigious bank in Nice, the Societe Generale.

The main portion of the bank has been modernized, but at the time of the great robbery the interior was resplendent in marble and old world charm. It was believed to be impregnable. That's why no one even considered installing high tech electronic equipment to protect the bank's safety deposit boxes. Albert would change all that.

Albert made his plans to rob the Societe Generale with the same patience required for a major military campaign. He rented a safety deposit box and studied the vault's layout. Four thousand boxes were housed in seven reinforced cabinets inside the large vault. To gain entry to the

vault, it was necessary to sign a log book. The signature was checked against a file signature. The customer was then ushered to his safety deposit box, where a guard inserted his key, as well as the client's, in order to open the box. The entire walk-in vault holding the 4000 boxes was closed at night by a 20-ton door.

There was no way to loot those boxes during banking hours, and there was no way anyone was going to get through that monster door to the vault. Ah, but there was another way - through the town's sewerage system. The plans of the sewerage system were readily available to anyone who cared to pick up a copy at the town hall.

Albert found out that he could drive a truck into the sewerage system by travelling down an inspection road. Access to this road could be gained from an underground parking lot. He estimated correctly that the equipment needed could be transported by truck to within 300 yards of the bank before it would have to be lugged by foot along a three foot high repulsive drain to the point where it would be necessary to dig a 25-foot tunnel. This would place Albert against the wall of the vault. If all went well, he figured he could get inside that vault and have a go at those 4000 safety deposit boxes over a weekend.

Albert went about forming a gang of specialists. It wasn't easy. Each man was hand-picked - men who knew how to build reinforced tunnels; men who knew how to go through cement walls. They were recruited not only for their skills, but also for their personalities. These men had to be compatible. Working conditions would not be ideal.

Equipment was of the utmost importance. It was purchased at large stores all over Europe. Albert knew the importance of procuring untraceable equipment in quantities that would not be noticed. An array of chisels was purchased individually; oxyacetylene torches, hammers, bricklaying tools, flashlights, electric drills - the list goes on. Nothing was left to chance. Waterproof clothing, rubber dingies, an extensive first aid kit and an industrial smoke extractor were considered necessities.

The amount of equipment became so extensive that Albert rented a villa in Castagniers, a few minutes' drive from Nice, to stash away his growing mountain of supplies.

It took two months to dig out the tunnel. The equipment was driven down into the sewer, then transferred onto inflated dingies and dragged through the stinking sewer. Two men worked at the tunnel, while another disposed of the earth. A fourth man shored up the roof and cemented the walls. Conditions in the tunnel were so disagreeable that each team worked only every third day. Work was carried on in ten minute intervals. May and June passed. In July, the men struck the concrete wall of the bank vault.

A week before the break-in, the whole scheme almost exploded in Albert's face. A woman, who had no connection whatever with the robbers, was convinced that her husband had secreted his mistress in the villa rented by the gang. The wronged wife decided to seek revenge. She told the owner of the villa that his property was being overrun by hippies.

The owner called police, who checked and found four gang members in the villa. The men were questioned, but were able to convince the gendarmes that they were doing nothing more sinister than arranging a party for that evening. They were merely waiting for female company to arrive. It was a close call, but the police accepted their story.

On July 15, an underworld doctor was paid to be on standby. The doctor didn't know why his services were required, but Albert wanted him available should any of his men require medical attention while working on the tunnel.

Next day, the heavy equipment was lugged through the sewers on inflated rafts. Once unloaded, it was dragged through the 25-foot tunnel to the wall. The gang had plugged into an electrical outlet at the entrance to the sewerage system. In this way, they had a supply of elec-

tricity right to the wall face. Working on their stomachs, it took the gang 19 hours of drilling and chiselling to get through that thick reinforced concrete wall to the back of the 30-ton cabinet containing the safety deposit boxes.

A hydraulic lever was used to move the cabinet inch by inch until there was an opening big enough for a man to crawl through. Albert was given the honor of being the first to enter the bank vault. After all, the whole thing had been his idea.

The safety deposit boxes were opened. It had been agreed that the gang was to take only gold, jewelry and hard cash - nothing traceable. But before business, a minor celebration. Albert had brought along expensive wines, goose liver pate, cheese and fresh fruit.

While enjoying their goodies, the gang was startled by a swishing noise from above. It turned out to be nothing serious. A gambling casino employee had just dropped the night's take in the depository. A bag, containing around a million francs, fell through a vent and landed at Albert's feet. It never rains but it pours.

As a precautionary measure, the gang soldered shut the vault door from the inside. No need to take a chance on being disturbed by a conscientious bank employee over the weekend.

By early Monday morning, the gang had opened 400 of the 4000 safety deposit boxes. It was time to go. All their equipment was left behind. Only the proceeds of the robbery were lugged back through the sewers on the inflated rafts and transferred to a waiting car. It was over.

On Monday morning, bank officials couldn't open their vault. An official from the security equipment company had to be summoned to gain entrance. The impossible had happened. The Societe Generale Bank had been robbed. Scores of clues were left behind, none of which proved of any value. Bottles of Margnat Village wine were sent away to be analyzed. The bottles were found to contain urine, which had originated from several individuals. That

Albert had thought of everything. Well, almost everything.

Those gendarmes who had followed up the lead given to them by the jealous wife wondered if the four men in the villa at Castagniers could have anything to do with the big bank job. A search of the villa uncovered spare burglary equipment and a case of Margnat Village wine. The four men, whose identity had been originally obtained by police, were now rounded up. At the same time, one gang member stupidly attempted to sell gold ingots legitimately. Stamped on each ingot was an identity number. He was readily apprehended.

Two members of the gang, Francis Pellegrin and Alain Bournat, confessed and named Albert as their ringleader. Albert was picked up and detained for questioning. The questioning lasted for months, right up until the day Albert jumped out of an open window of the Palais de Justice, landing on a ledge a few feet below. From the ledge he leaped onto the roof of a Renault 6. Albert hollered, "Au revoir!" as he rolled to the ground and made good his escape on a waiting motorcycle.

Later, when it became known that Albert had damaged the Renault to the tune of $625, the owner received an apology note and $625 by mail from our Albert.

The sum of $215,000 was recovered from the robbery loot. The gold bars one of the gang attempted to sell made up most of this amount. Only four members of the gang were convicted of taking part in the bank heist. None of these four spent more than six months in prison.

Claims totalling over $8 million were issued against the bank, making the robbery the largest in history. Many believe the true figure of the loot to be closer to $20 million.

And what about Albert Spaggiari? Rumors drift back to Nice. The former photographer is said to be dividing his time between several luxurious homes he maintains in South America.

Albert doesn't frequent sewers any more.

DUNGEONS
AND DRAGONS

James Dallas Egbert the Third was no ordinary young
ster. At the age of two, he could recite the alphabet. At
three, he was reading books. Dallas sailed through grade
school and completed high school in two years. As a high
school senior at age 13, he was offered scholarships to
several prestigious universities, including the Massachusetts Institute of Technology.

Dallas chose to attend Michigan State University in
East Lansing, Mich. because it had advanced special
courses for gifted children. At 14 years of age, he entered
M.S.U.

Dallas' IQ was measured at over 180, placing him in the
ultra-genius class. It is estimated that there are no more
than 300 individuals with IQs in that lofty range in the
entire United States.

Born in Dayton, Ohio, Dallas came from a fine upper
middle class family. His parents, Anna and Jim Egbert,
recognized that their son was special. As a result, they
demanded far more from him than parents might ask of a
child with average intelligence. The Egberts believed their
son should excel in everything he attempted. In the academic world, he rarely disappointed them.

On Aug. 15, 1979, Dallas Egbert disappeared off the
Michigan State University campus. Police were called in

to locate the missing sophomore. Gradually, the strange and troubled history of the boy genius emerged. It was learned that although Dallas excelled academically, he was socially ostracized by his fellow students. He was a slight, shy 16-year-old boy, attempting to mix with students far older. They found him annoying and childish.

Dallas was a lonely, depressed boy living on a hustling, bustling campus of 45,000 students. He found relief in drugs, often manufacturing his own from supplies available to him in the university's laboratories. There is also evidence that Dallas was a practising homosexual. However, while these activities may have provided a diversion, it was another aspect of his life which gave the troubled youngster relief from bouts of depression and, at the same time, stimulated him mentally.

Dallas was an avid Dungeons and Dragons player. The role playing game involves taking on characters which have assigned abilities, such as strength, dexterity, charisma, and so on. The players make life and death decisions while proceeding through a maze of obstacles. The object of the game is to slay enemies, avoid being killed, and to find a treasure.

Police discovered that students at M.S.U. were playing the game in a network of steam tunnels, which crisscrossed for miles underneath the campus. The students were extremely close-mouthed about their participation in the game. It was learned that while Dallas was an exceptional player, many of his fellow students found him childish. There was some evidence that they didn't want him as a participant in the dirty and extremely dangerous tunnels. Being ostrasized from the all-encompassing game must have devastated Dallas.

Eight days after the disappearance, the Egberts retained William Dear, a flamboyant private investigator, to locate their missing son. Dear figured that the boy genius had committed suicide. Dallas had left numerous clues as to his fate, one of which was an ominous note found in his room. It read, "To Whom it may Concern:

Should my body be found, I wish it to be cremated."

A cork bulletin board in the boy's room had a strange configuration of thumbtacks on it. An aerial photo of the campus indicated that the tacks resembled the layout of university buildings.

Investigator Dear, as well as the police, believed it was possible that this troubled boy was playing a real life game of Dungeons and Dragons. If the investigators proved successful, the clues would eventually lead to Dallas' body. If unsuccessful, the body might never be found. You may notice that the note read, "Should my body be found."

For 28 days, the hunt for Dallas continued. The tunnels beneath the campus were searched. Evidence of students enacting the characters of the Dungeons and Dragons game was confirmed, but no sign of Dallas was uncovered.

Investigator Dear and his team infiltrated the gay community and ingratiated themselves with those straight students who had had contact with Dallas, but still no concrete clue to the missing boy's fate was uncovered. However, the investigators found evidence which led them to believe that Dallas might possibly be alive. Those who had harbored him during the first days after his disappearance were fearful of coming forward with vital information.

By now, the bizarre disappearance and its unusual connection with the game, Dragons and Dungeons, had captured the imagination of the public.

The mystery was solved in a most prosaic manner. Dallas Egbert phoned William Dear out of the blue and revealed his whereabouts. He was holed up in a dilapidated old house in Morgan City, Louisiana. Dear flew to Louisiana and brought Dallas home.

Dallas and the detective became close friends. Although the boy was reluctant to reveal why or how he had disappeared for almost a month, he did confide in the detective. He told Bill Dear that he had been thinking of disappearing for almost a year. He felt no one really cared if he

lived or died and had often planned on suicide. His mother never seemed satisfied with his scholastic accomplishments. If he simply vanished, never to be found, he would, in his own way, punish his mother.

At other times, Dallas craved the simple life. A computer expert, he longed to work in a computer store explaining the intricate mechanism to potential buyers. In his heart he knew that neither his parents or society would hear of a bona fide genius working as a clerk.

Dallas explained that when he did finally run away, he wrote the suicide note in case he decided to kill himself. The thumb tacks on the cork board indicated the buildings on the campus and alcoves in the tunnels. The one pin that was missing was the one indicating the alcove where Dallas went when he first disappeared.

Down in the filthy alcove that first day, Dallas could see no way out. He was gay. He was on drugs. He had no real friends. He couldn't bear to tell his mother that learning and academic achievement were not his main aim in life. He decided to commit suicide then and there. Dallas had brought a quantity of quaaludes down into the tunnel. He took them all with a glass of milk.

The next night he woke up deathly ill. Walking and stumbling, he made his way to an acquaintance's home. He begged not to be sent to a hospital and remained there for a week. A policeman interviewed the acquaintance, who kept Dallas' secret, but told the frightened boy he would have to move. Dallas transferred to two more houses, staying stoned most of the time.

As the investigation into his disappearance intensified, his benefactors became nervous. They provided him with money and purchased a bus ticket to Chicago and a train ticket from Chicago to New Orleans. Now cast aside once again, Dallas attempted suicide in New Orleans. He mixed cyanide with root beer, only to wake up the next day, sick but still alive.

Now out of funds, Dallas discovered that oil fields could always use roustabouts. The jobs came with room and

meals. That's how Dallas ended up in Morgan City. He lasted only four days at the oil wells.

Why had Dallas called Dear after almost a month? He had kept in touch with the friend who had taken him in after his first suicide attempt. Back in East Lansing, it was becoming obvious that all the individuals from Dungeons and Dragons players to the three students who had sheltered Dallas, were about to get into all kinds of trouble. Several were seniors who stood in jeopardy of being expelled. The friend advised Dallas to call Dear and reveal his location before things got any worse.

After spending a month recuperating at an uncle's home, Dallas Egbert returned to his parents in Dayton. He enrolled at nearby Wright State University, majoring in computer sciences, but left the university in the spring of 1980 to work in his father's optometry store.

Three months later, unsatisfied with his home life, he moved into a furnished one bedroom apartment with a roommate, Kevin Bach. On Aug. 11, 1980, James Dallas Egbert the Third placed a .25 calibre pistol to his right temple and shot himself. With the aid of life support systems, he lingered for six days before the machines were disconnected.

IN THE
WRONG PLACE

All murder is reprehensible, but there is something particularly obscene when an innocent person becomes a victim for merely being in the wrong place at the wrong time.

Such a murder took place in April, 1947, in London, England. Three desperate young men ran into a jewelry store with pistols drawn. All three wore masks. One stood guard at the door, while the other two made their way into the store. Orders were shouted out to customers and employees: "Stand back and don't move!"

A young clerk moved one hand under the edge of a display counter until his fingers found the alarm button. The signal brought the manager on the run from the stock room. At a glance, he took in the situation and, not too wisely, attempted to knock the pistol from the grasp of one of the bandits. The other robbers saw what was happening and commenced to pistol-whip the manager about the head. During the scuffle a shot was discharged. Although no one was hit, the loud report frightened the three robbers, who quickly headed for the streets and their getaway car.

One man, obviously the preappointed driver of the getaway car, jumped in behind the wheel, closely followed by his two companions. As luck would have it, while the

men were in the store, a truck had parked directly in front of their vehicle. The three men wildly jumped out of the getaway car.

Several witnesses saw the men run down the street. The manager, blood streaming down his face, was in hot pursuit. Suddenly, a man on a motorcycle drove directly in front of the fleeing robbers. The driver of the motorcycle, Alec de Antiquis, attempted to dismount. A shot rang out and he slumped to the well-worn pavement of Charlotte St., dead, with a bullet in his head.

A witness to the shooting stuck out his foot and tripped one of the armed desperados. The robber went flying, losing his pistol in the process. The pedestrian jumped on the robber, but gave up the battle when a second bandit kicked him squarely in the head.

The three gunmen continued on their way and made good their escape. Back on the pavement, 36-year-old Alec de Antiquis lay dead. De Antiquis was a hard-working married man with six children. News of the daring daylight robbery and its tragic conclusion swept through London. Eyewitnesses were able to give vague descriptions of the wanted men. From these descriptions, Scotland Yard issued a bulletin.

Despite the descriptions, three days passed before the Yard came up with a solid lead. A taxi driver came forth with the information that on the day of the murder a young man with a handkerchief wrapped around his neck jumped on the running board of his cab. The taxi driver pushed him off. He noticed that the youth ran into an office building on Tottenham Court Rd.

Detectives canvassed the building. A 14-year-old office boy remembered a strange event which had occurred on the day of the murder. Two young men had dashed into the building, brushing him aside before going upstairs. When they left, the young office boy thought it strange that although both had been wearing raincoats upon entering the building, only one was now wearing a coat.

The office building was meticulously searched. Sure

enough, in a vacant upstairs office, police found a cap, raincoat and a piece of white cloth which had been used as a mask. The coat was traced to a manufacturer in Leeds, who was able to trace his sale to a south London shop. The shopkeeper remembered selling the coat, and was even able to come up with a sales slip, complete with name and address.

Police rushed to the home of a young south London couple, who readily admitted that the coat belonged to the man of the house. However, he had loaned the coat to his wife's brother, 23-year-old Charles Henry Jenkins. Jenkins was duly interviewed and proved to a tough cookie just out of Borstal. He would admit to nothing but, when informed that he would be placed in a lineup before two dozen witnesses, he declared, "I suppose it's because of the coat. If I am picked out, I will tell you about the coat, but I shan't tell you where I was until it comes to the last. I'm not an informer, but I'm not having this on my own. You surely don't think I would do any shooting?"

Twenty-four witnesses failed to pick Jenkins out of a lineup. Scotland Yard were compelled to release their man. Inexplicably, Jenkins volunteered to police that he had loaned the incriminating coat to a man named Walsh. Detectives were doubtful about this information, but were successful in tracking down Walsh and recovering stolen watches, the loot from a robbery which had taken place four days before de Antiquis was murdered.

Walsh, realizing that he could very easily be implicated in a murder, decided to tell all. He readily admitted to taking part in the earlier robbery. His companions had been Jenkins, Christopher James Geraghty, 20, and John Peter Rolt, 17. Walsh also insisted that he had had absolutely nothing to do with the robbery and subsequent murder of de Antiquis.

Police wanted to know why Jenkins had fingered Walsh. The reason became obvious. Walsh revealed that he had refused to split the proceeds of the earlier robbery with his companions. Jenkins was furious and decided to make

trouble for his former partner in crime.

Eighteen days after the murder, Jenkins, Geraghty and Rolt were taken into custody. Geraghty was the first to break. He admitted that he had fired the shot in the jewelry store and, much more importantly, had fired the shot which killed de Antiquis. "He got in our way. I fired, intending to frighten him," explained Geraghty.

When Rolt heard that his companion had confessed, he admitted to being the driver of the stolen getaway car. He and Jenkins had hidden in the office building, providing police with the raincoat which proved to be the first link in the chain of evidence leading to the killers.

Jenkins, Geraghty and Rolt were tried for murder at the Old Bailey. The jury deliberated only 50 minutes before finding all three men guilty.

Rolt was fortunate. Because he was under 18 years of age, he escaped the gallows. He was ordered "detained during His Majesty's pleasure." Jenkins and Geraghty were sentenced to death. Both sentences were appealed. Jenkins in particular thought he would never be executed as he had not fired the fatal shot. However, the law clearly states that if murder takes place during the commission of a felony, all taking part are equally guilty.

Five months after Alec de Antiquis was shot dead on the streets of London for being in the wrong place at the wrong time, Charles Henry Jenkins and Christopher James Geraghty were hanged in Pentonville Prison.

A CASE OF KIDNAPPING

Kidnapping of any kind at any time is a despicable crime. When a group of rounders decide to take it up as a vocation, disaster cannot be far behind.

Arthur Fried and his four brothers owned a garage in White Plains, N.Y. Times were tough in 1937 and the income from the garage barely supported the Fried families. That's why it was such a shock when, a few days before Christmas, Hugo Fried received a phone call advising him that his 32-year-old brother Arthur had been kidnapped. The caller demanded $200,000 for his safe return.

Hugo loved his brother dearly, but he and his other brothers had as much chance of raising that amount of money as a snowball has of not melting in hell. He told the kidnappers they must have abducted the wrong man. The Fried clan simply were not wealthy.

When advised of this shocking turn of events, the kidnappers commenced to haggle with Hugo. Finally, the bargain sum of $1800 was agreed upon. Hugo swore he wouldn't tell a soul. He would rendezvous with the kidnappers at precisely 10 o'clock that very night at a designated restaurant.

As soon as the conversation ended, Hugo made two calls. He informed Arthur's wife Gertrude that her husband was in the hands of kidnappers. Gertrude was

shocked and puzzled. Her biggest financial concern up to that point in her life was trying to dig up the rent money at the end of each month. His second call was to the police.

Somehow, newspapers got hold of the story and featured it in the evening edition. When Hugo went to the restaurant to meet his brother's abductors, they didn't show. Hugo feared that the newspaper leak had scared off the kidnappers. He was right. Arthur Fried was never returned.

The Fried abduction received wide publicity. As a result, five high school students came forward. On the night of the abduction they had seen a coupe cut off a sedan on the street. A man jumped from the coupe, waving a revolver. He got into the sedan and both cars drove away. It had all taken only a few seconds. The students could only add that the coupe's licence plate had started with 7N, while the sedan's licence had begun with the letters BM. Arthur Fried's sedan had a licence which began with BM.

Three months after Arthur disappeared, Benjamin Farber was kidnapped. Benjamin and his brother Irving owned a coal company. While they were not as poor as the Fried family, they were far from wealthy. Irving received a phone call demanding $200,000. Once again, the kidnappers were in for a surprise. Irving told them he had no way to raise such an amount. Some good old fashioned dickering took place. Finally, the sum of $2000 was agreed upon as a fair price.

Irving immediately called police. Because he had chatted for a lengthy period of time with the caller, he was able to describe the kidnapper's voice as distinctive and very metallic. After several more calls, a money drop was arranged. Irving was to take a package of money to the Williamsburg Bridge. He was to stand in a certain spot, toss the money so that it would fall onto South Fifth Ave. Irving did as he was told without police interference. Minutes after the money was dropped, his brother Benja-

min was thrown from a car in Manhattan.

When questioned, Benjamin could tell very little. His ears had been stuffed with cotton and his eyes had been taped from the moment he had been taken captive to the moment of his release. Four young men had been involved in his abduction. They had taken him to a hideout, which he had not had a chance to see. The FBI were stymied. They were obviously up against a gang who kidnapped on a regular basis. Nothing quite like this had ever happened before.

Four months passed. Two teenagers, Norman Miller and Sidney Lehrer, had just taken in a movie and were waiting for traffic lights to change when they were accosted by the kidnappers. A minute later, they were in the kidnappers' Packard coupe with tape stretched over their eyes. The two boys could hear Tommy Dorsey's band on the radio. The vocalist was singing, "A tisket, a tasket, I love my yellow basket."

After travelling several miles, the radio was turned off and the car came to a sudden stop. Sidney felt the barrel of a pistol in his back as he was roughly removed from the car. A dollar bill was shoved in his hand with the instructions, "Grab a taxi, buster. Tell Miller's old man we'll get in touch with him." Then the car sped away.

Norman's father, Charles Miller, was contacted. The familiar pattern was repeated. The kidnappers asked for an exorbitant amount of money, but were receptive to having the price lowered. This time, they struck a bargain at $18,000. Charles Miller paid off and his son was returned unharmed.

By now, the FBI had several clues with which to work. The Columbia Broadcasting Corp. had a transcript of Tommy Dorsey's live broadcast. The song had started at 46 minutes past midnight. Norman Miller gave investigators an approximation of how long he had driven in the car to the gang's hideout. In this way, agents were able to determine the outer extremities of a circle within which the hideout must be located. Norman also told the FBI

that, while being held captive, he had heard church bells and what he thought might be billiard balls striking each other. He also related that when the men received the $18,000 ransom, they were elated and mentioned that they first got the idea of kidnapping him when they saw his father at a racetrack.

While FBI agents searched for a pool hall within earshot of a church inside the boundaries of their suspect area, it was decided that the kidnappers might be regular horse players. Since the famous Saratoga meet was then taking place in upper New York State, FBI agents travelled to the famous old town to search for the kidnappers' car.

Sure enough, they spotted a Packard coupe with the licence plates 6C-6500. The ownership was checked out. The car belonged to Dennis Gula of Brooklyn, N.Y. The previous year's licence number was 7N-900.

Upon investigating Dennis Gula, it was learned that he was a hard-working, honest citizen who ran a bar/poolroom in the Ukrainian Hall in Brooklyn. One street away was a church. Gula was an unlikely suspect, but his son, Demetrius, who normally drove the Packard, was another kettle of fish. Demetrius earned a small salary assisting his father. However, he lived far beyond his means, often losing several hundred dollars a day at the racetrack.

The FBI kept Demetrius under surveillance. They soon learned of his three friends. Steve Sacoda was then in jail for parole violation. The other two men close to Demetrius were John Murphy and Willy Jacknis. All four men had police records. Sacoda had a distinctive metallic voice.

Despite seeing their abductors for only seconds, the kidnap victims were able to pick out photos of the four men from police mug shots. Demetrius was easily recognized, as he bore a striking resemblance to Buster Keaton, the famous movie comic.

The four men were taken into custody. Demetrius was the first to confess. The others made partial confessions.

All had one thing in common. They told the same story regarding the fate of the first kidnap victim, Arthur Fried.

The gang had panicked when they read accounts of the kidnapping in the newspaper. Arthur was being held in the basement of the Ukrainian Hall. As soon as Sacoda heard that the kidnapping was public knowledge, he shot Fried in the head at point blank range. The body was then placed in the furnace. The men waited four hours before peeking inside the roaring interior. There was not much left of Arthur Fried. More coal was heaped inside and soon there was no trace whatever left of Arthur Fried.

All four men were tried and convicted of murder. Each was executed in Sing Sing's electric chair.

BAD MEDICINE

I have always been a firm believer that one day a year should be set aside for mothers-in-law. Despite common belief, mothers-in-law, as a class, can be a fine group of ladies. Unfortunately, as individuals, they can be extremely annoying. What's even more exasperating, they are usually correct in their opinions.

Let's go back a few years across the big pond to meet Madame Dubizy and her future son-in-law, Edmund Pommerais, of Paris, France.

We'll start with Edmund, just for fun.

Ed was a tall, handsome lad of 24 when he arrived on the Parisian scene in 1860. Like many freshly turned out doctors, our boy thought it would be commendable to heal those on the bottom rung of the economic ladder. Before you could say syringe, Dr. Pommerais had a huge practice of non-paying, poor, sick patients.

This would have been just fine if the doctor hadn't had such expensive tastes. Ed was somewhat of a dandy when it came to clothing. He also maintained a lavishly furnished apartment and, in general, threw money around like it was going out of style.

As his debts rose, so did his longing for female companionship. Just when the doctor felt those old biological urges, who should come strolling into his clinic but

Madame Seraphine de Pauw. The poorly dressed but attractive lady had a husband in dire need of Dr. Pommerais' skill. Ed was more than willing to take on yet one more impoverished patient. Sadly, I must relate that despite the doctor's loving care, Mr. de Pauw was carried away to his great reward after several months.

Now, Madame de Pauw was ten years older than the doctor. Besides, she was encumbered with three small children, but as we all know, love or sex or whatever is blind. Madame de Pauw became Ed's mistress. Although deeply in debt, Ed managed to provide for her and the children.

Nothing wrong with all that, you might say, but darn it all, the bills kept mounting up. Ed was desperately in debt when, quite by chance, he met Madame Dubizy, who came complete with charming daughter. Ed did a double take. Dubizy was an old battle-axe, but the daughter was built like one of those sexy manikins on display at Galleries Lafayette.

When Ed found out that the Dubizy clan were loaded with francs, he decided to woo and wed Dubizy the younger. Despite the madame's open dislike for our Ed, he managed to court and finally marry her young daughter.

That's when Madame Dubizy showed her true colors. She fixed up her daughter's wealth so that Ed could not get his hands on any of it. That is, as long as Madame Dubizy lived. Ed made a mental note that it might not be that long.

Ed was a busy boy. Of necessity, he had to break the news of his marriage to Seraphine de Pauw and let her know that their private horizontal arrangements would have to undergo something of an adjustment. Seraphine sobbed, but Ed assured her he would send her enough cash to keep the wolf from the door. Let's give Ed his due - he sent a few francs for a couple of months. Then he quit. Out of sight, out of mind.

Ed was putting out fires as fast as they broke out, but

there was one blaze he couldn't quell. Those enormous debts kept piling up. Since he insisted that his wife have the best clothing and jewelry, his marriage, rather than alleviating his precarious position, only served to add to it.

That's when he decided to kill his mother-in-law. It wasn't that difficult. One evening Ed and the wife had dear Mama over for dinner. Ed liberally laced her favorite wine with poison. An hour after quaffing back half a litre, Mama felt ill. Not to worry. After all, her son-in-law was a doctor. Ed stayed with his stricken mother-in-law until dawn. Then he broke the sad news to his wife. Mama had departed this mortal coil.

Solicitous Ed comforted his wife, made all the funeral arrangements and signed the death certificate. He then got his grubby little paws on his mother-in-law's estate. The total amount conveniently wiped out Ed's enormous debts. Mama's death couldn't have been more timely.

Ed continued on his merry way. He gambled heavily on the stock market and lived lavishly. It was only a matter of months before he was once again over his head in debt. He attempted to borrow money through legitimate channels, but no bank would take a chance on him. Desperately, he tried money lenders, but they too wouldn't have any part of a man so deeply in the red.

At this juncture in Ed's life, who should write him a letter but Seraphine de Pauw. Seraphine could tear your heart out. She and her children lived in a hovel and were literally starving to death. She apologized for bothering Ed, but if there was anything he could do, it sure would be appreciated. Ed dropped in on his old flame. The situation was just as Seraphine had outlined in her letter. Ed produced 20 francs for food and became an instant hero to Seraphine and the children.

In the following days, Ed once more entered his old girlfriend's life. The flame, which had diminished over the years, once more burned brightly. Seraphine figured her lover was loaded. Quite the opposite was true. Ed was

dead broke and was delicately perched on the edge of bankruptcy and ruin. He did, however, have a diabolical plan.

He persuaded Seraphine, now completely under his influence, to take out a large insurance policy on her life. The face value was the equivalent of $150,000, a magnificent sum in the mid-nineteenth century. Ed would pay the first year's premium. Seraphine would then fake illness and call in her doctor, namely Edmund Pommerais. Ed would inform the insurance boys that their policy holder would be occupying a plot at the local cemetery within 12 months. Cunning Ed told Seraphine that the insurance company would offer her a cash settlement in order to avoid paying off the higher amount on her death. Ed explained that once they got their hands on the settlement money, they would be able to continue their relationship in style.

Seraphine de Pauw looked at the handsome young doctor who had re-entered her life like Prince Charming. She would do anything he asked. When Ed explained that he might have to give her some nasty medicine, which would make her feel slightly ill for a few days, she understood. After all, another doctor might be called in and it would be necessary to deceive him. Naturally, Ed was the beneficiary on the policy. To be on the safe side, he had Seraphine sign a will leaving everything to him. The poor woman had no idea what she was signing.

Ed's diabolical plot was put into motion. He scraped up the money to pay the first year's premium. Seraphine purchased the life insurance policy. After waiting a few months, she pretended to faint in front of neighbors in her tenement building. The rumor spread that she was in failing health. Finally, after one particular fainting spell, a neighbor called the doctor. Quick as a bunny, Ed was on the scene. He gave his patient some medicine, which contained small quantities of poison.

In the following days, neighbors visited. No question

about it, Seraphine was seriously ill. Each day, Dr. Pommerais made a house call. Nothing seemed to help.

While Seraphine suffered, she firmly believed that her discomfort would soon be over and yield her a fortune. During a visit from her sister, Madame Ritter, Seraphine confided that her sickness was a sham. She told her sister the entire scheme. The story was so convincing, Madame Ritter believed it and told no one.

On Nov. 17, 1863, Seraphine de Pauw died in agony. A neighbor called Dr. Pommerais. The doctor was at his lover's side during her final moments.

Ed wasn't a patient man. He was just itching to get his hands on that insurance money. He waited a week. On the day after Seraphine's funeral, he applied for the payoff. The insurance company acknowledged the claim and were about to issue a cheque, when who should show up but Madame Ritter with her unusual story.

Well, folks, the fat was in the fire. Seraphine de Pauw's body was exhumed and found to contain large quantities of digitaline. Ed was arrested and taken into custody. Madame Dubizy's body was also exhumed, but the exact cause of death could not be found. It didn't matter much.

Ed stood accused of murder. At his trial, Madame Ritter's story was enough to convince the jury that Ed had indeed murdered Seraphine de Pauw.

Dr. Edmund Pommerais was executed for his crime. He vehemently protested his innocence to the end. No one believed him.

THE DEATH OF JOHN KNIGHT III

John Knight III led two lives. As the grandson of John Knight, retired editorial chairman of the Knight-Ridder newspaper chain, he was a respected newspaperman. To the casual observer, the heir to the newspaper fortune had everything a 30-year-old man could desire. A graduate of both Harvard and Oxford, he held a responsible position with one of the family newspapers in Philadelphia, occupied a luxurious apartment, and had all the funds and intelligence with which to enjoy a full and rewarding life. He was also a practising homosexual.

Early Sunday morning, on Dec. 7, 1975, John Knight's world crumbled. The previous evening, which had started out pleasantly enough, was to end in death. John had shot pheasants in South Dakota earlier that fall and had sent them over to the swank La Truffe restaurant, where he was to host an intimate dinner party.

John's guests that night were a lady friend, Ellen Roche, Mr. and Mrs. Paul Janensch and Dr. and Mrs. John McKinnon. Paul Janensch was managing editor of the Philadelphia *News*, a paper owned by the Knight-Ridder chain. As such, he was John's boss. The McKinnons were friends of long standing. Dr. McKinnon had been John's roommate at university. The doctor and his wife had travelled to Philadelphia expressly to spend the week with

John as house guests at his luxurious Rittenhouse Square apartment.

Shortly after midnight, the party broke up. The Janensches and Ellen Roche left for their respective homes directly from the restaurant. John and the McKinnons returned to John's apartment. The dinner party had been a great success. There had been many toasts and much liquor had been consumed. Once at John's apartment, the two men continued drinking. Rosemary McKinnon, tired of listening to the good old university days, fell asleep on a couch.

Around 1 a.m. John received a phone call. Dr. McKinnon could only hear John's end of the conversation. He heard his host say, "I can't see you tonight. I've got houseguests." John explained that his caller was a pimp who supplied him with prostitutes. The McKinnons were rather embarrassed, but chose to ignore the remark. After all, their old friend was a single man. His sex life was his own affair.

The phone rang again around 3 a.m. John answered, and then advised his guests it was time to turn in. The McKinnons retired to their bedroom. Dr. McKinnon, while not staggering drunk, had had a lot to drink. He flopped into bed with his clothes on. Rosemary McKinnon undressed and retired.

An hour later, the doorbell rang. It was the man who had made the phone calls. John refused him entry. The man pleaded, "I love you, John. I must see you." When John opened the door, Felix Melendez, Steven Maleno and Salvatore Soli bullied their way into the apartment.

John was overpowered. His hands were tied behind his back and his legs tied together with socks and ropes. The three men wound his expensive silk ties around his head. Then they proceeded to punch and kick the helpless man. One of the men, probably Melendez, stabbed John Knight in the chest five times.

The three intruders ransacked the apartment. Tables were overturned, the contents of drawers spilled on the

floor until the place was a shambles. In the guest room, Mrs. McKinnon woke with a start just as the three men threw open the door. They ordered the nude woman out of bed. Her husband, in a heavy sleep as a result of the alcohol he had consumed, didn't budge.

Salvatore Soli, waving a revolver, forced Rosemary McKinnon to assist in the search for valuables. Felix Melendez stalked through the apartment like a madman with a scuba diving knife and a harpoon gun. Mrs. McKinnon was led into John's bedroom, where she saw her host gagged and tied hand and foot. She had no way of knowing if he was dead or alive.

When the apartment building's night attendant showed up at the door, Felix acted as spokesman. The attendant had received a complaint about the noise emanating from the Knight apartment. Felix apologized. The attendant went away, but his appearance had frightened Sal and Steve. They tied up Mrs. McKinnon, placed her under a sofa and took off with whatever loot they had gathered.

Now alone, Felix became even more tense and nervous. Rosemary McKinnon, despite the terror she had endured, kept her head. She talked Felix into untying her hands and feet. Once free, she dashed into the guest room, grabbed one of John's rifles, at the same time shaking her husband and placing the rifle in his hands. Quickly and concisely, she explained the situation to her half awake husband.

The doctor rushed into John Knight's room. There was the fully-armed Felix Melendez, standing on a bed shouting, "I didn't do it, I didn't do it." McKinnon grappled with Melendez, who finally broke free and fled from the bedroom.

Dr. McKinnon untied his host and attempted mouth to mouth resuscitation, but quickly realized John Knight was beyond help. While her husband was thus engaged, Rosemary McKinnon threw on a robe, ran from the apartment and pressed a button for an elevator. One can only imag-

ine her terror when Felix, still wielding his knife, jumped into the elevator with her.

Rosemary warded off Felix's attempts to stab her and was partially successful. Her fingers were cut and she received a slight wound around the left breast before the elevator stopped at the third floor. She was able to run out of the elevator and make her way down a fire escape to the main lobby. Meanwhile, Felix disappeared.

Why was John Knight murdered? We do know that Felix had been a lover of Knight's and had told his fellow conspirators that he had a wealthy friend who would be easy to rob. Felix was aptly rewarded for initiating the robbery, which culminated in the senseless torture and murder of John Knight. His companions blamed him for going berserk in the apartment. It was supposed to be a simple robbery. Now they were marked men.

They watched TV and heard the concise descriptions given to police by Rosemary McKinnon. That's when Sal and Steve decided to reward Felix. Under the pretense of burying some of the loot taken from the Knight apartment, they enticed Felix into a wooded area in New Jersey. Steve Maleno shot Felix Melendez dead.

Sal, accompanied by a girlfriend, fled to Miami, where he hocked the remaining stolen goods for $150. However, his girlfriend got cold feet and turned him in to police. Steve voluntarily gave himself up.

Salvatore Soli was found guilty of murder in the first degree, guilty of robbery, guilty of burglary and guilty of criminal conspiracy. He was sentenced to life imprisonment.

Four weeks after Sal's conviction, Steven Maleno pleaded guilty to the murder of John Knight, as well as that of Felix Melendez. He was sentenced to two consecutive life sentences.

AN INNOCENT MAN

Kenneth Miller, a 24-year-old Vietnam veteran, had the unbelievable experience of listening to a jury find him guilty of a crime he didn't commit. It was a nightmare.

On the evening of June 11, 1974, Janelle Kirby was alone in her Fort Worth, Texas garage apartment, when a man wielding a .22 calibre pistol walked in. He ordered Janelle to place her hands on her bed while he snapped handcuffs on her wrists. Janelle made a desperate lunge for the pistol. The pair grappled. Janelle kicked and bit at her attacker as they rolled on the floor.

Finally, the man wrenched himself free and stood over Janelle. Calmly, he aimed and started shooting. Five bullets struck Janelle in the head and face. Despite the horrible wounds, the terrified woman didn't lose consciousness. She watched as the man rifled her purse and left. Then she staggered down to another apartment for assistance.

This remarkable woman lingered between life and death for a week before gradually beginning to recover. When she was sufficiently strong, police had her scan mug shots. Two and a half months after the attack, she unhesitatingly picked out Kenneth Miller as her assailant. There was absolutely no doubt in Janelle's mind. She would never forget the man who had stood over her firing that gun at her head.

Police picked up Kenneth Miller. Miller had served with distinction in Vietnam. At the time of his arrest, he worked in a sporting goods store. He had handled guns most of his adult life. Now he stood accused of attempted murder. He was convicted solely on the victim's eyewitness identification.

Kenneth stood in the witness box and heard the guilty verdict. He was dumbfounded. Suddenly, he bolted from the courtroom, jumped into a friend's car and managed to escape from the courthouse. Another friend, Dianne Opperman, let him stay in her apartment for two weeks. During that time he learned that he had been sentenced to 70 years imprisonment.

Kenneth took off. He travelled to Michigan, then to Georgia. All the while he stayed in touch with Dianne Opperman. Dianne, a legal secretary, believed implicitly in Kenneth's innocence. She decided to join him in his life as a fugitive on the run.

With Dianne's total savings of $1000, the young couple attempted to carve out a new life. They travelled to Flagstaff, Arizona, where Dianne obtained a position with a law firm. Kenneth was hired as a mechanic with a large garage, although he knew precious little about his new vocation. However, he learned quickly on the job. Dianne and Kenneth were well-liked by everyone who came in contact with them, including several police officers with whom they socialized. For a year they were relatively happy.

Kenneth was always fearful that he would be captured. To alleviate his stress, he drank a bit too much. The least brush with the law caused him grave anxiety. A traffic ticket was enough reason to pull up stakes and move. Dianne and Kenneth tried California, returned to Flagstaff, and moved again to Las Vegas, Nevada.

Years passed. Dianne had little difficulty obtaining a good position with a law firm in Las Vegas. Using the alias Allen McGinnis, Kenneth worked hard, eventually ending up in the newspaper distribution business. His

income grew to $50,000 a year. This, coupled with Dianne's substantial salary, afforded the pair a more than comfortable lifestyle. They married and purchased a fine home, complete with swimming pool. They owned two cars, as well as a pick-up truck. On the surface, the McGinnis' had achieved the good life, but under the veneer of material possessions lay the ever present danger of discovery. Although they rarely discussed the past, Kenneth realized that if he were apprehended, his wife could be charged with being an accessory. Yes, it was a good life, but a fragile one.

Kenneth's parents died back home in Texas. He didn't dare attend either funeral. Frustrated and on edge, he drank more heavily. He and Dianne often bickered. Sometimes the bickering turned into shouting matches. When Kenneth struck her, Dianne decided to seek a divorce. In 1983, eight years after they fled from Texas, Dianne and Kenneth were divorced.

Without Dianne, Kenneth Miller's world crumbled. His drinking cost him his business, his fine home and eventually, his three vehicles. With little to hold him, Kenneth roamed the southwest U.S. as a drifter.

Meanwhile, back in Texas, Leonard Schilling was a cop with a long memory. He never forgot Kenneth Miller, the man he firmly believed fired five shots into Janelle Kirby's head. When Schilling became co-ordinator of a Crime Stoppers program, he placed Kenneth's name and photo on his "Ten Most Wanted" list. As a result, Kenneth's picture and description were widely distributed in newspapers, grocery stores, post offices and on TV. A reward of $1000 was offered for information leading to his arrest. On June 9, 1986, Kenneth was spotted and picked up in a Las Vegas appliance store.

Back in Texas, Leonard Schilling was delighted that after 12 years he had been instrumental in apprehending the man who had attempted to murder Janelle Kirby. The same week that Kenneth's capture was big news in Texas, Len Schilling received an anonymous phone call. It was

disconcerting. The caller said, "Miller didn't do it. Look for William Ted Wilhoit in the State Prison in Huntsville."

Next morning, Schilling dug into William Wilhoit's past. It wasn't difficult. Wilhoit had a long record of sexual offenses. He had also lived a few streets from Janelle Kirby at the time of the attempted murder. Besides, his physical description was strikingly similar to that of Kenneth Miller. Schilling realized that, other than Janelle's positive identification, Wilhoit was every bit as good a suspect as Kenneth Miller.

Wilhoit consented to be interviewed with the assurance that he would be immune from prosecution. Under this condition, he confessed to the attempted murder 12 years earlier. Wilhoit left no doubt in the minds of detectives and lawyers who were present at his questioning. Amazingly, he remembered the contents of Kirby's apartment, her clothing and jewelry.

There was no doubt whatsoever that he was telling the truth. Naturally enough, he claimed that the five shots were fired while he was grappling with Janelle, rather than while he stood over the helpless woman. Wilhoit even recalled that he lost the ejection rod from the cheap .22 calibre pistol he carried that night. Days after the attack, the ejection rod had been found on Janelle's carpet and had been turned over to the police. The ejection rod lay in an evidence box for 12 years. It now became the strongest piece of physical evidence linking William Wilhoit to the attack on Janelle Kirby.

Kenneth Miller was returned to Texas and, in due course, completely exonerated of any connection with the crime which had forced him to lead a fugitive's life for 12 long years.

THE HEAT
OF PASSION

Alma and Francis Rattenbury led interesting, adventurous lives before they met and married each other. Let's take Alma first.

Alma was raised in Kamloops, B.C., where she was something of a child prodigy. She was an accomplished pianist and violinist long before reaching her teens. In 1913 she met Caledon Dolling, and a short time later the pair married. Their marriage appears to have been a happy union until the outbreak of the First World War. Dolling enlisted and served overseas. He was wounded twice before being killed in action.

Alma, who had followed her husband to England, was devastated. In order to contribute to the war effort, she became attached to the French Red Cross and served as an orderly just to the rear of the front lines in France. Alma was wounded twice and received the Croix de Guerre from the French government.

At the conclusion of the war, Alma, a beautiful, charming woman, pulled herself together long enough to marry a former soldier with the great name of Compton Pakenham. The couple moved to Long Island, N.Y. To make ends meet, Alma gave music lessons. Her husband was an unsuccessful lecturer and book reviewer. Eventually, they divorced. With her son Christopher in tow, Alma returned

171

to her family back in British Columbia.

Let's have a review - two husbands, one son, one war, two wounds, one decoration from a foreign government. It should have been enough, but that simply wasn't Alma's style. There would be much more.

Francis Rattenbury was a British architect who emigrated to Victoria, B.C. in 1892. He was immediately successful in winning a competition for the design of the new parliament buildings in the B.C. capital. From that moment, Francis never looked back. He designed scores of fine homes and public buildings.

Around the turn of the century, he married Eleanor Florence Nunn. The couple settled into a large home designed by Francis. They had two children and led a happy, prosperous existence for some time. Francis continued to distinguish himself in his profession, designing the Empress Hotel in Victoria, as well as many other landmarks.

Then something happened to Francis Rattenbury. Maybe he had achieved too much too soon. Whatever the reason, he seems to have lost his ambition for his work as well as his affection for his wife. They lived together in their large home, but drifted apart.

One night Francis was introduced to Alma. He was completely enamored with the much younger, beautiful woman. From that moment, he worked toward one end - to divorce his wife and become Alma's husband. Francis was successful. At age 58, he married for the second time. The union, initially a happy one, did not meet with the approval of Francis' family. This, coupled with distasteful business deals, helped the Rattenburys make the decision to retire to Bournemouth, England. Money was not a factor. The Rattenburys were independently wealthy.

Francis Rattenbury didn't take well to retirement. He suffered from severe bouts of depression. In 1934, Francis was 66 and Alma was an extremely attractive 37. They lived in a large home called Villa Madeira, complete with servants and all the creature comforts. Francis consumed

a bottle of whisky each night. To alleviate what had become a boring existence, Alma now spent most of her time with her hired companion, Irene Riggs.

The situation was tailor made for an external ingredient to enter the plot. The ingredient was a rather simple, 17-year-old lad, George Stoner. Alma had advertised for a chauffeur/handyman and George applied for the job. Life would never be the same around Villa Madeira again.

Within weeks, Alma and George were hitting the sack at every opportunity. George, who may not have been a mental giant, was well above average in anatomical attributes. Alma realized that she had packed a full lifetime into the first half of her existence, but now knew she had been shortchanged in the sex department. George was making up for all that with youthful enthusiasm and God given natural ability.

Life in the large villa had something for everyone. George had a good job and plenty of sex. Rattenbury had his bottle. Alma had George. Even Irene Riggs wasn't doing too badly. She didn't have to hold Alma's hand any more.

Human nature is sometimes difficult to fathom. Unbelievably, George grew jealous of Rattenbury. The young stud couldn't stand the thought of Alma being in her husband's company. She assured him that she was now living with her husband in name only. To pacify George, Alma was able to get away with him for a weekend. They checked into an expensive hotel. Alma showered George with gifts and high living. The trip didn't have the desired effect. Once George tasted how the other half lived, he hated to return to his previous chauffeur/ handyman occupation.

When Alma told him that she and her husband were planning a weekend away from Villa Madeira the following day, George was incensed and swore he would do anything to prevent the trip.

Let's be fair to Alma. Whatever George's feelings were toward Alma, and there is some evidence that in his own

simple way he loved her, there is no doubt whatever that Alma truly loved George Stoner. Other than the obvious physical attraction, the odd couple had nothing in common. Alma was a sophisticated woman who had led a full, exciting life. By contrast, George, who was only 17, whose one big adventure was Alma.

On Sunday, March 24, at approximately 9:30 p.m., Alma kissed her husband good night and retired to her upstairs bedroom. Francis stayed in the drawing room sipping on his whisky and browsing through a book. Irene Riggs had the night off. She returned to Villa Madeira sometime after 10 p.m. and went directly to her upstairs bedroom. Shortly thereafter, she left her room to go to the bathroom. On the way, she met George Stoner. George, the only other live-in employee, was standing at the top of the stairs.

Irene inquired, "What's the matter?"

George replied, "Nothing. I was looking to see if the lights were out."

That satisfied Irene. She returned to her bedroom. A few moments later, Alma, who had always been very close to Irene, joined her for a chat in her room. Later, Irene would state that Alma was cheerful and told her that she was looking forward to spending a few days away from the villa with her husband.

Downstairs, in the Villa Madeira that night, George Stoner sneaked up behind the dozing Francis Rattenbury and clubbed him to death with a mallet. After the deed was a *fait accompli*, George dashed upstairs and into bed with Alma. Alma sensed that her lover was not acting in a normal manner. Finally, George blurted out that he had hurt her husband. Alma went downstairs and discovered Francis leaning back limp in his favorite armchair. His hair was caked with blood. Alma shouted, "Irene!"

Irene Riggs ran to the drawing room. Together, the two women washed the still breathing man's horrible head wounds. Stoner was sent to fetch a doctor. Francis lin-

gered between life and death for four days before expiring.

While ministering to her husband on that fateful night, Alma picked up Francis' bottle of whisky and took a few stiff drinks. By the time doctors and police arrived, she was almost incoherent. When questioned, she insisted that it was she who had attacked her husband. However, when Francis died, George confessed that he had killed the older man.

The strange love affair between the simple lad and the mature, cultured woman caused a sensation. Both were charged with murder. During the two trials which followed, George swore that he had acted alone and had not been influenced in any way by Alma. She, in turn, only withdrew her confession when she was assured that by doing so she would not be placing her lover in jeopardy.

On May 31, 1935, at London's famed Old Bailey, an English jury found George Stoner guilty of murder. He was sentenced to hang. Alma was found not guilty and released from custody.

Three days after the verdict was handed down, Alma took a train to New Milton, Hampshire. There, at the edge of a river, she calmly smoked a last cigarette before plunging a knife six times into her chest. Slowly, she slid into the water. Alma left a suicide note explaining that because her lover was to be hanged, she had no further reason for living.

An appeal was instituted by Stoner's lawyers and, within three weeks of Alma's dramatic suicide, his sentence was commuted to life imprisonment. In 1942, after serving seven years, George Stoner was released from prison. He joined the army, took part in the Normandy landings and survived the war. He later married and became a model citizen.

Alma would have been proud.

TO RUSSIA
WITH MURDER

Are the Russians concerned only with winning the Olympic games, sending cosmonauts into the stratosphere, and lining up for loaves of bread? Of course not. They are also deeply involved in murdering each other. What's more, like the citizens of all countries, they have the basic desire to get away with the dastardly deed.

Let's slip away behind the Iron Curtain to a cosy apartment on Moscow's Red October Street. The apartment is occupied by 22-year-old Margarita Tikhomirov, her husband Georgi, 24, and his parents, Valentina and Nikolas. Now for some brief historical notes. We'll get back to the apartment in a moment.

Georgi had suffered from tuberculosis as a youth and had spent some time in a sanitorium. He met Margarita when he was 16 and she was only 14. The two young people fell madly in love and were inseparable from that very first day. Pretty Margarita was a war orphan, who was supported and educated by the government. Her lowly status in life didn't sit well with Georgi's mother. She knew that in the Russia of the early 1950s, one of the only ways for a young man to obtain a dwelling of his own was to marry a rich girl.

After dating for two years, Georgi and Margarita were secretly married. They attempted to find rooms of their

176

own, but were unsuccessful. After being informed of the marriage, Valentina reluctantly took in her son and her new daughter-in-law. Valentina was just plain miserable to Margarita. Nothing satisfied the older woman.

Margarita realized that on her husband's salary at the brickyards, they would never get a place of their own. In desperation, she and Georgi decided that he would leave the brickworks and enroll in an engraving course. She would take instructions in midwifery. It might take a year or two, but at some point in the future they would see the financial light at the end of the tunnel.

Margarita's plan might have had an outside chance of success had she not become pregnant. The joy of giving birth to a healthy son was tempered by her mother-in-law's attitude towards the baby. Valentina would barely look at the infant, whom she considered an added inconvenience in the now grossly overcrowded apartment. The proud grandfather, Nikolas, showed some affection for the new arrival, but appears to have been completely under the domination of his wife.

When the baby was four months old, tragedy struck. The infant choked to death on his teether. Margarita and Georgi were not at home at the time. According to police reports, the child's grandparents had stepped out of the apartment for the briefest of moments. It was during their absence that the baby died. That's the official version of the baby's demise, but in light of future events, we can only guess at the truth.

Life went on in the apartment in its usual repressive way, with Margarita bearing the brunt of her mother-in-law's hatred. The two men in the apartment, her husband and father-in-law, seemed powerless to alleviate the abuse.

Had her depressing life driven the poor girl to suicide? That's what neighbors whispered when Valentina found her daughter-in-law hanging from a beam with a rope around her neck and an overturned chair at her feet. It was unfortunate that no one was at home that afternoon. Valentina and Nikolas were taking a walk, and Georgi had

not returned from his engraving course when Margarita came home from her midwifery instruction. The poor girl must have been depressed and decided to end it all. At least, that's the way it looked.

One thing bothered police commissar Gregory Arensky. When he examined the body at the scene, he noticed some slight bruising around the lips. A light flashed on in the deep recesses of Arensky's mind. At the time, he knew nothing of Margarita's history. It was just a detective's hunch that made him scan the apartment with thoughts of murder dancing through his head. When he saw two empty glasses on the kitchen table, he gingerly picked them up with a handkerchief and tucked them away.

Arensky proceeded to question the family. Georgi was devastated at the loss of the woman he had cherished since he was 16. Nikolas, as usual, went along with whatever his wife said. That good woman was as cool as a bowl of borscht. She emphasized suicide by saying over and over that she realized her daughter-in-law was losing her mind.

Arensky's computer-like mind was busy with addition. The bruises around the mouth looked suspiciously as if they had been inflicted by a hand placed over the struggling girl's mouth. Then there was the aggressive mother-in-law and the absence of anyone in the apartment. Could there be something rotten in the state of Russia?

When he questioned neighbors and found out that Margarita wasn't exactly the most popular member of the Tikhomirov family, Arensky felt his suspicions were well-founded. He had the glasses, which he had taken from the apartment, checked for fingerprints. One set of prints didn't belong to any family member. The plot, as they say in Russia, thickens.

Neighbors were questioned again. One remembered seeing Valentina enter the apartment on the evening of the murder with a strange woman. It took Arensky eight days to trace the stranger. She turned out to be Valentina's friend, Vera Rybakova, who lived in Khovrina. Vera

was the lady whose fingerprints were on the glass found in the apartment.

Arensky felt he had enough. In May, 1956, Valentina and Nikolas Tikhomirov and Vera Rybakova stood trial for the murder of Margarita Tikhomirov.

The crafty detective had dug up witnesses, who were now paraded before the court. From these witnesses, the prosecution was able to prove that Valentina had planned the murder for over two years. She had had some difficulty convincing her husband that she wanted Margarita out of the way for the good of the entire family and, in particular, for the benefit of their son. As usual, Nikolas acquiesced, but insisted that someone outside the family do the actual deed. Valentina remembered her old friend, Vera, who proved to be able and willing to do anything for 5000 rubles.

The treacherous trio chose a night when Georgi would be late. They waited. Nikolas became nervous. He and Vera had a drink of vodka out of glasses. Margarita walked in. Valentina and Vera were concealed behind curtains. Nikolas beckoned from the kitchen, "Come in and have a cup of tea."

Slowly, Margarita walked into the kitchen. Vera took the opportunity to attack Margarita from behind. She slipped a noose over her head and pulled. Margarita broke free and raced into Nikolas' arms. We will never know if she was dashing to what she perceived as protection or was involuntarily catapulted into the waiting grasp of her father-in-law.

Nikolas clasped his hand over Margarita's mouth to stifle any screams while Vera and her diabolical noose went to work. In moments it was over. The body was quickly hoisted up to the beam, the chair overturned and the suicide scenario set in motion.

During the trial, the unholy alliance began to crumble. Vera broke first. She admitted to being in the apartment at the time of the murder. She claimed she had poured the drink of vodka after having witnessed the murder by

the other two defendants. Heavens, she never even knew murder was about to take place until it was too late to do anything about it.

When Valentina heard Vera's story, she saw red. She blurted out that she hadn't paid 5000 rubles just to watch Vera drink vodka. As the accusations flew back and forth, it became apparent that all three defendants were equally guilty of murder.

Throughout it all, Georgi Tikhomirov sat quietly by himself. His mother and father were obviously guilty of murdering his wife. He now had grave suspicions that his little son had also been murdered. His entire family were either victims or culprits. He left the courtroom as the judge sentenced his parents to be shot by firing squad, a sentence which was later carried out.

ATTIC JOYS

Walburga Oesterreich had more moves than Wayne Gretzky on a good night. It wasn't her fault she was getting precious little opportunity to practise her various horizontal talents with her husband Fred. You see, Fred, despite his business acumen, was definitely deficient where it counts most - in bed.

Let's set the scene. Fred Oesterreich was a big man who had a big appetite and smoked big cigars. That's all Fred had that was big. In 1903, in Milwaukee, Wisconsin, he owned a thriving apron factory. Those were the good old days, when aprons were a hot item, something like pantyhose are today. Fred's wife, Walburga, was a gorgeous specimen of a woman. She had brown flashing eyes, full sensuous lips and a figure that would wake a corpse.

The Oesterreiches simply didn't get along. Oh, sure, they had been married for 15 years, lived in a large comfortable home and were quite wealthy. But there were problems. We already covered one of Fred's shortcomings. He also drank heavily, spent most of his time at the apron factory and, in general, neglected the gorgeous Walburga.

One fine day, Walburga was whiling away the time stitching something or other on her sewing machine when the darn thing jammed. It was only natural for her to call

Fred and have him send over one of the boys from the factory to repair the machine.

Seventeen-year-old Otto Sanhuber showed up. Little Otto stood just a smidgen under five feet, had a receding chin, buggy eyes and suffered from a severe case of acne. More often than not, his nose dripped. Folks, you could not call Otto an attractive man.

Who knows what chemistry takes place between us mortals? The exotic mixture of juices which ebb and flow in our veins ebbed and flowed that day when Walburga and Otto met. Before the day was over, Walburga was well aware that whatever deficiencies plagued her husband certainly didn't apply to Otto. As for Otto, he figured he had died and gone to heaven.

Walburga and Otto, the original odd couple, couldn't get enough of each other. No sooner did Fred leave the house each morning than Otto would sneak in to make love to the ever willing Walburga. While he was at it, Otto partook of Fred's abundant supply of liquor and food. The little rascal could eat up a storm.

For three years, this rather idyllic situation continued, but it was destined to self-destruct if left unchecked. Walburga couldn't think of life without Otto. To alleviate her fears, she came up with her bizarre and unbelievable idea.

Are you ready for this?

Walburga suggested that Otto move into her home and take up occupancy in the attic. She would have it furnished to suit his particular requirements. A candle, which could not be seen through the lone far window, could be used for light. Yes, there would be certain inconveniences, but the benefits far outweighed them. Otto would have the best food, Havana cigars, vintage wines and, not to be forgotten, as much sex as any man could desire. Rather coincidental, but nevertheless extremely convenient, was the location of the trap door to the attic - in the master bedroom, directly above the bed. Otto moved in.

The arrangement proved to be ideal for all concerned, if you don't count Fred. Otto, who had lived the anonymous

existence of an underpaid sewing machine repairman, now lived the strange life of having all his basic needs filled. The confinement wasn't quite as bad as it appears at first glance. Otto had the run of the house whenever Fred was out, which was often.

To pass the time when he wasn't performing at his specialty, Otto wrote adventure stories. Walburga typed them and sent them off to the pulps. Initially, all Otto received for his trouble was a drawer full of rejection slips. But let's give the little fellow credit. He persevered and soon started receiving cheques on a regular basis. Walburga opened a bank account for her lover and deposited the cheques.

Fred, now completely alienated from his wife, took to the sauce with a vengeance. As the years slipped by, he became a nag, always complaining about large food bills. His cigars were forever being depleted. When he complained of noises coming from the attic and wouldn't accept Walburga's explanation of mice scurrying about, she suggested he seek the help of psychiatrist. Fred soon became a regular on the couch. As a diversion, he often came home with a head of steam and took a few punches at his wife. Walburga was philosophical. It was a small price to pay.

In 1913, the Oesterreiches moved to a new home. Otto wasn't inconvenienced that much. He moved right along with the family. Walburga had made sure that her new home had a pleasant attic.

Naturally enough, there were some close calls. One day Fred came home unexpectedly and caught Otto raiding the fridge. Thinking that he had apprehended a sneak thief red-handed, Fred tossed Otto out of the house on his ear. He never for a moment realized that he was manhandling his wife's lover. Two hours later, Otto was nibbling on chicken cacciatore while he dashed off a China Seas adventure - in the attic, of course.

When Fred sold the apron factory in 1918 and bought into a garment factory in Los Angeles, it was a disruptive

experience for Otto and Walburga. However, Walburga managed to find a house complete with convenient attic. As usual, Otto moved in.

The weird lifestyle of Otto, Walburga and Fred sailed merrily along for the next four years, right up until the night of Aug. 22, 1922. That night, Fred came home loaded for bear. He commenced to punch out Walburga. Otto, who for all intents and purposes was now far more of a husband to Walburga than her legal spouse, saw red. The little fellow, who weighed only 105 pounds soaking wet, dashed down out of his attic retreat, grabbed a .25 calibre pistol off a shelf and unceremoniously ventilated Fred with more holes than your average Swiss cheese.

Walburga, a quick thinker on her feet, immediately took over. She snatched Fred's expensive diamond - studded watch off his wrist. She told Otto to get the hell back in that attic. Then she locked herself in a closet and slipped the key under the door into the room where her husband Fred lay so very dead.

A neighbor, who had heard the shots, called police. They released the hysterical Walburga from the closet. She told the police that she and her husband had arrived home and surprised a burglar. Fred resisted when the burglar attempted to relieve him of his watch. The intruder fired. He then tossed her in the closet and locked the door. Police had some misgivings, but reluctantly bought Walburga's story.

Fred's estate was valued at around $1 million, but there were many details to be ironed out before money trickled down to the grieving widow. Walburga hired a lawyer, Herman Shapiro, to handle her affairs. During one of her visits to Shapiro's office, she gave him a present, a diamond studded wristwatch. Shapiro remembered that a diamond studded watch had been taken from slain Fred's wrist. When he mentioned this to Walburga, she smiled and said she had been mistaken. She had found the wristwatch under a cushion in the living room and simply wanted Shapiro to have it as a gift.

A coincidence did Walburga in. It was a year after Fred's death. Detective Herman Cline, the officer in charge of the original inquiry into Fred's murder, dropped in to chat with lawyer Shapiro. He stood flabbergasted as he stared at the dead man's watch carelessly lying on Shapiro's desk. When asked, Shapiro related the story Walburga had told him.

Now, the fat was in the fire. Cline dashed over to Walburga's home and took the widow into custody. Walburga phoned Shapiro with explicit instructions, "Go up to the big bedroom in my home. Tap three times on the trap door in the attic. There's someone up there - a half brother of mine who is sort of a vagabond. Tell him I've gone to Milwaukee."

Shapiro did as he was told. Out popped Otto. His first words were, "Yes, I shot Mr. Oesterreich. It was an accident." Otto told all. Shapiro did what he thought best. He contacted a criminal lawyer, who suggested that Otto take a short trip out of the country. Otto tapped those dollars which had been accumulating from his stories and took off for Vancouver.

Meanwhile, back at the L.A. jail, police were in a quandary. They had no confession and no murder weapon. Reluctantly, Det. Cline released the widow.

Seven years passed. Walburga lived well on Fred's inheritance until 1930. That's when she and lawyer Shapiro had a falling out over financial affairs. Shapiro, fearful for his life, decided to go to the police with the real story of how Fred had met his end.

Walburga and Otto, who had returned to L.A. by this time, were both arrested and charged with Fred's murder. Otto was tried first and found guilty of manslaughter. As the statute of limitations had run out after three years, he was released from custody. Now 44 years old, the little stud wandered out of court and into oblivion. He had spent a total of 19 years in sundry attics.

Walburga didn't fare that badly either. At her trial, the jury failed to agree. She too was released from custody.

The 63-year-old Walburga left the courtroom with an abundance of money and sweet memories.

THEY KILLED
THEIR FATHER

Marie de Lourdes Rodrigues was a 20-year-old beauty when she met Richard Jahnke in Santurce, Puerto Rico. Marie was susceptible to the attentions of the confident American. She lived alone in a less than comfortable apartment and, as an operator with the local telephone company, earned only enough to get by.

On the other hand, the ambitious, serious Richard was a career army man. True enough, he was only a private, but he had a good book-keeping job at Fort Brooke. Besides, to hear Richard tell it, the book-keeping job was only the beginning. He was going all the way with the U.S. Army.

Marie was completely enthralled. She and Richard were inseparable. There was one thing which sometimes annoyed Marie, but at the same time was a form of flattery. Richard was extremely jealous. On occasion, his jealousy would cause a scene, like the time he flared up at a man who had done nothing more than cast an admiring glance at Marie on a bus. It had been an embarrassing scene.

On June 6, 1964, Marie and Richard were married. Nine months later, Marie gave birth to her first child, a daughter, whom they christened Deborah. That fall, Marie found herself pregnant once more. The pregnancy coincided with Richard's reassignment to Fort Ord, Calif. His three year

hitch in the army was up. Richard signed up for another six. On June 27, 1966, Richard John was born. Private Jahnke was elated to have a son. Five months later, the proud father was shipped to South Korea, where he spent 13 months before returning to his wife and two infant children. He was now Sgt. Jahnke. The army moved the family once more, this time to Fort Benjamin Harrison in Indianapolis.

By now, both children were active toddlers, who behaved no better or worse than average children. For reasons known only to himself, Richard believed them to be noisy and ill-behaved. He spanked both children often. Marie objected, but was overruled by her domineering husband. He told Marie that she was spoiling the children.

Once, when she objected strenuously that he was striking the children too severely, Richard hauled off and punched her in the face. Amazed at this turn of events, Marie threatened to call the base MPs, but Richard assured her that no one would believe her. He struck her again and hurled verbal abuse at her. For the first time in her marriage, Marie realized that her flattering army career husband had been disguising his true colors, that of a child and wife abuser.

The Jahnkes, a typical army family, relocated often in the ensuing years. A stint in Germany could have been a real adventure, were it not for the beatings inflicted by Richard. Rarely did a week go by that one or both of the children weren't severely beaten. Marie soon learned the rules. Long sleeves hid the children's bruises. Excuses made up for scraped knees.

Then there were the good days, when Richard behaved like a normal father to his family. Young Richard and Deborah would be lulled into a feeling of confidence toward their father, only to be brought back to earth by Richard's severe mood changes. It didn't take much. A noise while drinking soup could drive him into a tirade.

After his six-year stint, Richard left the army for good

and obtained a position in Cheyenne, Wyoming as an investigator with the Internal Revenue Service. As such, he carried a gun. Richard had a real affinity for guns and purchased a new one as the mood struck him. He kept many in his home at 8736 Cowpoke Drive.

The Jahnke children grew up in fear of their father. The months and years passed and the verbal and physical abuse continued. Richard and Deborah learned to live with the abuse, but hated to hear their mother being called a "fat spic" before receiving the full force of a punch to the face.

Young Richard joined the R.O.T.C. program at Central High School. He proved to be top cadet and became friendly with Major Robert Vegvary, the commander of the local R.O.T.C. program. In May, 1982, Richard was severely beaten by his father and decided to discuss the matter for the first time with an outsider. He talked to his superior officer. Vegvary strongly suggested that Richard report the incident to the authorities.

Reluctantly, Richard did as he was told. His scrapes and bruises were photographed. His mother and father were consulted, but in the end the incident was considered a "one incident occurrence." Richard Jahnke, Sr., treated the whole thing as a joke.

On the evening of Nov. 16, 1982, the lives of the Jahnke family living in the comfortable home on Cowpoke Drive would be changed forever. It was an anniversary of sorts for Marie and Richard. They had met in Puerto Rico exactly 20 years before to the day.

To celebrate, Richard took Marie to dinner at the Casa de Trujillo. Earlier that day Richard had fought with his son and daughter. Now Marie brought up the subject of counselling for the family. She suggested it might do them all some good. Richard agreed to give it a try, but swore that the whole thing was hopeless. His kids were rotten, and that was that.

Back at the house on Cowpoke Drive, 15-year-old Richard Jahnke waited for his parents' return. He was

well-equipped. He leaned against the front of the family station wagon cradling a 12 gauge pump-action Smith and Wesson in his arms. A Wesson .357 Magnum revolver fit snugly into his holster. Richard had also outfitted himself with a hunting knife. He was prepared for war.

Inside, acting as backup, Deborah nervously fidgeted with a M-1 .30 calibre carbine, waiting for the action to begin. She didn't have long to wait.

Marie and Richard drove into the driveway. Richard slipped out of his Volkswagen and was greeted by two loud roars from the 12 gauge shotgun. He would never strike any member of his family again. Marie ran to his side, then into the house and phoned for assistance.

As luck would have it, one of the first officers at the scene had been involved in young Richard's child abuse case some months earlier. He had a suspect in mind as soon as he arrived at Cowpoke Drive.

Inside the house, officers found weapons in a bedroom beside an open window. It appeared that the assailant had escaped through the window. A thorough search of the Jahnke house uncovered a total of 14 rifles, 12 hand guns and seven shotguns — 33 weapons in all. Many were loaded. One wonders, given the volatile personalities involved, why no one was killed earlier.

Young Richard had crawled out the open window into the bitter cold November night. After wandering for some hours, he made his way to the home of Donna Haese. He didn't know Donna that well, but he felt he had to talk to someone. Besides, it was so very cold. Donna's stepfather, Clarence Ketcham, let Richard in and listened as the boy told him simply, "I shot my Dad." Mr. Ketcham called police. Next morning, Deborah was picked up in a nearby park. She was far more substantially clad than her brother.

Richard Jahnke, Sr.'s estate amounted to over half a million dollars. Marie used some of that money to defend her children. Her lawyers were unsuccessful in having the Jahnke offspring tried in a juvenile court.

Richard was tried first, some two years after he had killed his father. He was found guilty of voluntary manslaughter. Deborah, who was tried separately, was found guilty of "aiding and abetting voluntary manslaughter."

Richard was sentenced to not less than five years or more than 15 years in prison. His lawyers appealed and gained his release on $5000 bail. The Wyoming Supreme Court upheld the court's sentence. However, the governor of the state, Ed Herschler, later commuted the sentence, enabling Richard to gain his parole on Sept. 9, 1985.

Deborah was sentenced to from three to eight years incarceration in a women's centre. She was released on $25,000 bail put up by her mother. The supreme court of the state also upheld her sentence. Once again, Gov. Herschler intervened, commuting her sentence to one year's probation.

Five days after both her children gained their freedom, Marie Jahnke married one John Druce. In attendance were her daughter Deborah, 20, and her son Richard, 19.

A MOMENT OF FURY

Edith Chubb wasn't a bad woman, really. Maybe a tad impetuous, but we all have our faults.

Edith, 46, lived in Broadstairs, England with her husband, Ernest, a plumber by trade. It wasn't an easy life; in fact, it was an extremely tough one. Let's look at Edith's lot that winter of 1958.

The Chubbs lived in a council house, together with Edith's mother and their five children. The eldest daughter, who was 16 years old, had a hole in her heart and wasn't expected to live more than five years. Then there was Ernest's sister, Lillian, who one day showed up for a week's visit and remained seven years.

A plumber's income didn't go far. True, Lillian worked, but she only contributed one and a half pounds a week to the family's income. It wasn't much.

To make ends meet, Edith took baby-sitting jobs, worked as a charwoman, labored as a cleaner in a factory and, three nights a week, worked as a practical nurse in a nearby hospital. Some nights the poor woman was able to catch only three hours sleep.

Month after month, year after year, Edith struggled. She never complained, but inside she seethed. She could take the housework; she could cope with the outside jobs, but she couldn't tolerate her sister-in-law Lillian. That

woman didn't lift a finger to help around the house. Many evenings, as Edith washed the dishes, Lillian would sit at the kitchen table, legs crossed, puffing on a fag, sipping a cuppa and making small talk. It was enough to drive a stronger woman than Edith to distraction.

Then there were the mornings that Lillian would consume a substantial breakfast and leave the house without moving a dish from the table to the sink. Edith boiled in silence until the morning of Feb. 6.

Edith had slaved for hours, preparing breakfast in shifts for her family, which totalled nine individuals. Gradually, members of the household left, until only Lillian and Edith. It was 8:40 a.m. Lillian put on her scarf and coat and prepared to leave the house for her work at a local store.

Edith took in the scene she had witnessed every morning for years. Not a hand of help, not a thank you. As usual, nothing. A rage, dormant for so long, sprung up within Edith Chubb. She rubbed her hands together, her eyes stared at her sister-in-law's back. Then she lunged.

Just as Lillian was about to walk out the front door, Edith's hands clutched at her scarf and pulled it from behind. She shook Lillian with all her pent up anger. That would show the ungrateful bitch to take her for granted. A good shaking would scare the living daylights out of her. One last strong pull on the scarf and Lillian fell back, striking her head on the stairs.

At that very moment, Edith heard the sound of footsteps approaching her front door. Her temples throbbed. What had she done? There lay Lillian, making gurgling noises on the floor. Surely she would be heard by the unknown person on the steps. Edith placed her hand over her sister-in-law's mouth for a few seconds. The person outside walked away and she removed her hand from Lillian's mouth. Lillian looked blue. Edith took her pulse. Nothing. Edith unwound the scarf. Surely Lillian would come around, but she didn't.

Edith sat on the stairs and waited, wondering what she

should do. Lillian was dead. She had to do something. Slowly, a plan formed in her mind. She fetched a wheelchair that had been used by her eldest daughter and struggled to lift the body into the wheelchair. Then Edith wheeled her macabre cargo out to the coal shed. That would do for now. She removed £12 from her victim's purse before throwing the purse into the stove. All that day and night, the corpse in the wheelchair reposed in the coal shed.

Edith later stated, "Next morning, after everyone had left the house, I pushed Lily in the chair over to Reading Street Road. She was covered with my travelling rug. I put her on the bank and went back home. It did not take me long."

That same day, the body was found. There were no signs of a struggle in the immediate area. The only indications of violence were the slight bruising about the neck and the bump on the head. It was obvious that the victim had been killed elsewhere.

Back home, Edith called her sister-in-law's place of employment and told them that she had not returned home that night. They advised Edith that Lillian hadn't shown up for work that morning either and suggested she call the police. Edith did as she was told. Soon, police were at her door with the sad news that her sister-in-law's body had been found not more than three quarters of a mile from the house. Edith feigned sorrow, informing the police that the last time she saw Lillian was when she left the house for work the previous day.

For a week police questioned every friend who might have given Lillian a lift to work. In fact, they questioned everyone who normally saw Lillian in the morning. All remembered seeing her each morning up until Feb. 6. On that morning, no one had seen her.

Detectives spoke to neighbors of the Chubbs on Hugin Ave. They learned that while Edith showed no outward animosity towards her sister-in-law, several suspected that she secretly hated Lillian. Many volunteered that she had

good reason to dislike lazy Lillian.

Police now suspected that Lillian Chubb had not left the house alive on the morning of Feb. 6. They turned to Edith for explanations. It didn't take long. Edith blurted out the whole story. "I killed her. It was just as she was going out the front door. Something just came over me. I pulled her scarf tight. She did not struggle. When I realized she was dead, I was horror-struck." She added, "Nobody knows what I've been through the last year. Lily was so smug and damn self-complacent. Nobody really knew what she was like."

In May, 1958, Edith Chubb was tried at London's famous Old Bailey. Forensic evidence bore out Edith's story of how she had strangled Lillian with the latter's scarf. Character witnesses testified that Edith was a conscientious, uncomplaining, hard-working woman. Her superiors at the hospital testified that she was one of the finest nurses in the institution.

A psychiatrist stated that, in his opinion, Edith had worked herself to the point where she was on the verge of a nervous breakdown. He testified that Edith had not intended to murder Lillian. She had tugged at the scarf during a moment of extreme mental irritation.

The jury obviously agreed. They found Edith Chubb not guilty of murder, but guilty of manslaughter. She was sentenced to four years imprisonment.

DEATH FARM

The plight of farmers in the U.S. has been well publicized. Almost everything utilized by farmers such as feed, fertilizer and farm instruments has risen in price dramatically in recent years, while the price of produce raised on the farm has remained relatively static.

On occasion, the frustration felt by the farmer churns within until it boils over into violence. An incident which exemplifies such frustration took place in Ruthton, a tiny community of 332 residents in southwestern Minnesota.

In 1977, 42-year-old Rudy Blythe fulfilled a lifelong dream when he purchased the Buffalo Ridge State Bank in Ruthton. Together with his wife, Susan, and 11-year-old son Rolph, he moved from Philadelphia into a life far different from that of the big city.

This was rural U.S.A., where everyone knew everyone else's business, where the banker ranked up there socially with the doctor, the lawyer and the mayor. All were men of importance, but none more important than the town banker. After all, the banker held mortgages on most of the homes in town and on the farms surrounding the community.

Rudy Blythe came to Ruthton with the sincere desire to loosen the stringent loaning restrictions enforced by the

previous owner of the bank. Rudy believed that the farmers were basically honest and hard-working. While his assessment of the farmers' character may have been accurate, they still had to have the ability to repay bank loans.

Rudy issued marginal loans. Gradually, over a period of five years, the bank itself was having difficulty in meeting its obligations. Rudy tightened up his loan policies and aggressively attempted to collect overdue loans. This new policy affected many farmers, including Jim Jenkins.

Jim owned a small 10-acre spread. He had first called at Rudy's bank a few years after Rudy moved to Ruthton. At that time, Jim had a few small loans with a bank in a neighboring town. He moved his business to Rudy's bank, consolidated his loans and obtained some extra money to take care of current expenses. This was more like it. The new bank manager was a great guy. Jim beamed at his good fortune and couldn't wait to get home and tell his wife, Darlene and teenage son, Steven.

Initially, Jim made his payments but, as financial conditions tightened, he had more and more difficulty in meeting his obligations.

Jim raised cattle. The hardest time of year was winter, when cheap feed was hard to come by. Long-suffering Darlene Jenkins had gone through many tough winters. By 1980 she had had enough. She left her husband. Steven stayed with his father, but spent a lot of time with his grandparents. Jim was devastated. His world was crumbling around him. With his wife gone, his son away most of the time and that heartless bank manager hounding him for back payments, his problems seemed insurmountable.

Rudy took a drive out to look at the Jenkins farm and cattle. He was shocked to find the farm deserted and all the cattle gone. Jim had sold off the livestock and skipped. Rudy was furious. He checked with the Lincoln County prosecutor and was advised that it was useless for a bank to initiate criminal charges against a farmer. It

had never been done in that part of the country.

Eventually, Rudy put the Jenkins farm up for sale. There were no takers. Jim Jenkins had even ripped out the bathtub and plumbing. The deserted farm soon became overrun.

The two men whose lives had become intertwined because of a mortgage on a farm were now both, in their own way, deeply troubled men. Rudy's bank was slowly failing. He was forced to hire a manager, Toby Thulin, to run the day to day activities of the bank, while he took a position with a financial institution in Dallas. Rudy commuted every two weeks to keep his hand in at the bank.

Jim Jenkins hitch-hiked through the Midwest, but eventually settled in Brownwood, Texas, where he gained employment as a mechanic maintaining school buses. In Jim's eyes, his misfortune was all the fault of banker Rudy Blythe. How come everyone had to work for what they got, everyone except bankers? They could just step in and take a man's farm. That's the way Jim Jenkins saw his predicament. Month after month, his hatred for Rudy Blythe simmered in his mind until it became an obsession.

Around 10 a.m. on Sept. 27, 1983, Rudy received a long distance phone call from Ron Anderson, a farmer who said he had seen the For Sale sign on the old Jenkins property. The banker and the potential purchaser made an appointment to meet at the Jenkins farm the next morning.

The following day, Rudy and Toby Thulin drove out to the Jenkins farm. Jim Jenkins was waiting. The first shot shattered the windshield of Rudy's car. The second smashed through Toby's neck, killing him instantly. Rudy ran from the vehicle. Crouching low, he desperately headed for the closest farmhouse, but he didn't have a chance. Two shots found their mark in Rudy's back, not more than an inch apart. By the time he sprawled to the ground, he was dead.

Jim Jenkins and his son Steven drove away in their white Chevy pick-up truck. They made their way back to

Texas, where, three days later, Steven walked into a police station in Paducah and gave himself up.

Steven told police that he had been behind a barn when the fatal shots were fired. After the shootings, his father had joined him, saying, "I fixed that son of a bitch Blythe." Steven went on to tell police that he and his father had quarrelled. Jim Jenkins had let Steven have the Chevy, but he took his rifle and left for nowhere in particular on foot.

Jim Jenkins wandered aimlessly for four days before stopping to write a note. After completing the note, he placed the muzzle of his 12-gauge shotgun into his mouth. His thumb closed on the trigger and squeezed gently like a good hunter should. Jim Jenkins was no more.

The note beside the body read: "I killed Rudy Blythe, the S.O.B. Steve leaving. Won't listen anymore. A guy might just as well be dead. Signed, James L. Jenkins."

On April 10, 1984, Steven Jenkins stood trial for murder in Ivanhoe, Minn. Almost all the participants in the tragic scenario were dead - Rudy Blythe, Toby Thulin, Jim Jenkins. Only Steven Jenkins was alive and the court had only his word that his father had killed the two victims, only his word that he had no hand in either shooting. The Minnesota jury apparently felt that Steven Jenkins was not an innocent spectator to the double murder, but an active accomplice, whether he pulled the trigger or not.

Steven Jenkins was found guilty of murder in the second degree in the case of Toby Thulin and guilty in the first degree concerning Rudy Blythe. Steven was sentenced to life imprisonment in the Blythe killing and 10 years imprisonment in the Thulin killing, the sentences to run concurrently.

Steven Jenkins will be eligible for parole in the year 2001.

THE PROFESSOR
AND THE HOOKER

Bill Douglas was a big, imposing man, who tipped the scales at 270 pounds. He was firmly entrenched as professor of anatomy and cellular biology at Tufts University's School of Medicine in Boston.

Bill and Nancy Douglas had been married for 20 years, had three fine children and a comfortable home in the suburb of Sharon. No question about it, the hard working PhD, at 42, had accomplished much in the academic world.

What the academic world didn't know, in fact, what no one knew, was that the respected Dr. Douglas was deeply involved with 20-year-old prostitute, Robin Benedict. Robin had been picked up by the professor in Boston's red light district, commonly known as the Combat Zone. Robin charged Douglas $100 per hour for her services.

While Robin considered the professor to be just another customer, Douglas fell hard. He wanted sex on a regular basis, but he wanted more. He enjoyed Robin's company and liked to take her out socially. They attended movies and plays together. Often they discussed the professor's career. Always, no matter what the occasion, Robin charged her best customer $100 per hour.

Douglas wanted to be treated differently than Robin's other clients. Most nights he worked late in his lab, which

afforded him a good cover story for his wife, who was quite accustomed to his odd hours. Robin would call Douglas after her last customer had left. He would then join her and, in this way, achieve some sort of satisfaction in the knowledge that he was the last one to sleep with her that night.

The strain of $100 per hour, which often added up to over $500 a date, took its toll on Prof. Douglas' income. In order to finance his love affair, he came up with a novel idea, which, for a time, worked rather well. He put Robin on the payroll as a lab assistant, representing her to the university as a graduate student from Massachusetts' Institute of Technology. Robin received a $200 cheque direct from the University each week. It wasn't much, but it covered two hours of the professor's time.

Despite the cost, Douglas took great pleasure in presenting Robin with expensive gifts. As a result, a steady stream of presents flowed to the prostitute from the professor. To cover these gifts, Prof. Douglas submitted fraudulent expense accounts to the university. He did little to disguise these expenses, which were readily detected by his own staff. Douglas received official notice that his expenses were being audited. The threat of detection didn't deter him. He placed fictional people on the payroll and turned their cheques over to Robin. In a little over a year, he defrauded Tufts out of $67,000.

During this time, Robin understandably lived well. She lavished gifts upon herself, which, when combined with those given to her by Douglas, made every day seem like Christmas.

In the fall of 1982, Nancy Douglas at last became suspicious. Her husband's nocturnal absences were now the rule rather than the exception. She faced Bill, who confessed that there was another woman. But all was not lost. He would break off with Robin and they would salvage their marriage. Bill lied to his wife. He kept on seeing Robin, at $100 an hour each and every hour.

Toward the end of the year, Robin managed to extract

$25,000 from Douglas which, together with a bank loan, enabled her to purchase a home in Malden. Two things incensed Douglas. First, Robin didn't want to tell him the address of her new home. Second, he learned she was living with her pimp in the house he had helped finance. Now that every ounce of blood had been drained from the sucker, Robin attempted to extradite herself from her relationship with Douglas. The professor didn't take the brushoff well.

Douglas managed to convince Robin to take a three day trip with him to Plattsburgh, N.Y. It wouldn't be cheap. The fee would be $1000 per day. When the trip was concluded, the professor had difficulty coming up with the $3000. As time went by, Robin insisted on payment and demanded an additional $2000 interest, making a total of $5000.

On March 5, 1983, Professor Douglas talked Robin into visiting him at his home while his family was absent, on the pretense that he had the full $5000 to give her. According to Douglas' later statement, Robin carried a two and a half pound hammer with her. However, it is quite possible that he had the hammer in readiness for Robin.

They met in a bedroom. According to Douglas, Robin hit him on the head with the hammer. He wrenched it away from her and brought it down on her head, crushing her skull and exposing her brain. Douglas dressed his own head wound before throwing his bloody clothing into a shopping bag, along with Robin's. The large hammer was put into a jacket pocket, but proved to be too big. The jacket was returned to a closet and the hammer placed in a bag.

There was a surprisingly small amount of blood about the room. Douglas wiped up the blood with bathroom towels. He then carried the body and the bags of incriminating material out to Robin's Toyota.

Douglas disposed of the garbage bag of clothing in a trash barrel along the highway. He continued driving into

Rhode Island, where he tossed Robin's body into a dumpster near a shopping centre. He covered the body with garbage and drove to Providence, where he parked the Toyota.

The next morning, Nancy Douglas met her husband at the bus stop in Sharon when he arrived home. He had called her to meet him. Although she begged him to tell her what he had been doing all night, he refused.

Later, Douglas retrieved the car and drove it to New York City, where he left it in a parking garage. He took the precaution of removing the licence plates. In effect, Douglas abandoned the Toyota.

A day after the bloody clothing had been deposited in the trash can, two men looking for empty bottles discovered the clothing and reported their find to police. The clothing was checked against missing persons. Robin's pimp had reported her missing. He informed police that she had been headed for Professor Douglas' house to collect a debt when he last saw her. He also told police of the long standing relationship between the professor and Robin Benedict.

When detectives knocked on the professor's door, he was already a suspect, although Robin's body had not been recovered. Much of the interior of the Douglas' bedroom was sent to a forensic lab for testing. Inside a jacket pocket, lab technicians were able to isolate a tiny particle of human brain, which no doubt had come off the head of the hammer when Douglas had temporarily placed it in his jacket. Bloodstained clothing found by the bottle gatherers was identified as belonging to the professor and Robin.

Professor Douglas was arrested and charged with murder. For a full year he claimed that Robin had left his home that night alive and well and that the incriminating evidence had been planted in his room.

Dramatically, on the morning his murder trial was scheduled to begin, Douglas confessed and pleaded guilty to manslaughter. He was sentenced to 18 to 20 years in

Walpole State Prison.

Robin Benedict's body has never been found. It is believed to be in a landfill site used by the trash collection firm, who collected the dumpster in which the professor had deposited her body.

MERCY KILLING

Anne Capute always wanted to be a nurse. It took her a long time and it wasn't easy, but she made it.

Anne was born and lived most of her life in Boston, Mass. Her father, a confirmed alcoholic, deserted the family and it was left to Anne's mother to raise the children. As each of the youngsters became teenagers, they took jobs, enabling the Caputes to survive.

At the age of 19, Anne married and proceeded to have children of her own. Barbara, Susan, Lori and Meredith kept the young mother busy. The dream of becoming a nurse was put on a back burner.

By 1975, Anne, who was now 38 years old, was living in Plympton, Mass. Her children were all of school age. Anne drove a school bus part time. It was now or never. She told her family of her lifelong ambition to become a nurse, an ambition she now wanted to fulfill.

Anne took Lemuel Shattuck Nursing School's entrance exam and passed. She entered an accelerated one year program and moved out of her home into one of the school's dormitories.

On Aug. 27, 1977, Anne Capute graduated in the top third of her class. She now was a licensed practical nurse and had no difficulty obtaining employment at Morton General Hospital. Anne proved to be an excellent nurse.

Her family was proud of what she had accomplished. She was doing what she always wanted to do with her life. She was happy and fulfilled. That is, up until Friday, May 16, 1980. That was the day Mrs. Norma Leanues died.

Mrs. Leanues broke her thigh bone as a result of a fall just before Christmas, 1979. Her personal physician, Robert Hillier, was an orthopedic surgeon on staff at Morton General. He discovered that cancer had weakened Norma's thigh bone. An operation followed and the tumor was removed. The tumor proved to be metastatic. It had spread to the thigh bone from elsewhere in the body. Extensive testing, lasting for weeks, failed to find the origin of the cancer.

When Mrs. Leanues lost feeling in her legs, Dr. Hillier concluded that a cancerous tumor was swelling in the spinal cord. Given the option of paralysis or surgery, the gravely ill woman chose surgery. Dr. Hillier removed most of the tumor. It too was metastatic.

For two weeks following the spinal operation, Mrs. Leanues was in extreme pain. Anne Capute and other nurses who cared for Mrs. Leanues considered her to be a terminally ill patient. She was given morphine to alleviate her excruciating pain. She often moaned and cried out.

On May 16, a conversation took place between the doctor and two nurses. The interpretation of the conversation is left to the reader's interpretation. According to Dr. Hillier, he was leaving the hospital when the conversation took place. He was informed by nurse Nancy Robbins that the morphine solution that Mrs. Leanues was taking did not appear to be effective. Anne Capute said Mrs. Leanues was still suffering considerable pain. Doctor and nurses decided to proceed with a shot that would be given in addition to the solution if the solution did not work. Dr. Hillier said, "I decided to go with 15 milligrams of morphine by shot every three hours, as needed, for pain, in addition to the oral solution, if the patient was in extreme pain. The shot was to be used only if the oral medication was not working and only at a frequency of every three

hours, no shorter than that. But it could be used, let's say, every eight or every ten hours."

Anne responded, "Don't worry, Dr. Hillier, we will take good care of Mrs. Leanues."

Dr. Hillier then left the hospital, called his answering service and transferred Mrs. Leanues to another doctor's care, as he would be away from the hospital for a week. On May 18, Norma Leanues died.

After Mrs. Leanues' death, it was noticed that nursing medication records indicated extensive amounts of morphine had been administered during the last days of the woman's life. This was reported to superiors. As a result, Anne Capute was interviewed by assistant administrator for nursing service, Maureen Costello. When asked to relate the conversation which had taken place between herself and Dr. Hillier on May 16, Anne's interpretation of the discussion differed in detail with that of Dr. Hillier.

She told her superior of Mrs. Leanues' agony, of her constant crying. Around 7:30 on the evening of May 16, nurse Nancy Robbins told Dr. Hillier that the morphine solution was not helping Mrs. Leanues' pain and asked if she could try some other medication. According to Anne, Hillier responded, "Sure, give her anything she wants, just make her comfortable. She'll be dead in 24 to 48 hours."

Nurse Robbins inquired, "How about morphine, 15 milligrams, subcutaneous, no time limit?" Robbins went to the desk to write the order. Anne proceeded to the medication closet to obtain the morphine and 10 milligrams of Valium, which Dr. Hillier had also ordered for Mrs. Leanues.

The drugs were administered and Anne went on to other duties. At around 10 p.m., she returned to Mrs. Leanues to find her screaming in excruciating pain. Anne gave her 30 milligrams of morphine. The next evening, at 5 p.m., Mrs. Leanues condition had deteriorated. Anne gave her 30 milligrams of morphine. At 7 p.m. she administered a further 30 milligrams; at 8 p.m., 30 milligrams;

at 9:15 p.m., 30 milligrams; at 10:15 p.m., 30 milligrams; 11:15 p.m., 45 milligrams.

Anne Capute was suspended without pay from her nursing duties. On Sept. 9, 1981, she stood trial for the murder of Mrs. Norma Leanues.

Dr. Hillier testified that it was often expedient for a doctor to give verbal orders to a nurse and sign the order form the next day. He had given such an order on May 16 concerning Mrs. Leanues. His verbal order had been "15 milligrams of morphine, I M every three hours, as needed for pain, p r n. To be given in addition to the morphine solution if that isn't effective."

However, the form presented in court read, "Morphine, 15 milligrams, sub-cu, p r n, no time limit. Make her comfortable. Give Valium I M." It was signed by Dr. Hillier. The doctor swore he never gave a "no time limit" order and that it was not his signature on the form.

Dr. Hillier also testified that he had not authorized or initialled the medical records for any of the numerous injections of morphine administered to the patient before she died.

Under cross examination, Dr. Hillier came under some criticism when it was established that he had the time to write out the medication order but was in a rush to leave the hospital for a week's holiday in Paris. He was also criticized for turning over the care of a critically ill patient to another doctor through a telephone answering service.

Defense attorney Pat Piscitelli's probing of administrator Maureen Costello elicited the information that at Morton General there had been a certain degree of laxity in following procedures. Several charts were produced which were not signed by doctors. Others were brought into evidence which did not have nurse's signatures. One doctor used a rubber stamp for his signature. In one case, medication was given to a patient 25 times without the doctor's signature in the designated area.

The defence made two points clear. First, that the gen-

eral procedure followed by other nurses in the hospital was no better than that performed by Anne Capute. Second, Anne's intention was to make her patient more comfortable and to allow her to die in dignity, rather than to cause her death. The jury obviously agreed. Anne Capute was found not guilty.

Attorney Pat Piscitelli advises me that Mrs. Capute has had her nursing licence reinstated and is presently employed as a private nurse.

LOVE ON THE RUN

By no stretch of the imagination could you call Tim Kirk a pillar of the community, unless that community was Bushy Mountain State Prison in Tennessee.

Tim started out bad and ended up bad. He was raised in Chicago and was an accomplished street fighter before he reached his teens. He attended school, but was absent most of the time until he dropped out altogether. His parents, hard-working decent folks, attempted to straighten out their boy. They sent him to Junior Military Academy in South Chicago. Tim hated every minute. His behavior was so bad, officials at the academy refused to keep him in the school.

By the time Tim was 15, he was holding up liquor and convenience stores. He had a steady girlfriend, Junine Fay, who sometimes accompanied him on his armed robberies. Not all his sojourns into crime were successful.

Sometimes he ended up in various Illinois correctional facilities for young offenders. Junine visited him and was always there when he was released.

When Tim and Junine were 18, they married. Junine worked as a welder. Tim worked at odd jobs, but most of his time was devoted to holdups and short sentences spent in prison. In 1968, he received his longest sentence

to that point - one year in the Missouri State Penitentiary.

Junine remained loyal to her man. Between robberies and prison sentences, Junine gave birth to three sons. She pleaded with her husband to go straight, but her pleas fell on deaf ears. After Tim struck her several times in a fit of temper, Junine left him for good.

Tim continued to pursue a life of crime. His police record grew. On several occasions he attempted to escape from prison. Finally, the system threw the book at Tim Kirk. He was sentenced to 65 years imprisonment. By 1980, Tim was incarcerated at Bushy Mountain, one of the toughest prisons in the U.S. The institution has received some notoriety as the prison which housed James Earl Ray, the assassin of Dr. Martin Luther King.

In February, 1982, Tim Kirk ended a long-standing feud between black and white prisoners. He killed two black inmates with a handgun.

This then was Tim Kirk: con artist, armed robber, habitual criminal and alleged murderer, when he met his lawyer, Mary Evans. Mary's life would never be the same. Her background was in sharp contrast to that of Tim Kirk.

Mary was born in Palmersville, Tenn. She was a good student who sailed through school. In 1972, she met Tom Evans, while attending the University of Tennessee. Mary and Tom married while both were still in university. Mary was taking law. For years she had thought of nothing other than becoming a lawyer, while Tom wasn't sure of his future career. During Mary's last year of law school, the pair realized the marriage had been a mistake. They agreed to an amicable divorce.

Shortly after her divorce, Mary met John Lockridge, a distinguished, good-looking man over 20 years her senior. Lockridge was married, but that didn't deter the couple from carrying on a protracted affair.

In June, 1981, Mary Evans graduated from law school and obtained a position with the law firm of Tipton and

Bell. For a year she worked successfully on minor cases before being given her first major assignment. She was made responsible for the defence of a habitual criminal, Tim Kirk, on a first degree murder charge. To lose the case could mean that her client would be put to death.

Mary drove to Bushy Mountain to introduce herself to her new client. Here was the well-educated, articulate lawyer on her first big case. Across from her sat a bearded convict, serving a 65-year prison sentence with a possible death sentence in his immediate future. Tim explained how he had been stabbed in prison, how a feud had developed, which festered and simmered for two years until, finally, following the rules of the prison, it came down to kill or be killed.

It is a phenomenon that no behavioral scientist can explain, but in the case of Mary and Tim, it happened. A strange chemistry was at work. Mary felt strongly attracted to her bearded client. Tim was enraptured with this charming, good-looking lawyer, who seemed to be sincerely concerned with his welfare.

In the following months, Mary visited Tim many times, sometimes as often as three times a week. Their meetings would last several hours. Guards got to know Mary well. Occasionally they would look the other way when the pair held hands.

In preparing Tim's defence, Mary had arranged to have him evaluated by an Oak Ridge psychiatrist, Dr. Gary Salk. Apparently, it was her idea to qualify Tim for a diminished capacity defence. Dr. Salk was a member of the Prison Aid Society of Tennessee and gave freely of his services to inmates.

A week earlier, Mary had called at Dr. Salk's office to set up the appointment. Casually, she examined the layout of the offices, explaining to the doctor that the guards accompanying the prisoner like to know in advance where to position themselves. Nonchalantly, she mentioned that she was sure the doctor wouldn't mind removing all

restraints from her client in order to enable him to perform the manual tests. Dr. Salk agreed.

Unknown to everyone, Mary and Tim had planned an escape. Despite Tim's warnings that although he had nothing to lose, she would jeopardize her career, family and even her freedom should she, as a servant of the court, aid a convicted armed robber to escape, Mary would hear none of it. She was determined to assist in gaining her man's freedom and to flee with him.

Three uniformed guards accompanied Tim Kirk and Mary Evans to Dr. Salk's office. The prisoner's handcuffs and leg irons were removed. Over two hours of testing took place before Tim Kirk slowly drew his .25 calibre revolver. He waved the weapon methodically and calmly announced, "All right, now, understand this, I don't want to hurt anybody."

The guards were disarmed and made to lie on the floor. Mary provided Tim with tape. As Tim secured the guards, he passed his revolver to Mary. Now there was no doubt in the witnesses' minds. Lawyer Mary Evans was an accomplice. Dr. Salk was made to join the guards on the floor. He, too, was tied and gagged.

Tim quickly took off his prison garb and donned civilian clothing provided by Mary. The pair dashed out of the building to Mary's Toyota and made good their escape.

Back in Dr. Salk's office, one of the guards managed to free himself after an hour. He hopped to a telephone. The word went out. Desperate Tim Kirk had escaped custody with the aid and assistance of his court appointed lawyer, Mary Evans.

The day after the escape, April Fool's Day, 1983, Mary's Toyota was found abandoned. Nothing quite like this had ever happened before. The news of the strange alliance made headlines throughout the South. The burning question - where was the wanted couple?

Mary and Tim kept moving. Mary had withdrawn her savings, which enabled them to stay mobile. Using aliases, they rented a car and drove to Florida. Once there, they

rented a house, bought groceries and settled in. It was a tense life, but Tim had his freedom and Mary had her man. A month passed. The couple thought it prudent to move.

As their money ran low, they planned a robbery. But as luck would have it, someone else with strikingly similar physical features to Tim held up a bank in Sarasota. Tim knew the place would be swarming with FBI agents. The desperate pair headed for the northeast coast of Florida. They managed to live off small loans wired to them by friends, but it couldn't last.

A Western Union clerk, Coreen Darcey, recognized Tim from a wanted poster. In minutes, Mary and Tim were in custody. The lovers had been at large for 139 days. Upon her return to Tennessee, Mary's licence to practise law was revoked. She would be eligible to regain her licence in five years. Mary was found guilty of aiding and abetting a jail escape and was sentenced to three years imprisonment. Ten months later, she was paroled.

While Tim was at large, he was found guilty of two counts of manslaughter in the cases of the two men killed in prison. He received a 40-year prison term in addition to the 65 years he was already serving. Tim Kirk will not be eligible for parole until the year 2048.

Separated from each other, it didn't take long for love to fade. On May 24, 1985, Mary Evans married Bill Evans, her former husband's first cousin. Two and one half months later, on Aug. 10, 1985, Tim Kirk married one Mary Paris in the exercise yard of Bushy Mountain State Penitentiary.

MYSTERIOUS MAIL

Sending human parts through the mail is definitely in poor taste. In Canada, our criminals rarely use Canada Post, no doubt firmly believing that any alternate mode of delivery would be less tardy. Not so in Europe, where the mails have often been used to advantage.

On April Fool's Day of 1926, the chief of police of Vienna, Herr Weitzel, was somewhat taken aback when he opened a personally addressed small package which had arrived by mail. It contained a human finger.

The Chief turned the distinctive digit over to his lab. No sooner had he finished his strudel break than the lab boys provided him with a full report. The finger was the first finger from a woman's right hand. It was slender, the nail being well-manicured and polished. The finger was free of callouses and was quite possibly that of a middle-aged woman. It had been recently severed with surgical skill.

The string and paper used to wrap the package was in common use and proved impossible to trace. The parcel had been mailed in Vienna.

Weitzel rubbed his goatee and thought of the possibilities. Of course, the distasteful parcel could be the prank of a medical student or mortuary employee, but the chief

215

couldn't take a chance. He had to assume a crime had been committed.

While the Vienna police were checking out missing persons and calling on mortuaries, Weitzel received another parcel. You guessed it, the package contained another human finger. It was the third finger from the same hand which had provided the previous finger. Examination of the nail indicated that it had the same polish. Medical examination revealed a rather disconcerting fact. The finger had been amputated with surgical skill while the victim was alive.

A plain gold ring was on the finger when it arrived. The ring was made of 22 carat gold. Tiny scratches or indentations on the underside of the ring had been made by the corrosive action of a diluted acid. The acid had many commercial uses, but the one detectives homed in on was its use in the removal of tattoos.

In order to find out if the amputated finger had ever been tattooed, it was necessary to remove the top skin. Once this was done, doctors were able to make out the image of a snake wound around the finger in the exact location covered by the gold ring. There was little doubt in the minds of the investigators that the acid used to remove the tattoo had made the indentations in the ring. But what did it all mean? Maybe the snake held some significance at one time, but had been displaced by the ring.

Tattoo parlors were canvassed, but police were unsuccessful in locating the one where the snake and been applied and removed. The ring also proved impossible to trace.

The story was leaked to the press, which caused Vienna police no end of embarrassment. Was a killer on the loose who took great relish in taunting the entire police force? Above all, could the chief expect further fingers to show up in his mail?

A week passed. The mystery deepened when a female body, *sans* head and two fingers from the right hand, was

found in a swamp outside Vienna. An examination of the torso shed no light on the identity of the middle-aged victim. However, it was noted that the two fingers had been removed with skill and the use of surgical instruments.

Police were able to make a plaster cast of a footprint found in soft mud near the torso. From the footprint, an anthropologist gave a description of the man who had made it. It was ascertained that he was over six feet tall, with broad shoulders and long arms.

Weitzel and his boys now had something to work with. They were looking for a tall doctor, most likely a surgeon. They came up with several in Vienna, but gradually all were eliminated. All except one.

Dr. Herman Schmitz was a surgeon who had a small practice, catering mainly to wealthy patients. A search of criminal records revealed that at one time Dr. Schmitz had been charged with malpractice, but had been found innocent by a jury. Despite the verdict, the doctor's practice had suffered. Eventually he gravitated to a small but lucrative practice. His patients obviously were unaware of his past.

A cursory investigation of Schmitz's family revealed that he had a wife and children. The children were of school age and Frau Schmitz seemed happy enough. That's what a cursory investigation indicated. An in-depth investigation uncovered the mistress. It was somewhat of a disappointment for the Vienna detectives to find out that she was alive and well. The victim had to be someone else.

Twenty-four hour surveillance teams were put on the good doctor, the dear wife and the willing mistress. The doctor stayed clean. So did the wife. But the mistress unwittingly led police to paydirt.

Detectives found a dress shop where the doctor's mistress had a charge account. In those long ago days before credit cards, kept ladies had their bills forwarded to their gentlemen friends every month or so. Vienna police, now

hot to trot, questioned the store manager. He told them that the doctor's current mistress was somewhat of a pain, unlike his previous mistress, Anna Stein. He explained that Anna had purchased far more dresses before the doctor had changed horses in midstream.

Police dashed over to Anna's apartment only to find that she had vacated the premises three weeks earlier. A survey of her regular haunts brought the same results. Anna Stein had disappeared. Police were pretty sure they knew the location of her torso and two fingers. However, they weren't sure about her head.

This puzzle was solved when they surreptitiously searched Dr. Schmitz's office. They found a small laboratory off the main office. There, reposing in a bucket of preservative solution, was the head of Anna Stein. Dr. Schmitz was picked up and charged with the murder of his mistress.

A meticulous search of the doctor's office turned up pieces of Anna's clothing, which had been partially burned. The doctor's current mistress was somewhat distressed to discover that several pieces of jewelry which had been given to her by Schmitz had once belonged to the deceased.

Witnesses were located who stated that Anna had been furious with her lover when she found out she had been replaced in his affections by a younger woman. They had argued fiercely, but the charming doctor sweet-talked Anna into bringing her belongings to his office under the pretense of taking a long holiday together in Paris. Anna fell for the ruse. Instead of a trip to the City of Light, she was first made helpless by dope, had two fingers amputated and was then murdered.

Dr. Schmitz admitted to quarrelling with his former mistress, but claimed she had thrown herself upon him and expired as a result of a heart attack. Examination of the body proved beyond a doubt that Anna had not died of heart attack. She had been administered a lethal injection of potassium cyanide. Police found a bottle of diluted

acid used to remove the tattooed snake from the dead woman's finger. This had been done to hamper identification of the victim.

Dr. Schmitz's trial for murder promised to be a sensation. The Austrian press carried little else on its front pages. But the drama of a sensational murder trial was not to be. Dr. Schmitz attempted to escape from jail. He made his way to the roof of the building and tried to jump to an adjoining lower roof. He didn't make it. He died on the ground after confessing to the murder of Anna Stein.

Why did the doctor send those fingers to the chief of police? It is believed he never forgave police for their investigation of the malpractice charge brought against him years earlier. He sent the fingers through the mail in an attempt to make the police appear foolish and incompetent. Instead, he drew attention to himself, which eventually caused his death.

FAMILY FEUD

A few years back, I flew into Houston, Texas to investigate Texas crimes for the Houston *Post*, then newly acquired by the Toronto *Sun*. I rented a car at the airport.

As I filled out the application form, the car rental agent couldn't help but notice my home address was Toronto, Canada. He bent over and confidentially gave me some advice. "You know, sir, it's different down here. Up where you come from, if you all have a tiny fender bender, you all get out of your vehicle and argue. Don't do that down here. Down here, the fella in the other car has a gun in the glove compartment. You start arguin' and he'll start shootin'. I don't want no trouble with my rentals."

I smiled. I had been in the state five minutes and I was being warned about guns. It really isn't that humorous. The truth is, most homes in the U.S. contain guns. They are literally everywhere. What follows is the story of a husband and wife, their son, and the accessibility of a shotgun.

Bill Keeler was a Texan through and through. Better still, he was a Texas success story. Bill obtained his engineering diploma at Texas A & M and joined the Atlantic Richfield Corp. in 1949. By 1973, he had worked his

way up in the company from junior engineer to Vice President, Research and Engineering. This was no small feat, for Atlantic Richfield is a huge organization employing hundreds of capable executives. The powers that be saw in Bill a tough but humanistic executive; a quiet man who worked hard and led an exemplary home life.

Bill's wife Anita complemented her husband in every way. She, too, was an achiever, who channelled her energies equally between her family and various charities. Anita was a tireless worker for the local Meals on Wheels program, as well as an active member of the United Methodist Women. The Keelers had four children; Barbara, 29, John, 25, Robert, 19 and the youngest, David, 14.

If ever a family prayed together and stayed together, it was the Keelers. They often went camping and fishing as a family. They attended each other's activities to contribute moral support. Probably the only ripple on the serene surface of the Keelers' idyllic domestic life concerned their eldest son, John. When he completed high school, he joined the army without his parents' consent. Upon being discharged, he immediately married; once again, a step which didn't meet with his parents' approval.

The entire family were steady church-goers. They attended the Schreiber United Methodist Church each Sunday. Bill belonged to the Brookhaven Country Club, where he golfed regularly each Saturday.

David, the youngest son, displayed the same drive and energy which had brought success to his father. He attended a prestigious private school, St. Mark's School of Texas, where his grades were consistently outstanding. He played the trombone in the school band, was a member of the football team and a member of the student council.

Yes, there is little doubt about it, you could look in on Bill Keeler's beautiful home in Dallas, complete with swimming pool, and believe that here lived a truly happy, successful man and his family.

Maybe that was true for a time, but affairs in the Keeler home took a tragic turn in the summer of 1981. At the time, the events which took place that summer appeared to be achievements which bring pride and happiness. Instead, they brought discord and tragedy to the Keeler family.

Bill was appointed president of the Arco Corp., Atlantic Richfield's largest subsidiary. The appointment culminated a lifetime of working for the organization. Bill had arrived. At the same time as his father was promoted, young David graduated from grade eight. He would be entering high school in the fall. The two happy events were celebrated by the family.

Bill Keeler had always wanted his family to be achievers. In a way, many of them were. But now, as the president of a major company, he expected perfection from his youngest son. Bill still retained his quiet calm in public, but privately he seethed at any minor fault on David's part.

Conversely, David, jubilant about entering high school, felt that parental restraints should be relaxed. Many of his friends took out girls and stayed out late. Bill Keeler felt that wasn't responsible behavior for the son of the president of a major company. He demanded perfection.

Early during that summer, David, who, like his father, kept things to himself, would sometimes sneak out of the house to be with his friends. He was still what most people would consider a good kid. He looked after the family pool and lawn, while at the same time holding down a summer job. Although he didn't say anything, he resented his nagging father.

On July 11, David and some friends caused a disturbance at Six Flags Over Texas, a local amusement park. As a result, the boys were taken to the park's security office, where they were found to have stolen souvenirs in their possession. The security police called David's father, who drove out, picked up the boys and took them home.

Bill Keeler held his temper and said nothing in front of his son's friends.

That evening, two other friends of David's, Debra Avant and her brother Don, were sleeping over at the Keeler house. Bill and Anita never even brought up the subject of David's behavior at the amusement park in front of his guests. Next morning, a Sunday, when the Avant youngsters went home to dress for church, Bill Keeler gave vent to his pent-up anger. Anita joined in.

We only have David's word for what transpired that morning, but there is no reason to disbelieve any of it. When Debra and Don Avant left, Bill immediately started to shout at his son over the shoplifting incident. Bill pushed David into his room and threw him onto the bed. All the while, Bill Keeler was shouting at his son. Anita joined in the tirade.

Eventually, Bill's temper waned and he told his son to dress for church. Together, the not so happy family attended church services. At the conclusion, Bill and Anita were delayed, as it was their turn to count the collection money. David left for home as soon as the services were over.

David went directly to where his father kept his semi-automatic shotgun. Fifteen minutes later, Bill and Anita arrived home. David met them inside the door. He fired seven shots into their bodies. Bill fell dead in the hall. Miraculously, Anita was still alive when her daughter Barbara showed up half an hour later to go for a swim in the family pool. Barbara went to her father's side and saw at a glance that he was dead. She turned to her mother, who whispered, "David did it." A few hours later, Anita Keeler died.

After shooting his parents, David jumped on his bicycle and drove away. He planned on running away, but changed his mind. About five miles from his home, he rode over to a parked police car and told the officers simply, "I just shot and killed my parents."

David was taken to a Dallas police station. He had no

intention of hedging about his crime. He told investigating officers that he had killed his father for being so strict and calling him a disgrace. His mother died because she had agreed with her husband.

Because David was under 15 years old, the state of Texas considered him to be a youthful offender, whose maximum punishment could not exceed incarceration in a detention centre beyond the age of 18.

At his sentencing hearing, David's lawyer claimed that David had always been urged to excel. When he fell short of his father's expectations, he was severely criticized. He repressed his emotions until they burst forth that fateful Sunday morning. Evidently, the presiding judge was swayed by this line of reasoning and felt that treatment was preferable to confinement. David was sent to Timberlawn, a private psychiatric hospital.

On Dec. 29, 1984, on his eighteenth birthday, David was discharged from Timberlawn. As the law of Texas stipulates, his juvenile record was sealed. Upon his discharge, he was able to claim his share of his parents' $1.2 million estate.

UNLUCKY IN LOVE

You could not call Evelyn Throsby lucky in love. Of her five husbands, she divorced two, a pair died, and the fifth killed her.

On Evelyn's first trip to the altar, she was accompanied by Walter Kiernan, a wealthy stockbroker and son of the Staten Island Kiernans, who made their mark in the coal game. Walt took more interest in the bottle than he did in Evelyn. The marriage broke up in something under two years.

Dr. Myrnee Lewis, a New York surgeon, was the next to share Evelyn's bed. He, too, couldn't stay away from the sauce for any length of time. The Lewises separated after seven years of marital disharmony.

Clement Pettit was the son of an extremely wealthy Milwaukee banking family. Clem was crippled by arthritis to such an extent that he could walk only with the aid of two canes. In 1930, he and Evelyn became man and wife. From all indications, this marriage was different. Evelyn truly loved and cared for her husband. He, in turn, worshipped Evelyn and was forever bestowing little gifts upon her. Oh, little things, like an apartment building in Milwaukee, diamond studded cameos and sapphire rings. Because Clem's health continued to deteriorate, he and

Evelyn decided that a move to sunny California would be for the best.

In 1935, the Pettits built a lovely home at 261 South San Raphael Rd. in Los Angeles. They enjoyed nine years of the good life, hampered only by Clem's arthritic condition, which was now complicated by heart problems. He died on Jan. 18, 1944, leaving Evelyn a wealthy widow.

Two years later, Evelyn, now 54, but looking 40, married for the fourth time. Norris Mumper was a retired engineer. He and the new Mrs. Mumper moved into the home built by and once occupied by Clem Pettit. On Sept. 3, 1948, a few days after Norris moved in, he died of a heart attack. He, too, left a tidy sum to Evelyn.

That pretty well takes care of Evelyn's four husbands. Now, let's get to number five. He was a real pip.

L. Ewing Scott was born in St. Louis. While still a teenager, he obtained a job as a clerk, then moved along to become a book-keeper with a stock brokerage firm. It was here that Scott learned that, in order to give the proper impression, one had to appear prosperous and be able to converse intelligently on a number of subjects. He studied the wealthy and powerful, how they dressed and spoke. Soon, he was pouring his entire earnings into jewelry and tailor-made suits.

The tall, ruggedly handsome Scott soon came to the attention of his employers. He was promoted to stock salesman. Elated, Scott proceeded to widen his sphere of social contacts by joining several service clubs and charitable organizations. He even took a fling at the stock business himself, but the L.E. Scott Co. soon failed.

In 1937, Scott married Alva Gagnier Brewer, the daughter of a rich Canadian publishing and mining magnate. Scott had no need to work. He took to the life of the idle rich like a duck takes to water. Luxuriating on an estate in the San Fernando Valley broke up the winters nicely. Extended cruises, memberships in the most exclusive clubs and plush parties were a way of life.

But Scott couldn't stand a good thing. He became so

abusive to Alva that her family finally bought him off. It is rumored that after five years of marriage, he walked away with a cool $50,000 in his jeans.

In 1949, Evelyn Mumper met 53-year-old Ewing Scott at a dinner party. Evelyn, at 57, looked much younger. She was slim, attractive, and what's more, was worth, give or take a few thousand, a cool million dollars. Scott, on the other hand, was making ends meet as a paint salesman, but never for a moment looked anything less than a cultured, well-dressed stock and securities wheeler dealer.

Before you could say gold digger, Evelyn and Ewing were married. Ironically, they were married on Sept. 3, 1949, the first anniversary of husband number four's death. The newlyweds moved into the house once occupied by Evelyn and hubbies number three and four.

For six years the Scotts led the life of the very rich. They toured Europe and South America. They cruised the oceans of the world. At home they were active in Los Angeles society, one of their close personal friends being singer Jeanette MacDonald.

Everyone who came in contact with Evelyn was impressed with her sincerity and charm. On the other hand, her husband was merely tolerated. Although he was handsome and debonair, there was something suspicious about the man, which acquaintances were quick to detect.

Gradually, Scott took over the management of his wife's financial affairs. From time to time, Evelyn would be seen with a slight bruise on an arm and occasionally a black eye. Rumors spread that Scott wasn't above keeping his wife in her place. By early 1955, Scott made no secret of the fact that he thought it wise to convert most of his wife's securities into cash.

On May 16, 1955, Evelyn and Ewing Scott test drove a Mercedes Benz. They told the automobile salesman, Ulrich Quast, that they were thinking of taking delivery of the new car in West Germany, as they planned on spending some time in Europe. They test drove the car, after which

Quast dropped them off at their home. He was the last person other than Ewing Scott to see Evelyn alive.

Strange things began to happen around the house at 261 South San Raphael Rd. The chauffeur, cook, and gardener, long-time employees of Evelyn's, were dismissed from service. Friends inquired after Evelyn. Often, there were no answers to their continuous phone calls. On rare occasions, Scott answered the phone, giving vague stories about his wife having a nervous breakdown and being confined to a sanatorium "back east." To some friends he confided that his wife was an alcoholic who was away taking the cure. No one was satisfied with these answers, and soon the dark suspicion that Evelyn had met with foul play dawned on her friends. They wrote to the district attorney's office. The D.A. reluctantly agreed to look into the matter.

The Scott affair was no ordinary complaint. While suspicious circumstances did exist, there was no proof that a crime had taken place. Ewing Scott had no criminal record. Mrs. Scott had been married on four previous occasions and had the means to move around the world. She could reappear at any time, causing a great deal of embarrassment to all concerned.

However, discreet inquiries were made. It was revealed that Scott attempted to gain entrance to Evelyn's safety deposit box after May 16, the date she was last seen. He also forged his wife's signature on traveller's cheques in order to deposit them in his own bank account. In August, Scott was questioned. He confided to detectives that his wife was an alcoholic cancer patient, who had simply left. She had taken about $18,000 with her when she went out for tooth powder on the evening of May 16 and never returned.

As summer turned into fall, Scott dated and continued to live the life of the genteel rich, minus Evelyn, of course. Unknown to him, his financial affairs were being monitored by the district attorney's office. It was apparent that Scott was using every means possible to acquire

his wife's fortune and continue his lifestyle with another woman.

In order to clear his name, Scott granted police permission to check his home. The interior of the house was meticulously searched inch by inch, but no sign of Evelyn Scott or any hint as to her fate was found. Outside, 10-foot steel poles were used to probe the earth. Nothing was uncovered.

Police officer Art Hertel had once been on a murder investigation where a man had buried his wife on his neighbor's property, believing that the police would never think of looking there. On nothing more than a hunch, he hopped the fence enclosing the Scott property. Hertel felt about the leaves at his feet. Sure enough, he came up with a partial dental plate and a pair of eyeglasses. The plate was identified by Evelyn's dentist as belonging to the missing woman. Her oculist positively identified the glasses.

Ewing Scott was picked up and indicted on 13 charges of fraud and nine counts of forgery concerning his wife's assets. Bail was set at $25,000, which was paid by Scott. He then fled to Canada. While a fugitive, he was charged with the murder of his wife.

Scott made his way to Barrie, Ont., where he stayed six weeks before moving on to Oakville. After two weeks in Oakville, he travelled to Midland and on to Penetanguishene. In Midland, he had become personal friends with the chief of police while his wanted poster hung in the Midland police station. All that summer and winter, Scott wandered throughout Ontario. In the spring, he was spotted entering the U.S. at Detroit. On April 16, 1957, he was returned to Los Angeles to stand trial for the murder of his wife.

L. Ewing Scott never confessed to his wife's murder, nor was her body ever found. However, his many lies about her disappearance and his subsequent looting of her estate, coupled with the discovery of her dentures, was too much for the jury to ignore. After four hours of

deliberation, the jury found him guilty of murder. He was sentenced to life imprisonment.

Over the years in prison, Scott could have been paroled, but on each parole date he refused to apply, stating that to apply for parole would be an admission of guilt. Finally, on March 26, 1978, he was awarded an unconditional discharge based on time served. He had spent over two decades in prison.

On Aug. 17, 1987, L. Ewing Scott, age 91, was found dead in his room at the Skyline Convalescent Hospital in Los Angeles. He died penniless, with no surviving relatives.

MARY ANNE COTTON

I knocked on the door of 13 Front St. in the village of West Auckland, England. An elderly gentleman answered my knock.

The village green faces Front St. On the other side of the green, neat row houses sit back from well-kept lawns. My research into the village's past had equipped me with the knowledge that the housing behind the green had not always been so neat and tidy.

When coal was discovered in this out of the way district of England over one hundred years ago, the miners who occupied the row houses were hard-working, hard-playing types who drank the hours away between shifts in the colliery.

But this was 1988. Robert House, the owner of the most infamous dwelling in town, invited me into his modest home. You see, Mr. House now lives in what was once the residence of one of England's most prolific mass murderers, Mary Ann Cotton.

I looked around the living room. Some things had changed over the past century, but in general the house is much the same - Mary Ann Cotton's home, where the plain miner's wife dispensed death in wholesale quantities.

Mary Ann was born in County Durham to Michael and Mary Robson. Her coal miner father was killed in an

accident when Mary Ann was only 14. Two years later she married a miner named William Mowbray.

The Mowbrays had two children in tow when they returned to County Durham in 1860, after living in several towns in the south of England. Mary Ann told friends that four other children had died before the family moved back. No investigation into these four deaths was undertaken, but in light of subsequent events, one can't help but wonder.

On June 24, 1860, the Mowbrays' four-year-old daughter, Mary Ann, died. The attending physician attributed her death to gastric fever. After the loss of their daughter, the Mowbrays moved to Hendon, where William gained employment as a fireman on a steam vessel out of Sunderland.

Mary Ann gave birth to another daughter, whom she christened Mary Jane. The sudden death of daughter Mary Ann had triggered the need for funeral money. The Mowbrays would never be caught short again. Mary Ann insured her husband and three surviving children with the British and Prudential Insurance Co.

In September, 1864, a son, John William, died. The attending physician signed the death certificate "gastric fever." Four months later, Mr. Mowbray, in the prime of life at age 47, came home on leave. He never returned to his ship. The doctor said it was that old standby, gastric fever. That May, Mary Jane, age four, died from the same illness. In each of the Mowbray deaths, Mary Ann received a few pounds for funeral expenses and a little extra to tide her over until the next tragedy.

Mary Ann gave birth to a daughter, Margaret, shortly after her husband's death. It was tough taking care of a new baby, but relief was only moments away. Mary Ann's mother took ill and asked her to move in. Unfortunately, mother was remarried to a George Stott. Four days after Mary Ann moved in to nurse her mother, Mrs. Stott died. Around Easter, 1866, baby Margaret passed away.

A girl has to make a living. Our Mary Ann moved to

Sunderland, where she obtained employment at the Sunderland Infirmary. One of the patients there, George Ward, a virile 33, had the misfortune to fall in love with Mary Ann. Upon his release from hospital, he married the woman of his dreams. In October of that year, he expired from gastric fever.

Still encumbered with the necessity of making a living, Mary Ann moved on. She answered an advertisement for a housekeeper. The advertisement had been placed by James Robinson, a widower with five children, living in the town of Pallion.

Let's see now. John Robinson, 10 months old, died in January; James, 6, left this mortal coil in April, just one week before the demise of Eliza, 8. Mary Ann was heartbroken over the children's deaths; so much so that Robinson fell for the sympathy act and married his housekeeper. Shortly after the nuptials, Margaret Robinson, age 3, passed away from gastric fever. Strangely, one of Mary Ann's stepsons managed to survive. Elizabeth Mowbray, 9, who had travelled with her mother to Pallion, also died that year.

The union of Mary Ann and James Robinson produced two children. Mary Ann dispensed with them via the gastric fever route in 1868 and 1869.

After the death of the second baby in 1869, Robinson discovered that Mary Ann, who ran the family's finances, had pretty well cleaned him out. Unknown to him, she had withdrawn all his savings, wiped out his credit with a building society and sold off valuable pieces from their home. Robinson was luckier than he could possibly have imagined. He walked out on his wife and survived.

Once again, what was a girl to do? Mary Ann met a widower, Frederick Cotton of Walpole. Fred had two small sons, but that didn't deter Mary Ann from moving in with him in July, 1870. In October, Mary Ann and Fred Cotton were married at Newcastle. One mustn't forget that Mary Ann was still married to James Robinson, but then again our girl was never one to concern herself with

details. Shortly after the marriage, Mary Ann gave birth to a son, Robert.

In 1871, Mary Ann, hubby Fred, and the three children moved into the house at 13 Front St., West Auckland, the home now occupied by Robert House.

Let's be fair to the medical and law enforcement personnel of the times. Mary Ann's crimes took place in some of the most unsanitary conditions in the world. It wasn't uncommon for epidemics to sweep through the poverty stricken mining areas, decimating whole families. The infant mortality rate was astronomical. Because of these abhorrent conditions, her crimes went undetected until she moved to the village of West Auckland.

On Sept. 19, 1871, Fred Cotton, 39, took ill in the mines and died. The insurance didn't go far. Strapped for cash, Mary Ann took in a lodger. The deaths continued. Stepson Frederick, age 10, died in March. Baby Robert, 14 months old, died a short time later.

It's lonely in West Auckland. Mary Ann bedded down with lodger Joseph Natrass. Joe gave up the ghost on April 2, 1872 after a short illness. He left his belongings, as well as £10 insurance money, to Mary Ann. Doctors were puzzled at Joe's death. Neighbors spread nasty rumors that Mary Ann had given Joe precious little nourishment during his illness, but had kept him well supplied with tea, which she perpetually brewed on the stove.

It was left to Thomas Riley to trip up Mary Ann. Riley, who was in charge of dispensing relief money to the poor of West Auckland, knew Mary Ann well. She complained to him that she had to take care of her surviving stepson, Charles Cotton, age seven. Riley was appalled when Mary Ann said, "I'll not be troubled long. He'll go like the rest of the Cotton family." A few days later, when he learned that the boy had died, Riley contacted police, the first person to do so in the over 12 years that Mary Ann had been busy dispensing poison.

Bodies were exhumed and found to be laced with arsenic. Mary Ann was arrested and taken into custody.

Her trial was delayed because she was pregnant. She gave birth to a healthy baby girl in January, 1873, after which she was brought to trial for the murder of her last victim, Charles Cotton. There was little doubt about her guilt. Mary Ann had sent Charles to the chemist to purchase arsenic shortly before his death. When the chemist wouldn't give the little boy the poison, she prevailed on a neighbor, Mary Dodds, to purchase it for her. Mary obliged, and told her story from the witness stand.

Mary Ann was found guilty of murder and was hanged on March 14, 1873. She was certainly one of the few criminals anywhere who killed her children, husbands, lover, and her own mother.

Have the good folks of West Auckland forgotten their most infamous citizen? Not by a long shot. It's been 116 years since the death of Mary Ann Cotton, but her picture is displayed in the window of the West Auckland Post Office to this day.

AN UNUSUAL GIFT

Devoted wives have been known to conjure up novel Christmas presents for their husbands. Would you believe several well-directed blows to the head with an ever-so-sharp axe? That's exactly the unusual gift allegedly presented to Dietlof Knott by his ever-loving wife Hester.

Up until the night Hester allegedly presented her husband with his unique gift, life was not that exciting for the Knott family. Hester, Dietlof and their three children lived in the village of Postmasburg on the fringe of the Kalahari Desert in South Africa. Postmasburg owed its existence to the West End Diamond Mine, located just outside the village. The closest real town was Kimberley, about 160 miles down the road. Life was dull. I mean *boring*.

It has been rumored that to break things up a bit, Dietlof occasionally used Hester as a punching bag. This currently frowned upon hobby was not considered that unusual back in 1925. Many of the miners struck their wives at the least provocation.

The morning of Dec. 23 began like any other morning. It was scorching hot, being the middle of summer in South Africa. Dietlof and his 15-year-old son Robbie went vegetable shopping. After they returned home, Dietlof helped his wife bake cakes.

That evening before supper, Robbie went into the garden and chopped firewood. Completing his task, he left the axe imbedded in the chopping block. Later, Hester went out to the woodpile and brought in some wood.

After supper, a few friends visited, but left after tea. It was an extremely hot, still night, a night when many South Africans in remote areas slept outdoors in their gardens or on their verandas.

A large spreading apricot tree grew in the Knotts' back yard. It provided some respite from the oppressive heat. The Knotts kept two double beds there for just such nights. At 9:30 p.m., husband and wife went to bed underneath the apricot tree. Robbie and the other two Knott youngsters occupied the second bed. The last thing Dietlof did before falling off to sleep was the unnecessary task of setting an alarm clock beside his bed. Soon, the entire family was asleep.

At 2:35 a.m., the Knotts' immediate neighbors, Mr. and Mrs. Venter, were awakened by Hester's screams, "Come, help, there is a robber in the house!" Mrs. Venter opened her door. There stood Hester in an agitated state, clad only in her night dress. First things first. Mrs. Venter gave her neighbor a slug of brandy, while Mr. Venter and his son Johann rushed to the Knotts' home.

They approached the house with a degree of caution, believing that they could be surprising a thief in the process of burglarizing their neighbors' home. Father and son thought they heard groans coming from the direction of the apricot tree. They lit candles. By the flickering light, they stared down at the body of Dietlof Knott. His head had been split open.

Let's have Mr. Venter tell it like he saw it. "His body was covered with a bedspread. He was lying on his back. I was horrified at the sight. While my son and I stood next to the double bed, I saw Robbie sit up, climb out of his bed, and come toward us. He was wearing his nightshirt. I told him to awaken the other children. He did so. They came around the bed and the little girl said, 'Look

at my poor papa.'"

Meanwhile, over at the Venters', Hester was explaining what had happened. She said she had been awakened by the noise of an intruder. She shook her husband, but he did not wake up. Desperate, she jumped out of bed and ran to the Venters for assistance. Hester added that she had noticed a stranger around her home for the previous few days and had mentioned it to her husband.

Police were called. Hester told her story much as she had told it to Mrs. Venter, adding that upon hearing the noise, she had entered her house via the back door and ran out the front to her neighbor's. That's where matters stood when the sun came up on the day before Christmas, 1925.

In the clear light of day, the police and Dr. Robert Vernon studied the crime scene. It was a gruesome task. Dietlof's bed was a mass of blood and bits of scalp. Detectives were able to ascertain that the killer had pulled the bedspread gently over Dietlof's head before striking the fatal blows with an axe. A total of five blows had been struck. One blow glanced off Dietlof's head and went through a pillow, causing an eerie rain of tiny feathers to cover the scene of violent death. The bloody axe, with tufts of Dietlof's hair clinging to the blade, was found beside the bed.

Detectives questioned everyone in the village. They soon found out that Dietlof often beat his wife. The last beating had taken place on Dec. 6, just 17 days before the axe fell. The reason for the fight had been Hester's accusations that Dietlof had been playing around with other ladies who were not particularly concerned that he was a married man with three children.

At the time Hester accused Dietlof, a neighbor had heard him yell, "I shall beat you until the devil is out of you. You do not know what is in you, but I will knock the devil out of you." It was revealed that Dietlof, a religious man in a weird sort of way, often accused his wife of sinful conduct if she even mentioned his dalliances with

other women. The beatings were his way of punishment.

When Robbie was questioned, he recalled his mother saying, "I will kill him and then they can hang me."

No one had seen Hester's mysterious stranger. If a stranger did exist, why would he not pick one of the far more affluent homes in the area to rob? Why would a robber choose a house with the whole family asleep outdoors? Why would he kill a sleeping man who posed no threat to him? If an intruder was around, why didn't Hester fear for her children, rather than dashing to the Venters' home, leaving them alone? Hester's story didn't add up. She had motive and opportunity. Police arrested our Hester and charged her with the murder of her husband.

On April 29, 1926, Hester Knott stood trial. One fact became obvious. The defendant was pregnant. She took the witness stand in her own defence and denied that she had ever accused her husband of infidelity or that she had ever threatened to kill him.

Hester recounted the minutes before disaster struck. "We went to sleep under the tree. I woke up and spoke to my husband. I said I heard someone walking. He remarked sleepily, 'Do not be frightened,' and went back to sleep. I saw something - I cannot say if it was a human being - at the gate leading to the road. I shook my husband. When he didn't respond, I ran through the house to my neighbors.'"

When Hester was asked why she didn't scream into her husband's ear, she replied, "I was afraid to speak loudly to my husband for fear the man would hear me." When faced with her son's incriminating statement, Hester claimed she and Dietlof had often talked about death in front of the boy and he had obviously misunderstood her meaning.

The prosecution made much of the fact that by the mere process of elimination, no one other than Hester could have killed Dietlof, nor did anyone have any reason to do so. The children slept soundly. As far as anyone

could ascertain, there was no robbery as nothing had been taken from the home.

Hester didn't have one drop of blood on her nightdress. The prosecution attributed this to her foresight in placing the bedspread over Dietlof's head before inflicting the deadly blows.

Defence counsel pointed out that all the evidence was circumstantial. No one had seen the killing. Fights between husband and wife were a common occurrence in Postmasburg. Just because no one had seen a marauding robber did not mean that one didn't exist. It was logical to believe that a robber, scouting what he thought to be an empty house, stumbled across the sleeping family in the back yard. Wanton killings by nervous and excited thieves had happened before.

The single most convincing piece of evidence for the defence was the fact that Hester had no blood on her nightdress. If she had struck her husband five times with an axe, the last four times she raised the axe over her head it was most probably dripping blood. Experts testified that it was in the realm of possibility that, if she were the killer, she could have escaped the shower of blood, but it was not probable.

Hester Knott was found not guilty. Before setting her free, the presiding judge voiced his personal doubts as to the validity of the verdict. One thing is certain - Hester livened up the little village on the edge of the Kalahari desert during the Christmas season of 1925.

BORN TO RAISE HELL

One of the most horrendous crimes ever committed was perpetrated by drifter Richard Speck.

Speck was born on Dec. 6, 1941, the day before the United States entered the Second World War. His early years were spent in Monmouth, Ill. The family moved to Dallas, Texas, when Mrs. Speck died in 1947. Richard attended grade school, and later Crozier Technical High School. During his teenage years, he was arrested ten times for burglary, trespassing and disturbing the peace. He dropped out of technical school after one semester, working as a laborer, truck driver, carpenter and garbage collector.

Richard married at age 20. His bride was 15-year-old Shirley Malone. The young couple had a daughter, who was placed in her mother's custody in 1966 when the Specks separated.

Early in 1966, Richard caught a berth on a Great Lakes ore boat. His brief career on the Lakes was interrupted when he was sent to St. Joseph's Hospital in Hancock, Mich. for an appendectomy. In June, recovered from his operation, he was hired by the Inland Steel Co. and served aboard the *Randall*. However, he was fired after a bitter argument with an officer.

Early in July, Richard Speck made his way to Chicago

with two purposes in mind. He sought help from a sister living in the city and desperately wanted to land a job on a boat headed for New Orleans.

Richard's sister, Mrs. Martha Thornton, gave him $25 and a lift to the National Maritime Union hiring hall. Each day, for four days, Richard attempted without success to obtain work on a ship.

The Union hiring hall was a half block from 2319 East 100th St., where eight student nurses lived in a town house owned by the South Chicago Community Hospital. One of the students, Corazon Amurao, was in bed when she was awakened by a knock on the bedroom door. She opened the door and stood face to face with a man holding a gun. The man was Richard Speck. The gun was pointed directly at Miss Amurao.

The young Philippine exchange student, together with her two companions, was ushered into a back bedroom, where three other student nurses were awakened. Speck assured the girls that he had no intention of harming them. He merely wanted money to get to New Orleans. The girls quickly complied by giving Speck whatever money they had in their purses.

The gunmen spoke deliberately and clearly, but reeked of alcohol. Speck told the girls to lie down. Methodically, he bound each girl, hand and foot, with torn bedsheets. All the while he assured them, "Don't be afraid, I'm not going to kill you."

Richard Speck untied Patricia Wilkening's ankles and led her from the room. A short while later, Mary Ann Jordan and Suzanne Farris arrived home and were made to join their fellow nurses. Ironically, Mary Ann didn't live in the house. She was just staying over for the night.

The two late arrivals were marched out of the room. Next to leave was Nina Schmale. A period of between 20 and 30 minutes elapsed between each girl's absence and Speck's return. During one of these periods, Corazon Amurao rolled under a bed. It was a move that was to save her life.

Merlita Gargullo, Valentina Passion, Patricia Matusek and Gloria Davy were individually led out of the room. All the while, Corazon Amurao lay quiet under the bunk bed in abject terror. She heard the muffled sounds of rape and murder. Finally, silence fell over the house.

At 6 a.m. Corazon Amurao ran from her hiding place. She hopped over the bodies of her colleagues to a second-storey ledge which ran along the front of the house. Miss Amurao screamed, "Help me, help me! Everybody is dead! I am the only one alive on the sampan!" In her terrified state, she thought for a moment she was back in the Philippines.

The strange sight of the hysterical girl screaming soon brought passers-by to the house of horror. Corazon Amurao was the only one of the nine girls to survive Richard Speck. Her eight companions were dead, all raped and either stabbed or suffocated to death. One of the girls had been stabbed a total of 18 times.

Corazon described Speck to police. His description and the details of the heartless multiple murders received wide publicity. Twenty minutes after a bulletin was released to patrol cars, police learned that a man matching the description had left two bags at a gas station. He had mentioned that he was looking for work at the National Maritime Union. A check at the union confirmed that one Richard Speck was seeking a berth aboard a ship headed for New Orleans. Speck's photograph was on file with the U.S. Coast Guard. Corazon picked his picture out of a group of police photographs.

The FBI were able to tell Chicago police that Speck's left forearm was tattooed with the words, 'Born to Raise Hell.' His fingerprints matched several prints taken from the nurses residence.

Speck made his way to the 90-cent a night Starr Hotel on West Madison St. in Chicago's skid row district. He registered as B. Brian. Speck read an account of the murders and then slashed his right wrist and left elbow. As his blood poured on the floor, he yelled through the

paper thin walls to the man in the next room, "Come and see me, you've got to come and see me! I done something bad!"

The man in the next room didn't respond. Speck staggered out of his room, dripping blood. A desk clerk called police. Speck was rushed to Cook County Hospital.

Dr. LeRoy Smith looked down at the man admitted as B. Brian and thought he closely resembled the man everyone was talking about who had killed eight nurses. The doctor washed away some of the caked blood covering a tattoo on his patient's arm. He uncovered the words, 'Born to Raise Hell.' Dr. Smith leaned over and asked, "What's your name?" He received the faint reply, "Richard Speck." The hunt was over.

Richard Speck recovered to stand trial on eight charges of murder. An Illinois jury took only 46 minutes to find him guilty on all eight charges. He was sentenced to death.

In 1972, when the death penalty was outlawed in the U.S., Speck was residing on Death Row. He was resentenced to from 400 to 1200 years in prison. Despite the seemingly insurmountable number of years stipulated in the formal sentencing, Speck has come up for parole a total of six times.

His latest hearing, before the Illinois Prisoner Review Board, took place in September, 1987. Once again, he was denied parole. Parents of several of the murdered student nurses are actively involved in seeing that Richard Speck never be freed. So far he has spent 21 years behind bars since the night he systematically took the lives of eight innocent young women.

CHEATING
THE GALLOWS

Come along with me now to another time and place, to Marion County, Mississippi before the turn of the century. At that time and in that place, the Ku Klux Klan was an organization every bit as powerful as the state's law enforcement agencies. The Klan controlled several organizations, could pack juries, bribe policemen and fix elections.

Will Buckley and his brother James were members of the Klan. They were well aware of the power of their white-hooded brethren, but when the arrogance and inhumanity of the organization touched them personally, well, that was a horse of a different color.

For no apparent reason, maybe just to have a little fun, Klan members severely beat up the Buckley brothers' black servant, Sam Waller. Will and Jim were incensed. The beating was a cruel, senseless attack. To their way of thinking, it was an attack on their property which had to avenged.

The morning after the beatings, Will and Jim hopped onto their trusty steeds and rode into Columbia, which was then little more than a village. In no uncertain terms, they let it be known that they wanted the perpetrators of the outrage to be punished. Otherwise they would take matters into their own hands. If they weren't satisfied,

they would divulge the secrets of the Klan. The brothers then hightailed it out of town and waited to see if anyone would comply with their demands.

The Klan took the attitude that the boys were just blowing off steam. No one was foolish enough to mess with the Ku Klux Klan. The Buckleys would cool off and the incident would soon be forgotten. They were wrong.

A few days later, the two brothers rode up to the Columbia courthouse with Sam Waller. They marched in while the court was in session and made an unsolicited speech. Jim named Sam's attackers and demanded that they be punished. Then the two brothers rode off slowly on horseback. They had to move slowly; Sam was on foot.

The Buckley farm was some miles outside Columbia. Because Sam was trudging along on foot, they were travelling at a snail's pace through uninhabited, lonesome terrain. A shot rang out from behind some bushes. Sam ran for his life. Will fell to the ground, mortally wounded. He died an hour later.

Jim carried only a knife. When two men emerged from behind the bushes, he attempted to take his brother's revolver from its holster. Unfortunately, he had trouble turning Will over to remove the weapon. In desperation, he faced the two men. Evidently, they lost their courage and ran into nearby woods.

The county sheriff was soon on the case. He followed the assassins' tracks to a stream, picking them up again where one of the men left the stream near a small settlement. Will Purvis, 19, a known and avid member of the Ku Klux Klan, lived in one of the houses. Neighbors who did not belong to the Klan were more than willing to attest to Purvis' arrogant and cruel ways. Two days later, when bloodhounds led the sheriff to Will Purvis' home, he was taken into custody and charged with murder.

In August, 1893, Will Purvis stood trial for murder. The trial was strange in many ways. Hundreds of honest, God-fearing citizens wanted a conviction and a hanging. Yet

they felt that a member of the Klan would never be put to death.

As the evidence unfolded, it was apparent that there was a very strong case against Purvis. The tracks leading from the murder scene corresponded precisely with boots owned by the defendant. Purvis' neighbor, Jeff Hanton, testified that Purvis had come to him before the killing as he worked his fields, saying, "If anything happens tonight, I want you to testify that I was here."

Hanton was a respected citizen. His testimony went a long way toward convicting Purvis, but it was still not as strong as that given by the dead man's brother. Jim testified that he had stood face to face with the murderer and recognized him immediately as Will Purvis. There was absolutely no doubt in his mind.

About the only thing in Purvis' favor was the evidence of several of his field hands, who swore Purvis was working in the fields with them at the time of the murder. As they were employees of the accused, they had a vested interest in his acquittal. They were not believed by the jury.

Purvis was found guilty and sentenced to hang. All appeals failed. The governor of the state refused to intervene and the accused man, still professing his innocence, prepared to meet his maker.

Nineteen-year-old Will Purvis walked up the steps to the improvised scaffold placed in front of the Columbia courthouse. Executions were public events in those days. A large crowd had gathered to witness Purvis' hanging.

The doomed man walked briskly to the trap door. A noose was placed over his head. The door sprung open and Purvis plunged through it. His full weight bounced as the rope grew taut. Then the rope snapped. Purvis, pale as a ghost and shaky on his feet, rose and looked around. Realizing he was neither in heaven or hell, he mumbled, "Let's get it over with," as he made his way to the steps of the scaffold.

Someone shouted, "This man's been hanged once too

often already!" Other members of the crowd took up the cry. Instead of being executed, Purvis was taken to his cell.

Eventually, the supreme court ruled that the execution had to be carried out, but Will Purvis was not to die at the end of the hangman's noose. On the day of his second date with death, he escaped from custody. His case became a hot political issue. When politicians who had championed his cause came to power, he surrendered, received a reprieve and was released from jail. Purvis was something of a novelty as one of the few men in history who was hanged and lived to tell about the experience. But his case was far from over.

After Purvis gained his freedom, many expressed the opinion that he knew who the real murderers were, but, true to the code of the Ku Klux Klan, refused to reveal the killers' names. Once the Klan knew this, they decided to let him hang. It was also the belief of many that respectable Jeff Hanton had told the truth. Purvis had gone to him to manufacture an alibi for the time of the murder, because he knew it was going to take place and wanted to protect himself. Purvis did not necessarily mean that he was the one who was going to ambush the Buckleys.

What about the positive identification by Jim Buckley? Surely, if he had been able to identify the killer at the time of the murder, it would not have been necessary for the sheriff to employ bloodhounds to follow tracks two days later. Was it possible that the murdered man's brother had been caught up in the mood of the day and wanted someone he thought was guilty to pay for his loss?

It took 27 years for the truth to come out. A man whose name we cannot use, for he was never convicted of the crime, came forward during a religious service and confessed that he was one of the two men who had ambushed the Buckleys 27 years earlier. He swore that Will Purvis had been chosen to be one of the killers, but

had backed out of the scheme. Purvis had been willing to hang rather than reveal the names of the two killers. This man's confession was thoroughly checked. It was proven beyond any doubt that he was telling the truth.

Twenty-eight years after the ambush, Will Purvis was awarded $5000 compensation, a rather paltry sum for going through the traumatic experience of being hanged.

MURDER OR SUICIDE?

The vast majority of murder cases are elementary; the motive obvious, the method self-explanatory and the perpetrator quickly apprehended, tried, and convicted. However, there are those rare cases which appear to be routine, if murder can ever be called routine, but in hindsight hold all the ingredients which fascinate connoisseurs. Let's look at one which has held the interest of criminologists since it occurred back in 1884.

The village of Wrangle in Lincolnshire, England, is not known for the exciting lifestyle of its inhabitants. Over a hundred years ago, the village, without reservation, could be called quiet.

William Leffey, a 59-year-old farmer, lived in apparent harmony with his wife Mary, who was ten years his junior. The childless couple owned a nice little cottage.

Early on the morning of Feb. 6, Mary left her home to travel to a nearby town to sell butter, which the Leffeys produced on their farm. Will climbed aboard Sam Spence's cart and accompanied his wife for about a half hour. Then he walked back to his cottage.

Several Wrangleites saw and chatted with Will that morning. They later reported that he acted normal in every way. At 3 p.m., Will Leffey staggered out of his cottage, down the street to the home of the local doctor,

who was stuck with the memorable name of Dr. Bubb.

Unfortunately, Dr. Bubb was not in, but maid Elizabeth Hill offered the doctor's sister as a substitute. Will told Liz that Miss Bubb would do in a pinch. When that kind lady appeared, Will extracted a basin from a basket he was carrying. The basin was about half full of rice pudding. Will got right to the point. "I have been poisoned," he said. Then he staggered out into the yard, vomited and collapsed, moaning, on a mound of straw. He begged the two women to fetch the doctor.

They advised him that Dr. Bubb's replacement, a Dr. Faskally, was expected momentarily. Will responded to that comforting statement with, "That won't do. I want to see him in one minute. I'm dying fast."

Dr. Faskally arrived on the scene and immediately agreed with Will's diagnosis. Once again, Will stated that he had been poisoned when he ate that obnoxious rice pudding. Dr. Faskally treated his patient as best he could. He then solicited the help of bricklayer Robert Chapman to assist Will to his home. Dr. Faskally would follow.

While Chapman was helping Will, he engaged one of the ladies of the village, Mrs. Longden, to give him a hand. They were soon joined by another volunteer, Richard Wright. No question about it, Will's sudden illness had caused quite a stir in the otherwise sleepy village. Finally, the entourage succeeded in getting Will Leffey into his own bed.

Around 6 o'clock that evening, who should show up but Mary, back from her successful commercial butter enterprise. Mary went directly upstairs to the bedroom. She took one look at her everloving husband and assorted hangers on. She could only blurt out, "What's the matter? What's all this about?"

Will stopped retching long enough to raise his head and respond in a rather nasty fashion, "You know all about it, my dear. Go down and don't let me see you any more."

Mary was hurt to the quick. She spun on her unfashionable muddy shoes and left the room in a huff, without

uttering another word. A few minutes later, Richard
Wright came downstairs for a spot of tea. He encountered
Mary, who contributed the rather illuminating statement,
"I suppose he says he's been poisoned. We haven't any
poison in the house to my knowledge and haven't had any
for years."

Richard had to dash upstairs without responding to
Mary, because inconsiderate Will began retching again.
When Mrs. Longden came downstairs, Mary offered her
some tea and remarked that she herself had felt squea-
mish all day. She went on to say by way of explanation,
"I put the sugar and rice together for the pudding and
left my husband to put the milk in."

At 8:30 that same night, Dr. Faskally advised Mary
that her husband was surely dying. Mary, the blabbermouth, replied, "If he's been poisoned, I'm innocent. People don't know he went out the other night and wanted to
hang himself. If he's been poisoned, I don't know where
he could have got it." Three quarters of an hour later,
Will Leffey left this mortal coil, in agony to the end.

Later that same night, police questioned Mary. She told
them her husband was perfectly normal when he climbed
down off Sam Spence's cart and walked home. She had
prepared the rice pudding in the basin so that Will could
cook it whenever he pleased. There was nothing unusual
in this. She prepared rice pudding each week when she
went out to sell butter. Mary elaborated, "If he got any
poison, he must have taken it himself, for I know nothing
about it. I've not had poison in the house for years."

The day after Will's untimely demise, Mary was
arrested and charged with his murder. On May 7, 1884,
Mary stood trial with her life in the balance.

The evidence against Mary was overwhelming. Arsenic
was found in Will's body. The half basin of rice pudding
contained 135 grains of arsenic. Two grains is considered a
fatal dose. Portions of a hard crust along the side of the
basin were almost solid arsenic. In fact, the pudding contained so much arsenic that it had formed a creamy paste

on the bottom of the basin.

All the villagers who had attended Will during the hours before his death testified to Mary's various statements. Three other witnesses gave evidence insinuating that the murder might have been premeditated. They stated that Mary had told them she wished Will were dead and out of the way in the days immediately before he died.

Defence counsel came up with a nephew of the dead man, Will Lister, who testified that he had slept over at the Leffeys' a few days before his uncle died. During the night, his uncle had joined him in bed and told him he had just tried to hang himself. The defence presented suicide as an alternative to murder. They also touched on the unlikely theory that some outsider could have put arsenic in the pudding before Will returned home.

The Lincolnshire jury deliberated only 35 minutes before finding Mary Leffey guilty of murder. Mary was sentenced to death and was hanged on May 26, 1884.

After Mary's execution, the entire case was studied in an objective manner. No arsenic was ever found in the Leffey home, nor was Mary seen to place arsenic in her husband's food.

When Will staggered from his home, he passed several cottages before arriving at Dr. Bubb's residence. Many believe that it would have been more natural for him to have sought assistance at a neighbor's cottage at the first sign of feeling ill.

Arsenic was commonly used as a rat poison at that time. Most cottagers knew what constituted a fatal dose. Surely Mary knew that such a mammoth quantity would be readily detected. It would seem likely that Mary would have placed a much smaller amount of arsenic in the rice pudding in an attempt to avoid detection.

Is it possible for a man to consume one half basin of rice pudding without detecting the taste and appearance of arsenic? After all, he ate rice pudding each week and should have known the difference. If Mary had poisoned

her husband, would she not have had a ready made story to relate rather than stupidly running around professing that she hadn't poisoned anyone?

At no time did anyone ever prove that Mary and Will didn't get along. Motive, that most important ingredient of all murder cases, was absent.

Young Will Lister testified that his uncle had admitted attempting to hang himself. He had no earthly reason to lie. What if Will Leffey was mentally deranged and poisoned himself in order to end his life and wreak revenge on his wife for some imagined wrong?

We will never know for sure, but many believe that Mary Leffey, who mounted the scaffold protesting her innocence, may have been hanged for a murder that never took place.

THE
BRUCE CURTIS CASE

Any parent would appreciate a well-behaved, studious son like Bruce Curtis. Bruce attended prestigious Kings-Edgehill in Windsor, Nova Scotia, the oldest private school in Canada. He was a member of the debating team and led his class academically in his graduating year. In that summer of 1982, Bruce, 18, had been accepted by Dalhousie University in Halifax, where he planned to study astrophysics.

He had no way of knowing that soon he would be incarcerated in the Bordentown Youth Correctional Institution in New Jersey, serving a 20-year sentence for manslaughter. Something went wrong, drastically wrong.

During that summer, Bruce received several long distance phone calls from a school chum, Scott Franz. Scott had graduated with Bruce and was planning to attend Mount Allison University in New Brunswick. In the meantime, he invited Bruce to visit him at his home in the village of Loch Arbor, New Jersey. Scott painted an extremely attractive picture of life in Loch Arbor, alluding to cars, servants and a large home overlooking the ocean.

Bruce succumbed to Scott's verbal picture of a fantastic visit. It would be Bruce's first trip out of Nova Scotia by himself. His parents consented to the trip. The boy deserved some kind of a break before embarking on his

university career. Bruce left his family's 750-acre property in Mount Hanley, near Middleton, N.S., for New Jersey.

From the moment Bruce's plane landed at Newark Airport on June 29, everything went wrong. The plane was late. Scott's stepfather, Alfred Podgis, was irritable and soon let his feelings be known. He was an avid collector of baseball cards and evidently had missed an appointment with a dealer in order to meet the plane.

The Podgis home at 401 Euclid Ave. was far from a happy one. Bruce, who had been raised by loving, caring parents, found himself in the midst of intense family arguments between stepfather and son. Al Podgis and his wife, Rosemary, also argued incessantly. Police had been called to the Podgis home over 100 times in the previous 14 years.

On the evening of July 3, Al Podgis was in such a state the boys decided to stay outdoors. The two friends spent some time that night walking to pass the time. When they returned, Al and Rosemary Podgis were still up and about, arguing. The boys ducked under the front porch and listened to the argument. Finally, Al went to bed. Mrs. Podgis came outside and suggested that the boys sleep on couches in the living room.

According to Scott, the next morning, Independence Day, he ventured upstairs to fetch Bruce's travellers cheques and suitcase. He fled the house when his stepfather fired at him. The two boys spent the day away from 401 Euclid Ave., but still had the practical problem of getting their belongings out of the house. Bruce had only purchased a one way ticket to New Jersey. He and Scott had planned to drive back to Nova Scotia together.

That evening, the two boys watched fireworks before returning to Euclid Ave. Scott knew his father had hidden firearms in the family's International Harvester Scout van. He took out two Winchester 30-30s and entered the house. The boys went to sleep on the downstairs couch with the weapons at their side.

Early on Monday morning, shots reverberated through-

out the house on Euclid Ave. and Al lay dead in an upstairs bedroom. His son admits shooting him. According to Scott, he killed his stepfather as he was reaching for a .22 rifle.

Downstairs, Mrs. Podgis was preparing French toast for breakfast. Startled at the shots, Bruce grabbed the 30-30. At the same time, Mrs. Podgis heard the shots and dashed around the corner, colliding with Bruce. The gun went off and Rosemary Podgis lay dead at Bruce's feet. In the exact words quoted in Bruce's original statement to police, "I don't know whether when I jumped back, my hand moved too and I pulled the trigger or if it just went off. It was just a blur."

Scott ran downstairs and was confronted with the sight of his mother's body. He could only ask, "What happened?" Bruce replied, "I shot your mother."

The two boys cleaned the house of blood. They lifted the bodies of Al and Rosemary Podgis into the family van and made their way to Pennsylvania's Ravenburg State Park, where the bodies were unceremoniously thrown over an embankment. When they drove back to Loch Arbor, they observed police cars on Euclid Ave. and decided to keep going.

The rifles were disposed of down a storm drain. Ammunition was thrown out of the window of the van as the vehicle sped down the highway to Atlantic City. The boys stayed overnight at Harrahs, the famous gambling casino. Next day, they arrived in Washington, where they did some sightseeing, then on to Knoxville, Tenn. Scott had some vague notion that his sister, Rosie, who lived in Texas, would be sympathetic with their predicament.

On Tuesday evening the bodies were found at the base of the embankment by two men walking along a path in Ravenburg State Park. Al Podgis' nude body had been stuffed in a trunk. Rosemary Podgis' body was wrapped in a sleeping bag.

Meanwhile, back on Euclid Ave., the Podgis' married daughter, Barbara Czacherski, couldn't locate her parents.

She called police, who investigated the now deserted home. When they found bloodstained bed clothing and weapons, they assumed that murder had taken place in the home. Their suspicions were confirmed with the discovery of the two bodies and the information that Scott, Bruce and the Scout van were missing. Scott and Bruce were picked up in Texas and returned to New Jersey.

In the months between apprehension and trial, several events took place which played havoc with Bruce Curtis' story of accidentally shooting Rosemary Podgis.

On the advice of his attorney, Scott was persuaded to plead guilty to the murder of his stepfather. It was pointed out to him that the physical evidence and expert testimony indicated that his father was not killed from across the room while sitting up reaching for a weapon, but was killed at close range while lying on his back with his head on the pillow.

Scott agreed to plead guilty and testify against Bruce in return for a reduced sentence. Gradually, he added small but pertinent changes to his story. He claimed it was Bruce who wanted to bring weapons into the house. It was Bruce who wouldn't let him call police after the shootings. It was Bruce who suggested getting rid of the bodies.

On March 14, 1983, Bruce Curtis stood trial for the murder of Rosemary Podgis in Monmouth County Courthouse in Freehold, N.J. Scott Franz was the chief witness for the prosecution. He readily admitted that there was extreme animosity between himself and his stepfather, but insinuated that Bruce enjoyed the murders. According to Scott, Bruce smiled and joked as he cleaned up the blood after the killings. Bruce cleaned off the weapons before discarding them.

After deliberating over 11 hours, the New Jersey jury found Bruce Curtis not guilty of murder but guilty of aggravated manslaughter.

Scott Franz pleaded guilty to the murder of his stepfather and was given the minimum sentence of 20 years

imprisonment with parole eligibility in 10 years. He was placed in a medium security institution, but because of disciplinary problems has been transferred to Rahway Prison, one of the toughest in the U.S., where he is presently serving his sentence.

A month after his trial, Bruce Curtis was sentenced to 20 years imprisonment with eligibility for parole in 10 years. This is the maximum sentence possible for aggravated assault.

The relative sentences of the two boys outraged many who had followed the case. Put simply, one boy who admitted shooting his stepfather in the head while he lay in bed, received exactly the same sentence as one who professed that he had killed accidentally and was found guilty of a far less serious crime.

For five years the Curtis family exhausted every legal avenue open to them to gain some semblance of justice for their son. Gov. Thomas Kean of New Jersey rejected Bruce's plea for clemency, after a year's consideration.

The Curtis family then concentrated on efforts to have Bruce serve his time in a Canadian institution. It was a frustrating process. Although the U.S. ratified an agreement in 1978 whereby prisoners may be transferred to Canada, each state had the choice of ratifying the agreement individually. New Jersey took eight years to ratify this agreement.

It took Bruce Curtis' lawyers six months to obtain the one page form entitled "Intention to Apply for Transfer." The application was duly submitted and finally approved in 1988.

Bruce Curtis is presently serving his sentence in a jail in Nova Scotia.

MISSISSIPPI BURNING

The movie *Mississippi Burning* is a fictionalized account of events which took place during the turbulent summer of 1964, when scores of civil rights workers arrived in the state of Mississippi to promote voter registration in the black community.

Opposing their efforts, local white officials did their utmost to instill fear into anyone who sympathized with the "Northern agitators."

On the night of June 21, 1964, a group of men, some of them officers of the law, committed an act which was to send shock waves throughout the nation and the world. That was the night they murdered civil rights workers Mickey Schwerner, 24, James Chaney, 21, and Andrew Goodman, 20.

Mickey Schwerner didn't have to scour the back roads of Mississippi attempting to change the world. He didn't have to join the Congress of Racial Equality (CORE), and later the Council of Federated Organizations (COFO). He didn't have to live on $9.80 a week. Mickey Schwerner chose to do so, because he had the idea that the color of a person's skin shouldn't predicate their station in life.

After graduating from Cornell University and completing post-graduate studies at Columbia, Mickey set out to right certain wrongs. On Jan. 19, 1964, he and his wife

Rita arrived in Meridian, Miss., with the task of converting five empty rooms into a community centre. He also carried a list of young blacks who had indicated their desire to join the fight for freedom.

One of the names on the list was that of James Chaney.

It was hard work, but little by little, the young idealistic couple whipped the dilapidated rooms into an office, a library, and classrooms, where they taught subjects varying in content from children's stories to instructions on how to register to vote.

Mickey and Rita had difficulty finding a place to live. Appreciative blacks took them in for one or two nights, but they were always asked to leave. Pressure had been put on their hosts. Subtle and not so subtle threats proved to be a difficult obstacle. Despite the problems, the efforts of the Schwerners resulted in some headway. Young blacks volunteered to join the movement. They passed out pamphlets and visited with black leaders. The white community took notice. They didn't like what they saw. "What's the Jew Commie with the beard agitating our blacks for anyway?"

James Chaney proved to be a valuable worker at what was now called the Meridian Community Centre. CORE even provided the centre with a blue station wagon.

Soon, James Chaney was devoting his full time to the movement. On several occasions, he and Mickey ventured into the neighboring town of Philadelphia, Miss., a 36-mile trip. Their mission was to feel out the black population, knowing full well that Philadelphia had the reputation of being a danger zone, vehemently opposed to integration of any kind. The town sheriff, Lawrence Rainey, had run for office on the promise that he'd "handle the niggers and the outsiders."

Chaney had been successful in talking the officials of Longdale's Mount Zion Methodist Church into letting Mickey Schwerner speak at a Sunday service. They even

voted to approve the establishment of a freedom school in the church.

On June 16, Mickey, Rita and Chaney headed to Oxford, Ohio, where hundreds of volunteers were in training to go to Mississippi later on that summer. They planned to pick one top-notch volunteer to help Chaney in the Longdale Freedom School.

That same night, four automobiles pulled up to Longdale's Mount Zion Methodist Church. Ten gallons of diesel fuel were poured inside. One of the men lit a match and the church burned to the ground.

On Sat., June 20, 1964, Mickey Schwerner, James Chaney and Andrew Goodman drove back to Meridian. Rita remained in Oxford. It is estimated that 200 students would travel to Mississippi that summer devoted to helping blacks register to vote.

There is evidence that by this time Mickey was a marked man. Times were tense. Gov. Paul B. Johnson stated, "This action is repulsive to the American people. Turmoil, strife and bloodshed lie ahead." George Wallace declared, "It is ironical that this event occurs as we approach celebration of Independence Day. That day we won our freedom. On this day, we have largely lost it."

Next morning, Mickey was anxious to visit the burned-out church in Longdale. He had heard that the mob who had torched the church had also beaten up the blacks who had been holding a meeting in the church that night.

By mid-afternoon, the three boys arrived at the burned-out church. One of the men who had been beaten ominously mentioned to Mickey that he heard members of the mob were looking for him. Unknown to Mickey, a plot was afoot to "kill the Jew with the beard."

As the three boys drove down the road, Dep. Sheriff Cecil Price, a member of the Ku Klux Klan and Sheriff Rainey's right-hand man, stopped their blue station wagon. Price radioed highway patrolmen Poe and Wiggs. He told them he had taken three men into custody and required help in transporting them to jail.

By the time the two officers arrived at the scene, the three civil rights workers were changing a flat on their station wagon. Price told the two officers that he had arrested the boys for "speeding" and "suspicion of arson" in the burning down of the Longdale Church.

The three boys were lodged in the Neshoba County Jail in Philadelphia. It was stifling hot. That day the temperature reached 101 degrees. What did Andy Goodman think of what was happening around him? It was his first day in Mississippi. But things were looking up. The three men were freed a little after 10 p.m.

Killers were waiting 10 miles outside Philadelphia. It was they who had given the signal for the three to be set free. Their leader was none other than Deputy Cecil Price. He was accompanied by other men intent on keeping Mississippi "free and pure."

Price intercepted the station wagon. Mickey, James and Andrew were placed in an official Neshoba County car and transported to unpaved Rock Cut Road. All three were shot to death and buried in an earthen dam under construction. One of the conspirators operated a bulldozer.

In minutes, Mickey Schwerner, James Chaney and Andrew Goodman ceased to exist. Their station wagon was burned with diesel fuel and deposited in Bogue Chitto swamp several miles from the dam. The men then gathered at the courthouse square in Philadelphia, shook hands and congratulated each other on a job well done.

The three civil rights workers were immediately missed. FBI agents, headed by 37-year-old John Proctor, were dispatched to find them. They received little in the way of cooperation from Sheriff Rainey and his deputy, Cecil Price.

As the days passed and the search for the missing young men intensified, tempers grew short. There was even talk that the whole thing was a hoax. Locals said the missing trio was in Chicago drinking beer.

A week after the boys went missing, their station wagon was removed from the swamp. It would take 44

days before the bodies were recovered from the dam. To this day, no one knows who informed on the conspirators. It was rumored at the time that the informer was paid $30,000 to reveal the location of the bodies.

Mickey Schwerner's parents wanted their son to be buried beside James Chaney in Mississippi. No white undertaker could be found who would accept the job. The body was cremated. Andrew Goodman was buried in Mount Judah Cemetery in Brooklyn.

Two months later, on Aug. 16, a memorial service was held for all three victims amidst the ashes of the Mount Zion Methodist Church at Longdale. The 11-year-old brother of James Chaney looked beyond the crowd at Sheriff Rainey and Deputy Price, who watched the service from a distance. The little boy made a speech. He closed by shouting, "We ain't scared no more of Sheriff Rainey!"

Several of those involved were tried for conspiracy and denying the victims their civil rights by killing them.

Cecil Price received a six-year prison sentence for conspiracy. He was released after serving four years. He now is employed as a safety officer for a trucking firm.

Six others received sentenced of three years to ten years imprisonment. Many still reside in the Philadelphia/Meridian area.

Jimmy Jordan pleaded guilty and was sentenced to four years. It was Jordan who eventually revealed most of the details of the killings to the FBI.

John Proctor, the veteran FBI officer in charge of the case, is now retired. He operates a detective agency in Meridian and often bumps into the men he helped convict.

Sheriff Lawrence Rainey was acquitted of all charges. He is now employed as a security guard at McDonald's Security Guard Service. His employer, Mr. E.E. McDonald, is black.

Ben Chaney, the 11-year-old who shouted, "We ain't scared no more of Sheriff Rainey," has led a strange life since the murder of his older brother. Andrew Goodman's parents provided a scholarship for young Ben at a small

private school in New York City.

The culture shock was too much. At age 17, Ben, with two companions, was involved in a total of four murders in Florida and South Carolina. In each case, Ben did not kill anyone and could have walked away from his companions at any time. He received three life sentences and spent 13 years in prison before being paroled. He is now free and is attempting to set up an organization to assist black voter registration in Meridian, Mississippi.

TED BUNDY'S LONG ROAD

The delays had come to an end. Theodore Robert Cowell Bundy had a date with Florida's electric chair.

In January, 1989, Florida's governor, Bob Martinez, signed the official death warrant shortly after the U.S. Supreme Court turned down Bundy's final appeal. Sternly, the governor stated, "Bundy is one of the most notorious killers in our nation's history. He has used legal manoeuvrings to dodge the electric chair for ten years."

Ted Bundy was brought up in Tacoma, Washington. There was nothing in his youth to indicate that the handsome charmer would become a notorious serial killer, known simply as "Ted" to the law enforcement agencies of four states.

He graduated from Wilson High School with a B average, attended the University of Puget Sound, switching to the University of Washington for his sophomore year. In 1972, Ted graduated and, for a short time, worked for the King County Law and Justice Planning. While thus employed, ironically, he wrote a pamphlet on rape.

Ted entered the University of Utah Law School. A few months later, young girls began to disappear without a trace. Lynda Ann Healy, 21, a University of Washington student, vanished from her apartment. On March 19,

Donna Munsen, 19, a student at Evergreen State College, disappeared on her way to a musical recital. A month later, Susan Racourt, 18, left Central State College at Ellenburg to take in a movie. She was never seen again. On May 6, Roberta Parks, 22, walked out of the Student Union building of Oregon State University and vanished.

Ted, who by now had quit law school, obtained employment with the Emergency Service in Olympia. Girls continued to disappear. On June 1, Brenda Ball, 22, vanished after leaving a bar with the express intention of going home. Georgann Hawkins, 18, left her frat house at the University of Washington. She, too, was never heard of again. Slim, handsome Ted Bundy continued to counsel troubled individuals all that summer down at Emergency Service.

In August, Ted left his job to continue his law studies in Salt Lake City. Soon, girls in that area began to vanish. An old girlfriend of Ted's back in Seattle read about the rash of killings in Utah. She was troubled. Witnesses claimed that a young man who called himself Ted was known to have attempted to pick up girls. He would approach them, wearing a plaster cast on one arm, and ask for assistance placing a small boat on top of his tan Volkswagen. The Ted she had known in Seattle drove a tan Volkswagen.

With many misgivings, she called police. After she told them of her suspicions, they decided to check out Ted Bundy at the University of Utah Law School. Their cursory check of Ted's records and application at the school indicated that the former girlfriend had either made a mistake or was one of those vindictive women who was seeking revenge. After all, this guy had a recommendation letter on file from no less a personage than Washington's Governor Don Evans.

On Nov. 8, 1974, something happened to Ted that had never happened before. One of his victims escaped. Carol Da Ronch, 18, was approached by a young man who claimed to be a police officer. He told the girl that

someone had been apprehended burglarizing her car and asked her to accompany him to the police station to identify the stolen goods. Carol got in the Volkswagen. She then asked the police officer to identify himself. Instead, the man pulled out a pair of handcuffs and a pistol. He threatened, "Be still or I'll blow your brains out."

Carol didn't hesitate. She jumped from the car, stumbled and fell. Her assailant had also left the car and now stood over the fallen girl. Carol got up, scratching at her attacker's face as he attempted to control her. The terrified girl ran to the centre of the street and managed to hail a passing motorist. Her potential abductor raced to his Volkswagen and sped away.

Now that they had a surviving witness, police were anxious to show photos of suspects to the badly frightened girl. Carol failed to pick anyone who resembled her attacker. Inexplicably, she was not shown Ted Bundy's photograph.

Ted moved on to Colorado. Soon after, Julie Cunningham, 22; Denise Oliverson, 23; and Melanie Cooley, 21, vanished. At the Wildwood Inn near Aspen, a Michigan nurse, Caryn Campbell, 23, disappeared from the corridors of the inn. Her terribly mutilated nude body was found some ten miles away months later. A brochure from the Wildwood Inn would later be found in Ted's Volkswagen. Also, credit card purchases would indicate he had been in the area when all four women disappeared.

Police attempted to find Ted, now wanted for questioning, but it would be nine months before he would be taken into custody by a highway patrol officer whom Ted attempted to evade. Inside his car, Ted had little goodies, such as a crowbar, handcuffs, a nylon stocking and an ice pick.

Ted Bundy was arrested. Current photos were taken of him and, together with other photos, were shown to Carol Da Ronch. She pulled out Ted's photo without hesitation. "This is the man!" she shouted.

Ted Bundy, now a likely suspect in the murders of girls

in Washington, Colorado and Utah, as well as in the kidnapping of Carol Da Ronch, was released on $15,000 bail.

Law enforcement agencies of three states were sure they were all looking for the same man, yet they didn't have any direct proof. This changed when the material vacuumed from the floor of Ted's van revealed pubic hair which matched that of Melissa Smith, the murdered daughter of Midvale, Utah's police chief. They also found hair which matched that of Carol Da Ronch and Caryn Campbell. Together with the Wildwood Inn pamphlet and credit card purchases from Colorado, police felt they had enough evidence to proceed with the prosecution of the Colorado killings.

Meanwhile, Ted was tried and found guilty of the kidnapping of Carol Da Ronch. He was also sentenced to 60 days in jail for evading a police officer. While in custody, he was charged with the murder of Caryn Campbell. At the time, Bundy stated, "I have never killed, never kidnapped, never designed to injure another human being. I am prepared to use every ounce of my strength to vindicate myself."

Charming Ted was now a prime suspect in a grand total of 32 cases involving missing and murdered women. Over the years several decomposed bodies were found and identified. Others have never been found.

Ted informed the court that he wished to represent himself in future court appearances. As a result, he was given access to the Glenwood Springs Library. One day, left alone to pore over law books, he jumped out a window to the pavement 20 feet below. Ted managed to steal a Cadillac, but was soon picked up and hustled back to jail.

Ted wasn't through escaping from jail. His second attempt was far more successful than the first. He managed to lose a great deal of weight in a short time. Now slimmer than usual, he squeezed up into the false ceiling in his cell and crawled to freedom.

In the following weeks, Ted travelled by car, bus and

plane, making his way to Chicago. On New Year's day, 1978, he took in the Rose Bowl game on TV in a bar in Ann Arbor, Mich. His old school, the University of Washington, won the game.

A week later, the most wanted man in America made his way to Tallahassee, Florida, and took a room a few blocks from Florida State University under the name Chris Hagen.

It was killing time in Florida.

In the wee hours of Jan. 15, Nita Jane Neary returned to her university dormitory after a date. A man, clutching a two by four piece of wood, brushed past her on his way out. Nita rushed upstairs in time to see 21-year-old Karen Chandler, soaked with blood, stagger out of her room. Nita looked into her friend's room. She saw Cathy Kleiner lying on her bed with blood gushing from her head.

Soon, 40 coeds were milling about, ministering to their wounded friends. There was more. Margaret Bowman, 21, lay motionless in death. A maniac had crushed her skull and twisted a pair of panty hose around her neck. Lisa Levy, 20, had been sexually attacked and beaten to death. Her killer had bitten deeply into her breasts and buttocks.

Ted Bundy became unnerved at the police activity taking place so close to his rooming house. He left that very night, checking into a Holiday Inn in Lake City, about 100 miles down the road from Tallahassee. Next day, 12-year-old Kimberley Leach disappeared from her school. No one connected her disappearance with the slaughter which had taken place in Tallahassee.

Five days later, an alert Pensacola police officer picked up Ted in a stolen Volkswagen. He claimed to be Kenneth Misner, a Florida State student. He had 22 credit cards to prove it. Next day, the real Kenneth Misner called police to report his wallet and credit cards stolen.

When Ted's photo appeared in the paper, he was recognized in the rooming house back in Tallahassee as Chris Hagen. A fellow roomer had seen the man he knew as

Chris enter the rooming house at 4 a.m. on the morning of the killings. Fingerprints identified the bogus Kenneth Misner and Chris Hagen to be escaped convict Ted Bundy.

Florida authorities didn't want to release Ted to another state. They endeavored to build an airtight case against their man. They managed to do just that.

Dental technicians were given teeth mark impressions taken from Lisa Levy's body. They matched in every detail impressions taken from Ted's teeth. The Florida jury which heard the Bundy case took only six and a half hours to find him guilty. They recommended death in the electric chair.

In February, 1980, Ted stood trial once more for murder, this time for the murder of 12-year-old Kimberley Leach. Once again, he was found guilty and sentenced to die.

For ten years, Ted has danced around Florida's infernal machine. He has had several dates with death, on occasion coming within days of being executed. The story of his life, and his killing spree, was dramatized in a made-for-television movie starring Mark Harmon.

At 7 a.m. on Tuesday, January 24, 1989, Ted Bundy was executed in Florida's electric chair.

Printed in Canada